UNDER THE MAGNOLIA MOON

A Novel

McAnally Publishing

New York Ska Dale Houston Sugar Bee Los Angeles

UNDER THE MAGNOLIA MOON

A Novel

DANI DENALI

McANALLY PUBLISHING

McAnallyPublishing@gmail.com

For information: danidenali072@gmail.com
Cover Design by Mark McAnally
Library of Congress Cataloging-in-Publication Data has been applied for.

ISBN-13: 979-8-218-38333-6 Paperback
ASIN: B0CTHNYVV2 (eBook)

FOR TOBIN

"Yuck! This book is so old that it smells…"

—Billy Galloway

PROLOGUE

It was dark now, and the expectations of the night were definitely out of the ordinary. His senses felt heightened as he kept a watchful eye out for them. For they could arrive at any moment, and he needed to be ready.

There was an incident the night before, when everything that had transpired in his life had culminated in one breakthrough moment. It felt similar to a dam, which had broken inside of him, and a deluge of sanguinity had spread into his crestfallen soul. A feeling of freedom ensued, and for the first time, he felt hope in his heart.

He never believed he could live up to the normal standards of society. Because he always felt like a square peg trying to fit into a round hole. At one point, he wondered if he would ever amount to much, and at his lowest, he had almost given up.

But he had a fighting spirit, and even as the dark well of hopelessness tried to swallow him whole, there burned a spark inside of him that would never relent. Not ever.

He now had the realization that there was a place for him. A place where he could grow into the man he had always wanted to become. He knew he was clever, and being clever, he knew that there was always more to learn.

As he worked, he remained vigilant. His heart felt lighter with a clear vision of his future, yet it lingered, heavy with the task at hand as sweat trickled down his spine.

It was time. Time for him to become a man. Time to put away all childish things and become the warrior that he was meant to be.

He saw it! The menacing shadow weaved in and out of sight in the darkness. With stealth and speed, his hands reached for his weapons. Then he ran towards the fight.

CHAPTER 1

1845

The physician had left long ago, and William was in an agitated state.

"Why her?" The phrase kept swirling in his mind like a rabid tornado. Anger, frustration, and fear of the unknown kept him on guard as he marched through the house with one purpose: to secure the doors and barricade the windows. He feared this day would come, but it had come way too soon.

Three things were on his mind, while hauling the dining room table up onto its end and shoving it towards the window. The first being Mary. Poor sweet Mary was lying in their bed. She was sleeping under the beautiful handmade quilt she had crafted last spring. Second, being the imminent danger, and third was the guilt he carried. The burden of knowing her demise was his fault.

William moved through the house, picked up a lantern, and stared into the flame. Horrific memories surfaced about that summer long ago. The dreadful day he made a mistake. The morning, he had taken his men and rode into town in a rage. Shaking himself from his thoughts, he looked around the room in a paranoid state. Something wasn't right.

Had he heard a noise? If so, it was a miniscule sound, like a mouse getting into the cupboards. He knew the damage those tiny teeth could do. Still, he prayed for a mouse. William scanned the soft pine floors, peering into every corner of the room, but nothing looked out of place. Darkness enveloped him as he blew out the flame and sat the lantern down.

Fear and heartache kept him awake while he slipped into their bedroom and turned the skeleton key to lock them safely inside. In the fireplace, the embers were turning to ash. He added wood to fuel the fire and blew the bellows to fan the flame.

While doing the mundane chore, William thought about what the physician predicted and fell under a dark cloud of futility as he despaired.

The doctor's words were a reminder of what had to be done soon, as he remembered every word verbatim.

* * *

William impatiently waited as the doctor rode up outside.

"What happened?" Dr. Grant asked as he steadied his horse.

William hurried him inside as he explained the accident. "Mary rode to town by wagon and bought supplies for the farm. On her way back home, the hitch pin snapped, and the horses ran away, leaving the wagon and Mary behind. She lost control of the wagon and when she used the brake; it broke as well. I found her beside the wreck, and I believe she was crushed."

Dr. Grant nodded as he put on his spectacles. "Please, leave the room while I assess the patient."

A while later, the doctor looked sorrowful as he stepped from the bedroom with his hat and medical bag in hand. He shook his head and said, "I'm sorry William…but she will die soon. Her body is broken beyond repair. I made her comfortable with laudanum until she passes. You better say your goodbyes soon."

William prayed as he struggled to accept her fate. Then he turned toward the bed.

A breathy moan eluded her lips while he stood guard over her body. It felt odd as he studied her face because she looked at peace while she slept. Even while dying, she was beautiful. The laudanum Doc Grant administered helped settle her down and cut the pain.

It remained of no comfort for him because he knew what came next. William sat down on an old wooden chair and leaned forward to observe the rise and fall of her chest. The chair groaned under his weight, and he reacted by jolting up out of the seat to scrutinize the darkened room. Even though he realized the noise was his fault. He sat down again, and after checking on Mary, he leaned back and relaxed.

For a moment, he felt at peace. Then a sense of foreboding plagued him. A nagging sensation came to a head as the edges of his dream broke apart, and reality came crashing through. He bolted upright and realized they were here.

They were in the dining room snarling and growling. Wood splintered and windows broke. Things were skittering across the floor, while a heavy glass lantern shattered when it hit the stone fireplace.

Did he smother the fire? If not, they both might not survive the night.

He prayed while chaos loomed, and then he heard it. A long scratching noise scraped down the door. It reminded him of teeth scraping against a metal eating utensil. He gritted his teeth until his jowls ached. His ears tingled, and then the feeling shivered around to the base of his skull and traveled like lightning down his spine.

"William," she whispered his name in a weakened state.

"Shh, I am right here, my dearest." He comforted her, while wishing she remained quiet.

William reached for her soft, dainty hand. The burden of guilt he carried for so long grew heavier with each breath she took. It should have been him lying on his deathbed, not her. He needed to tell her.

How did the thick wooden brake handle split in two? It was near impossible. But a broken metal hitch pin reeked of something more sinister. It had to be.

As absolute chaos continued, and the scratching on the other side of the door became frantic. William leaned in and spoke the words he had kept from her for years.

"Mary, I am sorry. I have brought a curse upon this house. Please forgive me?"

~Present Day~

CHAPTER 2

THE TOWN

"Boy howdy, Mable. It sure is a beautiful morning," Betty said, while smiling at her long-time friend. Betty carefully stepped down from the front porch, where she had been patiently waiting for Mable to arrive.

She enjoyed the alone time and the peaceful moments of the morning, while she listened to the birds sing and flitter about as the sunlight bloomed from the east. Betty passed the time relaxing in her favorite rocking chair, as the fragrant flowers greeted her from several large electric blue pots. The soft colorful petals were happily bursting out of the containers and falling to the sides like a pastel waterfall.

Today, Betty was dressed for comfort. She wore a yellow T-shirt and a pair of pink capri sporty pants. Her shoes were no frills and had the added comfort of orthotics. She noticed Mable was wearing something similar, and she had to smile at that. They were like two peas in a pod. Except for today, Mable had her hair pulled back with a ball cap slapped on it. Betty knew what that meant. Mable hadn't slept well last night.

"It sure is," said Mable, as she pulled her ball cap down over her eyes and aimed her body in the direction, they walked every day.

"And I certainly enjoy stretchin' my legs with you," Betty said, as she paired up with Mable. Together, they began their morning routine.

While they strolled down the sidewalk, Mable felt concerned as she asked, "How's James doing this mornin'?"

"Oh, fair to middlin'. He's going to see the doctor again this week. That nasty spider bite sure did a number on his leg. If he would've just let me call the plumber, he wouldn't have been under the house in the first place. He's gettin' too long in the tooth to be messin' 'round under there. I sure was worried there for a bit. It was growin' bigger and gettin' deeper by the minute."

"Maybe you should've told him that, after all those doctor bills, it would've been cheaper to have called the plumber."

"He'd wring my neck if I told him that!"

As they giggled, they both simultaneously hopped over the uneven crack in the sidewalk.

With a mouthful of gab, Betty, and Mable turned the corner and walked the rest of the block toward the heart of their community.

* * *

They lived in the quaint town of Sugar Bee. But any self-respecting town-folk called it Shugabee. As a small southern speck on the map, it was a respectable, and upright, place to live. Beautiful magnolia trees grew along the east side, which hid the little community from the busy highway. The fragrant trees blossomed all the way down to the slow-rolling Big Leaf River. They had a mill, a church, and several small businesses, and were the proud owners of the State Championship High School football trophy. Go Stingers!

Sugar Bee had the most charming little flower garden, right in the middle of town. Where the lush plants meandered the whole block long. There were many varieties of flowers and bursts of bright colors everywhere. From the yellows and pinks of the Black-eyed Susan's. To the soft blooms of the Vincas, with their red, white, and purple petals, contrasting with their emerald, green foliage.

It was a place where you could sit back on a shady bench, drink an ice-cold lemonade, and people-watch. The children of the town popped up lemonade stands in the park almost every day. The little entrepreneurs made decent money at it too. They borrowed their mama's prettiest, white laced tablecloths, and fancy glass pitchers. Which raised the price of the drink, even if the lemonade was a little sour.

The flowers showed blossoms all summer long, and the Hosta's grew as big, and as wide, as a dinner table.

A round little fountain sat on the north side of the park, where the children played and enjoyed the respite from the dreadful summer heat.

Right in the center of the square, there stood a grand wooden gazebo. Freshly painted bright white and adorned with intricate latticework, the gazebo stood like a beacon for the whole town. It was a wonderful place for the community to gather. It became a busy little area in the morning, with book clubs and such. But it glowed in the evenings, on a romantic summer night, with string fairy lights and live music.

The church, which was located across the street, on the north end of the park. Held a barbecue and ice cream social, once a month, on a Sunday afternoon. You could hear the soft tone of the church bell every Sunday morning throughout the town.

The people of the town took great pride in their little slice of heaven. The place was downright picturesque. Even with the bustle of foot traffic, there was no litter to be found.

Little storefronts sat across the street, on three sides of the park. The massive window displays were painted in various colors, and little signs were hung to welcome their customers into their stores. Several proprietors created shading by adorning a variety of awnings, which kept their patrons out of the oppressive summer sun and the cool winter rain. It was early in the morning, and the stores were still closed. But that didn't deter Betty and Mable as they took a quiet stroll through the garden.

"My, oh my! Just look at those hydrangeas, Mable! They're even prettier than they were yesterday." Betty ogled the flowers with a pang of jealousy. "Cooper Daniels has the greenest thumb in all of Pope County."

Mable made a noise as she yawned, and Betty eyed her friend with concern. Before she could say a word, Mable covered another, even longer, yawn.

Then she waved her hand like she was shooing a housefly away, and said, "I'm sorry, Betty. The sun rose before my body felt rested. I hardly slept a wink last night."

"Well, you better be careful," Betty chuckled, "you're gonna catch flies."

They slowed their pace as they strolled close to the middle of the park, enjoying the beaty around them with each step.

Since Mable knew Betty as well as she knew herself. She prepared to explain why she was so plumb tuckered out.

But Betty interrupted her as she whispered, "Hey, look over there."

Mable looked at her friend and saw her line of sight as she turned her head in the general direction. "What are you seeing, Betty?"

"There's a man over yonder, in the shade. He's right next to 'Luther's Hardware and Feed Store.' Do you see him?"

Mable squinted her eyes. She really needed a new pair of eyeglasses.

"No, I…" then she saw a slight flutter from his long jacket. "Oh," she whispered, "I do see him."

They picked up the pace, and pretended disinterest, as they watched. But he slipped around the corner away from them and their watchful eyes.

Flustered, Betty whispered under her breath. "I've never seen that man 'round here. But if he hangs 'round long enough, Sheriff Halsey will run him right out of town."

The pair stepped to the corner of the park and walked in the opposite direction, away from the storefronts and the stranger. They were now entering one of the older neighborhoods, and the houses were dilapidated.

Normally, they walked in the other direction. Because John Parker's brand-new house was being built, and it appeared almost finished. It was a little thing that they both enjoyed, and they grew excited when he began to landscape his front yard. To them, it was the icing on the cake. But today, for safety's sake, they went a different way.

"Well, spill the beans, Mable. What's goin' on with you?"

Mable took a deep breath and sighed. "I had a bit of excitement last night."

"Oh my, what happened?"

"Remember how I was tellin' you that the microwave had been actin' up?"

"Sure, I remember."

"Well, it caught fire!"

Shocked, Betty's eyes grew wide as she gasped, "Hush yer mouth!"

"Do you recollect when I said that it was buzzin' and growin' louder?"

"Yes, go on!"

"Well, I warmed up some fried chicken for supper. Walked out of the kitchen and went into the livin' room. You see, I was gettin' my teacup for a refill. Then it buzzed like it was goin' to explode! I hurried back to check on it, and smoke had filled the kitchen! There was a loud *Bang!* Then a little flame shot out from the side of it!"

"Well, I declare! What did you do?"

"I snatched a potholder from the counter, and pulled the plug, of course! I thought that wretched contraption was goin' to electrocute me!" Mable exclaimed, as she tossed her hands into the air.

"Then I threw a bath towel over it and waited for a few minutes. I wanted to make sure that blasted thing wasn't gonna go up in flames. It didn't, of course. Thank the good Lord!"

"Land sakes!" Betty exclaimed, "I'm sure glad that you're alright!"

"After all the excitement, I opened the microwave, and smoke billowed out. But the chicken looked perfectly fine, so I ate it." Mable looked at Betty with a straight face.

Betty chuckled, "Sounds about right."

"What can I say? I was hungry." Mable laughed. "I figured I better save my money since I took that death trap outside and chucked it into the trash."

They continued for a few blocks and walked past Auntie's place. She had the cutest little yellow house, but the yard needed to be mowed, and the bushes needed trimming. A white picket fence surrounded the front of the home and had seen better days.

Auntie was outside feeding the neighborhood cats. She was busy cooing at them in a sweet little way as Mable and Betty walked past. They smiled and waved when she looked up and stopped fussing with the cats. Then Auntie gave a neighborly wave and went back to minding her own business. She dropped her last handful of kitty food, turned back toward her screen door, and went inside her house.

"Good Lord! Have you ever seen so many cats all in one place?" asked Betty.

"No, I don't believe I have. How many do you think there were?"

"I bet there were at least fifty."

"Nah, I don't think there were that many."

Exasperated, Betty eyed her friend. "Mable, when are you goin' to stop complainin' about getting a new pair of eyeglasses, and just buy them already?"

"Well," she thought for a moment, "right after I buy a brand-new microwave."

Betty shook her head and laughed. "Sounds about right."

CHAPTER 3

JP

JP, otherwise known as John Parker, pulled up to his brand-new house. He was the sole owner of Parker's Saw and Lumber Mill, located on the south side of town, along the Big Leaf River.

Since he created the plans for his home and worked with the contractors to make it a reality, he was mighty proud of his new place. It was an enormous challenge.

John wanted to add a dash of character to the backyard, so he made plans for a brand-new deck and firepit. He could envision a crisp fall night enjoying the heat from the fire, as he relaxed in his own backyard.

But at the moment, his thoughts were elsewhere. He had just come from the mill where there had been a problem with the woodchipper. Rats were the culprit. They had chewed the wires on the control panel completely in two. JP thought about yesterday morning when he showed up to check on production and remembered seeing them scurrying around. Now, he thought, he may have an infestation.

With the crisis averted, he decided a few cats roaming around the mill should fix the rodent issue. So, he made a few phone calls. One call was to Mia at the Sheriff's department. Surely, they would know of someone who might let go of a few fuzzballs to help him out.

John pushed the button to the automatic garage door opener and tapped his finger on the steering wheel as he watched it ascend. He planned to work on the railing of the deck and surround the trees with a rich brown mulch. When the garage door opened, he noticed the table saw was sitting askew. It wasn't placed up against the wall as it should be. Maybe a contractor had stopped by and used it, he thought.

John slid his athletic frame out of the truck and walked into the garage. Smelling that fresh paint smell made him feel a little giddy. He straightened the table saw and went back to unload the lumber and heavy bags of mulch. As he hauled everything into the garage, John whistled a catchy hit song from the radio.

With a pep to his step, he put on his tool belt and pulled out the tape measure. Happily, getting ready to smell some sawdust. His plan was to cut the posts first, before taking them to the backyard.

After hoisting the cumbersome wood up onto the table saw, JP measured the lumber. He flipped the power switch to turn on the blade, and the sound it made had him jumping back in surprise.

"What in the hell?" he yelled.

The blade was bent as it screeched against the steel frame and shot sparks at him. He immediately shut it off and picked up his trusty skill saw as he muttered, "There's more than one way to skin a cat."

JP measured one last time before cutting. He put the blade to the lead pencil mark while gripping the post tighter, and with his index finger, he pulled the power trigger. But nothing happened. JP took the blade away from the wood and pulled the trigger a few more times. Again, nothing happened.

"Someone must've unplugged it," he growled with frustration, as he set the skill saw on the table. He grabbed the cord with both hands and started to follow it to the outlet on the wall. But it felt loose in his hands. Then he realized there was no plug at all, as he noticed wires sticking out at the end of the cord. Looking around for the missing piece, he wondered if someone had used the table saw and accidentally lopped off the skill saw cord, there by bending the blade.

John had put pressure on the contractors to get things done, and there were quite a few late nights. They were busy hammering and sawing away, to have the house completed in time. Maybe he had ticked off a neighbor.

Worried, he might find something worse. He dropped the black cord, forgot about the plug, and went to check the interior of the house. He was hoping nobody had broken in and vandalized the place. Upon opening the door, he sighed with relief. Nothing was amiss, and JP made sure the doors and windows were locked up tight as he walked through the house.

"Well, apparently today is not my day," his voice echoed into the empty house. "I guess I need to stop by the hardware store," he said as he felt his blood pressure spiking.

Thinking about the fact that most of his belongings were packed into moving boxes, and the frustration he felt from this incident, John decided, "Screw it! I'm moving in by the end of this week!"

John took off his tool belt, slipped the cell phone from his back pocket, and made a call. He walked to his truck as he heard a smoky voice answer, "Kate's Interior Design."

"Yeah Kate, it's JP. I'm gonna need an ETA on when that paint is going to dry. I need to start moving into the house here in the next few days."

Paranoid, he looked around toward the other houses to see if any neighbors were watching him, but no such luck.

CHAPTER 4

THE SHERIFF, MAX, AND THE THROWDOWN

Jake Halsey's massive hand hit the alarm button on his digital clock as he sat up in bed. Dog-tired, he scrubbed his face with both hands and measured the stubble on his chin by touch.

He swung his enormous feet off the bed, and they hit the floor with a thud. He sat for a moment staring with bloodshot eyes at the wall until he smelled the cheerful notes of coffee coming from the kitchen. It was time to get up and get ready for work. His wife would be nagging at him soon if he didn't get a move on.

He readied himself by pinning his badge to his shirt and placing the military-style utility belt around his waist. Then he unlocked his gun case, and after checking it over, he holstered his weapon and walked into the kitchen.

Jake's wife, Cheryl, was at the kitchen sink washing dishes. She picked up a dish and said, "Hello husband."

"Hello wife," he said, as he walked up behind the love of his life. He wrapped his enormous arms around her and kissed her neck.

"Your coffee is already in your to-go cup. It's sitting next to your keys."

He walked over to take a sip of the hot concoction and showed his appreciation as he said, "Hmm-mm, that is a good cup of Joe."

Tired of doing the dishes by hand, Cheryl reminded him. "Don't forget—"

"I know, pick up the part for the dishwasher," Jake interrupted her.

"Thank you. I really miss the dishwasher." She stepped next to him and retrieved a tea towel from a drawer to dry her hands.

"I miss her too." He quipped with an ornery smile and tugged at her golden ponytail.

"You better git!" she laughed, as she wound up the tea towel and gave him a snap at his retreating backside.

Jake hopped into his Ford Ranger pickup and stopped at the park before he went to work. The word around town was that a football game was happening this morning, and he wanted to watch them play before hitting the grind. As he pulled into the parking lot, he saw little Billy Galloway and his friends. They were busy cheering for Dick Sanders' boy, Dean. He was running for a touchdown, and the boys were jumping up and down, yelling in excitement for their buddy.

There stood a long rivalry between the Sugar Bee, Buzz Cuts, and the Binder Blades. The two competing saw and lumber mills sponsored the teams, and it always made for a lively game. The score was 24-21, and it looked like the Buzz Cuts were going to win. He would have enjoyed watching the game until the very end, but he needed to check in at work.

Jake drove the short distance to the Sheriff's department. He really enjoyed working for Sugar Bee and the surrounding area. It was a pleasant reprieve from working as a city cop.

In the city, the hours were long, and the stress was putting a strain on his marriage. So, he looked for employment elsewhere. He wanted to work at a job he had always loved, and to have a happy wife. One morning, he found the opportunity online, and he never looked back.

Jake smiled as he walked up the sidewalk with a spring to his step. The red-bricked building was new, and so was the Fire Department next door. Cool ventilated air greeted him as he opened the door and walked inside.

The color scheme in the main office depicted shades of light creams and dark browns. Kate's Interior Design decorated it, and she did a wonderful job, making the department a pleasant place to work. The entrance was adorned with wooden framed pictures of law enforcement in full uniform. They were standing in groups in front of the old department. Portraits of a few retired sheriffs hung on the wall, with recessed lighting which highlighted their faces. Kate added just a touch of greenery from wide leaf plants, which created a lush oasis next to the front counter.

"Morning, Sheriff." Deputy Mia Romero greeted him as he entered the building. She turned to collect a stack of mail placed on the counter, as her light brown ponytail swished to the side. Mia typically had a smile on her youthful face, but this morning was different.

Her expression was serious as she got to the point. "We've received a few calls about a stranger walking around town." With her petite hand, Mia handed him a list of complaints and phone numbers.

"Someone vandalized a few vehicles, over on Third Street."

"Okay, I'll look into it," Jake said, as he rolled up the paper and headed for the key box. Halsey slipped the key ring off the metal hook and walked to the back door. They had only two cruisers for all of Pope County, and they sat, at the ready, in the garage attached to the Sugar Bee, Sheriff's Department. He wanted to check out the vandalized cars first, since he recognized Cooper Daniels' name on the complaint.

Jake folded himself into the car and quickly realized that Mia had forgotten to slide the seat back. His body felt cramped in the small confines of the car, and like a big man in a little coat, he struggled to get out of the seat. The gear on his belt made it impossible to reach the adjustment bar on the front of the seat near the floor. But Jake was determined. He refused to yell for help to get out of the dang cruiser. He maneuvered the items around on his belt, which took some time, and a few choice words. But after a few minutes, he slid out of the seat to freedom. Jake chuckled, while adjusting the seat to the farthest position from the steering wheel and deemed it safe to get back into the car.

He turned the ignition key, and it fired up with a hefty rumble. With a brawny hand, he slid the car into gear and rolled out of the garage. After fixing the seating issue, the car fit like a glove. Jake loved driving the Dodge Challenger.

He appreciated the fresh strip of mulched plants and flowers that ran between the curbs of the adjacent parking lot for the Fire Department. They were Cooper's handiwork. Cooper sure did a great job maintaining the public lawn and gardens there in S.B.

He drove out into the street and headed over to Third. Mia spoke over the CB radio. Her voice sounded small, as if she were speaking through a tin can, as she said, "Jake, we have a 10-59 over at 'Luther's Hardware and Feed Store.'"

Picking up the microphone, he gave a solid reply, "10-4, on the way." Halsey flipped the switch to light it up, and with a slight push of his big toe, the car growled and leaped forward with momentum.

The Sheriff pulled up and saw two young men throwing down in front of the store. He noticed Max Galloway as the aggressor. Max's ornery sidekick, Jeff Trowbridge, was standing by watching the action.

Jake jumped out of the cruiser and grabbed Max by the scruff of his neck, as he said, "Knock it off, Max, or you'll be in more trouble than you already are!"

"What the—" Max then realized Halsey had a hold of him and he put his hands up to show compliance. "Okay alright, I'm done!" Max was annoyed as he irritably straightened his T-shirt and leaned against the cruiser. He pointed to the kid, who was sprinting away, and accused, "That guy stole my phone!"

"Were you going to beat the phone out of him?" Halsey asked.

Max sulked as he said, "He deserved his ass kicked."

"I think it's time for you to come with me," said Sheriff Halsey, as he turned Max around to handcuff him.

"Seriously?" Max asked, exasperated.

"Seriously," Halsey replied sarcastically. "You need to learn to call the Sheriff's department when you have a problem. We are going for a ride, and you are going to cool off and think about your choices. If you don't straighten up and start using your head, you will end up in jail." Halsey placed Max into the back of his cruiser and shut the door.

Then, with a look of contempt as he raised his eyebrow, he turned his attention to Jeff and said, "You better get home and suck up to your mother. I suggest you mow the lawn and take out the trash, because in about an hour, I'm going to be calling her."

Jeff promptly about-faced and went straight home.

Halsey got back into his vehicle and while he drove over to Third Street, he counseled Max on his decision-making.

"Let me impart some wisdom. You and Jeff have been without father figures for a long time, and your mothers are doing the best they can for you." Halsey looked in the rear-view mirror and saw Max roll his eyes.

Irked, Halsey yelled, "Hey! Eyes on me!" He watched as Max stared at him in the mirror's reflection.

"It's time to grow up and make better decisions. You need to help your mom out and start becoming the man of the house." Halsey eyed Max for a moment, stressing his point.

"If you don't change your ways, I'll have to take you to jail, and I don't want to do that. The kid you were roughing up, could very well decide to press charges. Then, the next thing you know, I will be at your door."

Max slumped tight-lipped in the back seat. Then, a minute later, he leaned forward and stuck his nose to the window to get a closer look as they pulled up to the scene.

Halsey saw the broken windshields on the two vehicles in question, and asked, "Do you know what happened here?"

Max fell back against the seat with a thump. "I don't have a clue what you're talking about, and I don't go around busting windows out of cars. Man, talk about being railroaded," he pouted.

Halsey got out of the vehicle and walked up to Coop's house. He knocked on the door and waited, but nobody answered.

Hearing the commotion, the long-haired neighbor, Lyle Mayhew, stepped outside onto his front porch. He looked a little more than half-baked as he walked up to the Sheriff and watched him with a dazed expression.

Halsey was busy surveying the damage as he walked around the vehicles and observed the shattered windshields and ruined paint. They had deep grooves and scratches covering them, and it looked as if they had been driven through a forest of nail-riddled trees. He noted the two bricks which sat in the gutter, right next to the curb.

Lyle stood with his arms crossed, and watched as Halsey took down the vehicle's information.

Halsey looked up, and nodded, and gave him his full attention. Before Lyle spoke, he cleared his throat and Halsey prepared himself for the bong breath. The sing song whine of his voice was always thick and slow, like molasses in January.

"Hey man... I wanted to let you know... Coop got a ride from his boss. Soo... he isn't here right now. The car parked behind...uh... Coop's truck... is mine. I heard a loud smash! So, I got up... and looked outside the window." He pointed with his thumb, over his shoulder like a hitchhiker, towards his house.

"Then it sounded like... a metal trashcan... being knocked over in the alley... over there... but I didn't see anyone," he said as he alluded to the alley on the other side of the street.

The alleyway sat right in between both vehicles. Mature overgrown trees shaded the area, and two large leaning bushes, heavy with dark green leaves, encroached on both sides of the entrance. Which made it almost hidden.

Halsey noted the stoner's name and home address for the umpteenth time. Then he asked him a few questions, as Lyle tried to stay calm.

As the fog cleared from his mind, Lyle was growing more frustrated by the minute, as he gave Halsey the lowdown. His high had diminished enough for him to realize how much it was going to cost to fix his car. "Oh man… this kind of damage is really going to hurt the old wallet," he whined.

As he slipped his pen and notepad into his front shirt pocket, Halsey replied, "They will consider both vehicles totaled, and I'm sure your insurance will help with the loss. Meanwhile, I will do everything I can to sort this out."

Lyle thanked Halsey, then hung his head as he walked back up to his house.

Max listened to Lyle's stoner drawl and shook his head as he whispered, "Man, that guy is such a burnout."

Halsey got back into his cruiser and took Max home. They were on the other side of the high school, and a few blocks past that was Max's house. He had to get back to the shop and fill out paperwork.

As Jake pulled up to Max's house, he paused before getting out of the car. "Hey, think about what I said earlier, because soon you'll be turning eighteen. I promise I'll look into the phone issue for you, so don't go pressing that kid again."

"Yeah, yeah. I'll leave him alone." Max said and almost looked sincere. But then he smiled, which looked more like a smirk. The light pink scar next to his mouth, courtesy of his old man, turned white.

Halsey got out of his cruiser and opened the door for Max. While he took the cuffs off, he said, "I want you to do some chores around the house and take out the trash for your mom. And while you're at it, cut the lawn. Why don't you make her life a little easier. Because God knows, she's trying to do it all by herself."

Frustrated, Max started walking toward the house.

When Halsey hollered, "Oh, and by the way, later on this evening, I'll be driving by to make sure you got it done."

Max rolled his eyes as he walked up to the door. Now he had chores to do.

Halsey had responsibilities of his own. He had to figure out who was vandalizing his town. Was it the new stranger who's been seen roaming around? Or little troublemakers running around late at night? Either way, he was determined to figure it out.

CHAPTER 5

COOPER DANIELS

"Son-of-a—" Cooper cut his explicative short when he heard a low growl come from the old dog laying on the ground.

"Hush now, Sadie." Coop knew Sadie was alerting him to something. He scanned in the general direction that she pointed with her long, blonde, scruffy nose.

To his surprise, he saw a man getting out of a black dusty sedan. Tired, Cooper climbed down off of the tractor. He hiked up his slim waisted, long-legged Levi's, and readjusted his ball cap.

"He sure parked, far enough away. I suppose he saw the ruts in the driveway and thought better of it," he mumbled to the dog. Cooper gave a half-hearted wave, as he watched the stranger make his way up the long stretch of, part gravel but mainly, dirt road. Cooper was at the barn, which was built next to the old white farmhouse. Both buildings sat back on the property, far from the county road. The stranger moved with purpose, towards his general direction, but he favored his right leg with a limp, and it slowed him down a tad.

Curtis's farm was located northwest of town. Highway 109 ran north and south a few miles east of Sugar Bee, and the traffic always culminated in that general direction. There weren't many strangers that visited out here.

Coop took the rag out of his back pocket, wiped the grease from his hands, and unceremoniously shoved it back into place. There was no time for visitors. He was behind schedule already, and this damned tractor was working on his last nerve.

With suspicious green eyes, he watched as the stranger made it to about the halfway mark, and now he could discern a few features. The fella didn't dress like he was from around here. The man wasn't exactly in business attire, either. He wore a light gray, long-sleeved shirt, which was pulled up on his forearms, and black utility-pants with big pockets on the thighs. Coop noticed the black, military-style boots as he drew closer. Maybe he was an insurance agent coming out for a visit about his truck.

He still wasn't sure how he was going to explain the damage that had been done. It looked like a tornado, filled with saw blades, had picked it up, and placed it right back where he had parked it.

"Stay right there Sadie, and don't growl," Cooper said, as he patted her head. He smiled and walked out to meet the stranger. He held out his hand and gave the man, with

29

the light olive complexion and straight long nose, a firm handshake.

"Hi, I'm Cooper Daniels, but my friends call me Coop. What brings you out this way?"

The man shook his hand with a disarming smile and said, "I was on my way to town, and saw you were working on that tractor. Since I'm not in a hurry, I wondered if you could use some help?"

Coop eyed the man suspiciously, as he thought, maybe the guy was into selling tractors. He thought it mighty strange, but Curtis wasn't exactly around to show him what to do. So, he welcomed the help.

Coop respected old Curtis Cartwright and hoped he was making the right decision by allowing a stranger onto his property. After college, where he studied Agricultural Science, and botany, he couldn't seem to find a job. Thanks to being what Curtis liked to call "a hellraiser."

But Curtis, and the town council, were willing to take a chance on him, and he was bound and determined not to disappoint them.

Coop sighed, and with a half-hearted nod, replied, "Since Curtis isn't around right now, I sure could use a hand."

"Alright," the man squinted his light blue eyes, "the first thing I would check is the safety switches.

"Right before you got here, I noticed something chewed the dead man's switch in two."

"Let's look it over and see if any of the other switches are faulty before you leave to buy that part."

They worked together and found the neutral safety start switch was missing. The wires were there, but the switch was gone.

"I can't believe it's completely missing," Coop said, frustrated, as he shook his head.

"Are you having problems with things disappearing or being broken?" the man asked.

"Well, yeah, I have. This morning someone broke my windshield and completely ruined the paint job on my truck. Then I came to work, and this heap won't start. Curtis likes to call it gremlins. I don't know what the heck is going on. But I'm having one helluva day," Coop shrugged, as he took a breath and let out a long whistle, like the sound of a bomb dropping.

"Well, it looks like everything else is in working order," Coop said, as he handed the stranger the red oil rag from his back pocket.

"Thanks." he took the old rag, and wiped his hands clean, then handed it back to Coop.

"No, thank you," Coop replied, as he shook the man's hand. "I wouldn't have found the problem without your help."

"You're welcome. I'm glad we figured it out." He grinned as he looked at his watch. "Well, it's time to get back on the road, and I hope the rest of your day goes better."

"Thanks," Cooper replied with a smile.

The man turned to walk back towards his car, and Coop felt a sigh of relief. Coop was glad he had made the right decision about accepting the stranger's help. Realizing that the man had never introduced himself. Coop hollered, "Hey, I never got your name!"

The man turned around and walked backwards a few steps. "The name's Midnight," he said as he smiled and turned back around without missing a beat.

CHAPTER 6

MIDNIGHT

The sun hung heavy in the late afternoon air while he studied the shattered windshields on the vehicles. Both automobiles were ruined, as scratches ran deep on the fenders and doors. This was going to be a problem. They were already spreading.

Hanging around town might be a gamble, but he needed to find out if this was the place where the 'cursed one' lived. The local hardware store was closed earlier this morning, which was a minor inconvenience. Pumping information from the proprietor would have made things easier. But that was a no-go, at least for right now. Cooper Daniels might be there, and he didn't want to make his presence known all over the small town.

Midnight got back into the rental and drove around town to see if he could find the telltale signs that he was close.

CHAPTER 7

THE BOYS

The gray, two-bedroom home on 1311 Black Willow Lane was small and unassuming. Except for the black and white skull and crossbones flag, which hung inside the front window facing the street. The house wasn't special, in any way, shape, or form. Although, the yellow house next door looked similar in shape and size. Years ago, it was painted gray with black trim and definitely needed retouched. At the front of the house, directly in the middle, sat the front door. It was painted black and had two concrete steps which led up to it. There were two matching windows, also framed in black, which hung on each side of the entrance.

An old, cracked, concrete driveway ran along the right side of the house and ended abruptly a few feet past the back corner of the home. There used to be an old, slanted garage at the end of the drive, but it had been gone for years. To the right of the driveway, a tall, weathered privacy fence separated the adjoining properties.

An old wooden shed sat perched on a slab of concrete in the far-left corner of the backyard.

The back of the home mirrored the front. Except the backdoor was accompanied by two sunken steps, where a few steppingstones led to the driveway.

The view from the backdoor was breathtaking. Where the backyard ended, the Big Leaf National Forest began. The mature trees grew tall, lush, and green, and nothing obstructed the beautiful view.

Billy sat down on a lawn chair next to his tent. He watched and waited for his older brother, Max, to finish mowing the yard. Billy and Max had several similarities, except Max was taller and had a scar. They both took after their lovely mother and her Mexican ancestry.

Billy wondered why Max was mowing. It wasn't like Max to do his chores without a huge argument from their mom. Something shocking was happening. There was no way Max was becoming a responsible adult. Had he done something wrong? Either way, Billy felt like he was in the Twilight Zone.

Max finished pushing the noisy lawn mower over the last section of overgrown grass and killed the engine. As it died down, he turned and saw Billy staring at him.

"What," said Max. It didn't come out as a question, but more of a statement, so Billy ignored it.

"Nothing," replied Billy. His older brother was a tool, and he didn't want to be tortured by him.

"Then why are you giving me the stare down," Max smirked.

Billy turned away from him and hoped that Max would soon grow bored and go away.

"Now you're giving me the side-eye," Max mouthed off, as he walked over and picked up his bottle of water. He uncapped the lid and yeeted it with a flip of his fingers at Billy.

"Ow!" Billy faked injury, ready for his brother to leave.

Max took huge gulps of water and poured the rest over his sweat-soaked head. Then he tossed the empty water bottle aside, as he ripped off his T-shirt and stuck part of it into his back pocket.

"You're lucky that I'm busy taking care of man stuff, or I'd come over there and kick down your tent," growled Max.

Billy grabbed his pillow and sleeping bag and tossed them into the tent. His temper was getting the best of him, and as he crawled into the tent on his hands and knees, he whispered to himself. "Who has the grumps? Does Maxi-Pad have the grumps?"

He then realized his first mistake. He turned his back on Max. Suddenly, both of his ankles were grabbed and pulled outside of the tent, and, with a thump, his belly hit the tent floor.

"Dang it, Max, leave me alone!" Billy shrieked. Then he was flipped over, like a McDonald's hamburger, onto his back, and yanked out of the tent onto the damp grass. Because of the instant terror of what was going to happen next, he put his hands out to defend himself. His brother grabbed his wet T-shirt hanging from his back pocket and rubbed it all over his face.

"Oh, does little Billy need his dirty face washed?" Max snickered.

Now, Billy's face was wet, and it smelled of arm pit. He slapped Max's hands away with a tiny windmill effect and yelled, "Aww! That's so freaking nasty!"

Bored with torturing his little brother, Max chuckled as he stood up and walked off.

Billy was left lying there, like a dead man. He didn't move for a good long minute. He knew when to play possum. It was a natural survival instinct for him, and he wasn't ashamed of it either. Max could get mean. So, he learned to pick his battles. But someday, he was going to get him back. He had to wait for the perfect moment.

Billy waited until Max shoved the lawnmower into the shed and slammed the door. But the door didn't remain shut. It swung back open, and Max slammed it shut again. As if it were mocking him, it creeped back open. Max executed a high kick karate maneuver, and it swung open a third time. Then, with great patience and his pointer finger, he pushed it shut.

Billy snuck a glance over at Max and stifled a small giggle. It was quite comical to watch Max when he was trying to be such a badass. But Billy didn't dare move until Max was out of sight. Even then, as he watched him walk into the house and slam the door, he remained laying on the ground.

Troy yelled toward the backyard, "Hey Billy! Are you back there?"

Billy hopped up, scrunching his nose from the smell. While brushing off his clothes, lawn clippings fell to the ground as he walked over to the outside water spigot. Revolted by the stench of armpit, he picked up the hose and turned on the water to wash his face.

"Yeah! I'm here. Come on back," Billy yelled, as he let the water rush out and then begin to cool. Billy gasped when he stuck his head under the stream of water. It felt freezing cold on his hot scalp and face, and it shocked his system for a second. Then he felt relief as he rubbed his face clean.

Troy walk around the corner pushing his bicycle. He leaned it up against the house and waited for Billy to shut off the hose. Troy was tall for an eleven-year-old, which made him skinny as a beanpole, and he had sandy blonde hair which curled at the ends.

"Well, I made it, and it looks like I'm the first one here," said Troy, as he looked around while readjusting his wire-rimmed eyeglasses.

"Hey, if you want to," Billy pointed to the tent, "you can throw your stuff in there."

The tent had a lower room on the front of it, making it look like a big green igloo, but farther inside, it grew spacious. It sat at the back of the property, where it met the forest. Troy walked over and sat his backpack inside.

A well-worn path ran next to the tent and sloped off into the woods. It went up and down as it lowered through the thick forest and stopped at the Big Leaf River.

Close to where the path ended sat an old, single lane bridge made of stone. Billy liked to fish there because it was quiet. Naturally, trees and bushes encroached upon it since it had been abandoned by the town long ago. Billy figured there must have been a road leading to it, once upon a time, and someday he was going to see what was out there on the other side of the river.

Together, Butch and Dean walked around the corner of the house.

Butch nodded, "Was sup."

Dean mimicked Butch when he asked, "Was sup?" with a nod.

Butch wore mirrored Ray bans, and Dean wore sunglasses that wrapped around his circular face. They were pushing their bikes and dropped them to their sides onto the ground at the same time.

Butch slipped his sunglasses up onto his spiky, bleached blonde hair. It was so full of gel; it bounced right back into place.

Dean took his backpack from his shoulder and dropped to the ground. He had heft to him and played football every chance he got. At only eleven, his size was a force to be reckoned with on the field.

Billy was excited! Camping with his friends in the backyard was something he had always wanted to do. While everyone was busy putting their gear into the tent and talking. He walked over to the shed and took out three foldable lawn chairs. Billy set them up in a circle around the fire pit, which was built of stone.

Since he was the oldest, by one year, he took his responsibilities of being the leader to heart. He refused to ask his mom for money, since she was single and struggled to keep them afloat. So, he took the old lawnmower out and cut several lawns. He was quite successful with his endeavor and made enough cash to buy a cooler full of ice, pop, and food for the sleepover. Plus, one more thing.

Billy walked behind the shed. He couldn't contain his excitement for one more minute. He wanted to show them what else he had bought. It sat hidden behind the shed next to a pile of old dried wood. Billy pulled the brand-new brown tarp from it and stared at it with pride. "Hey guys, look at this!"

His friends, hearing the excitement in his voice, hurried around to the back of the shed where he stood. They stopped and stared at it with awe. The boys rang out a mixture of, "Nice! Sweet!"

"Hey that's lit! When did you get it?" Butch asked.

"I bought it yesterday." Billy grinned as he grabbed the cushioned hand grip and pulled it from the wall of the old wooden shed. "It's an Elite BMX Freestyle 20-inch. I thought maybe later we could go for a ride."

"Those gray and black camouflage wheels are killer!" Troy drooled.

"It looks badass, with the matte black paint." Dean nodded his approval.

"Ha, how cool is that? It matches your house," laughed Butch.

Billy beamed; he knew his friends would appreciate his brand-new bike. Then he covered it back up to hide it from Max.

Next, everyone went to the cooler. They grabbed a cold can of pop and took a seat around the fire pit to rest awhile.

"Hey, I heard someone went crazy last night and broke the windshields on a couple of cars over on Third street. Let's ride over there and check it out," said Butch.

The boys drank their cans of soda as fast as they could. Racing each other with each gulp of the sweet drink.

Billy emptied the fluid from his soda can with one final, long pull. He brought it away from his lips, and while his neck worked a swallow. He crushed the aluminum can with his hand and took a deep breath. Expelling air from his stomach while working his mouth into an 'O' shape, like a fish gasping for air. Billy stuck out his chest with pride as he made one long, echoing loud burp. "BLOWAHOHOHAAAA!"

They laughed and followed suit with a chorus of belches, then crushed the cans and threw them to the ground to smash them.

Excited to show off his new bike, he ran behind the shed and ripped off the tarp. He mounted it and put his foot down on the pedal, but it dropped toward the ground with no pressure from the chain. His chain had popped off and was now hanging loose. He got off and slipped it back on, pushing the pedal around to secure the chain back onto the rear wheel cog.

Billy pushed his bike around the corner and said, "Hold up guys, I need to tighten my chain. Then we can go."

They leaned against their seats, with their hands on the handlebars of their bikes, and waited patiently for Billy to fix his bike. Billy loosened the bolts which held the back wheel onto the frame and moved it back to tighten the chain.

Billy made quick work of it and tossed his tools back into the toolbox in the shed and hopped on his bike, as he said, "Let's go!"

His friends were turning their bikes around as he pushed past them and rode to the driveway. He turned his head and made sure they were catching up as he pedaled out onto the street and down the hill.

He felt his first taste of freedom as the late afternoon breeze blew past his face. His new bike rode so smooth on the hot pavement, and the twenty-inch tires ate up more ground, which made it faster than his older bike. So, he slowed to a crawl to wait for everyone to catch up. As he waited, he almost salivated at the thought of riding the bike path Max had created behind their house in the forest. He couldn't wait to ride his new bike there. His friends caught up, and they pedaled past the Sugar Bee High School and turned left at the corner onto Third street.

When they arrived, a stunned silence fell over them, as they stopped in the middle of the desolate street.

Billy came upon the scene first as he rolled to a stop and dropped his foot down to the ground for balance. "Oh man, that is messed up."

"Holy shit!" Dean's mouth hung open in disbelief.

"Wow, whoever did that is psycho," said Butch.

"Holy shit!" Dean said again.

The windshields were spider webbed and the body of each vehicle was trashed.

Billy looked at the scratches on the vehicles and said, "I wonder what made those?"

"What do you mean?" asked Troy.

"Besides the crushed windshields. What does it look like to you?" asked Billy as he pushed his bike up to the truck. Then placed his hand with fingers spread over the scratches and made a swiping gesture.

"Holy shit!" Dean was so freaked out that he could only form two words.

"It looks like claw marks," Troy said.

"Holy," Dean repeated, and everyone finished his thought together, "shit!"

They looked at the totaled vehicles for a few minutes longer until they grew bored and talked amongst themselves about the football game Dean had won that very morning. Everyone agreed Dean was MVP, and the Binder Blades had never stood a chance. The air grew stagnant and hot around them as they stood on the street with no shade.

"Hey, do you guys want to go to the square?" asked Billy, while wiping the sweat from his brow. "Let's mess around at the fountain for a little while," he suggested.

"Sounds like a plan," Butch agreed.

The rest of the boys nodded in agreement as they turned their bikes around and pedaled their way to Sugar Bee Park.

It was a hot summer's day, and their energy levels were in full force. The thought of the crisp, cool water from the fountain had them in high spirits.

When they entered the town square, Billy noticed a girl that he liked was sitting by the fountain. They quickly rode up to the concrete pool of water and dropped their bikes. While his friends ran toward the blue water and splashed each other, Billy walked around to the far side of the fountain.

He sat down on the white painted ledge of the pool away from the war zone and tested the water with his fingers. It felt just as cool as he thought it would be. He glanced over to see if she was looking his way, but she was busy looking down at her phone.

Katie Daniels was the new girl in town. The rumor was that she and her mother moved here because her parents were getting a divorce. She looked so cute sitting there with her long, straight, blonde hair parted in the middle with tiny white butterfly clips holding her bangs from her suntanned face. She was wearing a white tank top, matched with a pair of light blue denim, overall shorts, and white flip-flops.

Billy glanced over her way again and noticed that she looked sad. He had never talked to her before and his whole body was heightened with nervousness as he walked up to her and asked, "Are you okay?"

She glanced up at him with tear-filled eyes. She had the greenest eyes he had ever seen, and when she looked at him, it made him feel like someone had punched him right in the gut.

Embarrassed that someone had seen her crying, she wiped away the tears that had slipped onto her cheeks. "I'm okay," she sniffed.

With butterflies in his stomach, he stood facing her for a moment. Then sat down next to her on the wooden park bench.

She sighed, then said, "It's just, well, it's my dad. I was supposed to stay the night at his place, but he never showed up at my house."

She blinked, and Billy saw a tear slide down her cheek before she caught it and swiped it away.

"He didn't even call me and tell me he wasn't coming. So, I texted him, and I've been waiting for a text back for over an hour," she frowned.

"I'm sorry that happened to you. He could have lost his phone. It happens."

With a shrug, she said, "Maybe."

She looked over at Troy, Butch, and Dean. They were now sitting on the ledge of the fountain looking over at them and laughing.

"Are those guys your friends?" Katie asked, changing the subject.

Billy shrugged. "It depends on the day. But most of the time, yeah."

"I'm Katie," she said with a small smile.

"I'm Billy Galloway, and that's Butch, Dean, and Troy."

She waved at the boys, and they waved back.

Acting like a goofball, Dean waved. Then he stiffened with his hand mid-air, and with a frozen goofy grin, fell over into the pool of water. They both laughed at his antics, and, with that, they relaxed a little.

"Listen, I haven't been around my dad in a long time and from what I can remember. He wasn't that nice of a guy. So, I'm okay with it. You know, with him not being around," said Billy, as he shrugged with a tightlipped grin. "It sounds like your dad cares. Give him a chance to make it up to you. If he's a good guy, he will make it right." He shrugged and then explained, "Sometimes, you just have to wait and see."

Then, her phone made a small metal ringing sound, like a bicycle bell.

She looked down at her phone and then looked up with a smile and said, "It's my dad."

She stood up to walk away, but then she stopped and turned toward Billy.

"Hey, thanks for talking to me. I was so bummed out and, well, it helped."

Billy smiled at Katie and replied, "I'm happy that he texted you. Hey, are you going to the concert at the gazebo? The one that is coming up soon?"

"Yeah, I saw a flyer for it. Maybe I'll see you there." Katie smiled bashfully, then gave a little wave as she continued to walk away.

Katie left the park and Billy, filled with glee, ran over to the other side of the fountain, and splashed the guys with great vigor.

They, of course, all ganged up on him and made sure that he was just as soaked as they were. After they settled down, they headed back to Billy's house for roasted hotdogs from the fire pit.

CHAPTER 8

AUNTIE AND HER DILEMMA

Dressed in a light blue nightgown with her comfiest house slippers, Auntie DeLeon murmured in a sweet voice to the cats. She scooped kitty food and placed it down on the old, cracked sidewalk in a straight line. It was growing late in the evening, and she stood there listening for a moment.

She thought it strange that the usual sounds of cicadas, which were almost deafening this time of year, were nonexistent. Their song seemed to intensify with the warmth of the season.

"Hmmm, not a peep in this heat," she thought aloud. But then she heard the meowing from the little beggars for their dinner and as she looked toward her overgrown yard, she gave a surprised laugh. "Oh my, where did y'all come from?"

She noticed them staring at her as they watched her every movement she made. When the next tiny kibble dropped to the pocked marked concrete, they rushed forward for food.

"Is it my imagination or is there more of you?" Bewildered by the sight, Auntie didn't trust her own eyes. The massive number of cats mulling about in her backyard had become ridiculous, and her neighbors were definitely going to notice.

"I have an army of cats!" Auntie said, as she giggled at her situation, but then she felt overwhelmed and a little dismayed. "What am I going to do with all of you?"

Watching the moggies, she cupped more food and added it to the line as she backed up toward the house.

The ferocious felines were coming out of the woodwork. They ran around the old forgotten car which had been parked in the backyard for years. It had been broken down for so long, bushes had crept up around it.

They came in droves from the forest behind the old wooden shed. It had been painted yellow to match her house, but now it was peeling and chipping away. At one point, she was going to have the shed demolished. But a set of security lights were attached to it, and when she turned on her back porch light, they lit up the whole backyard. She liked being able to see if she was going to run into a bear, so she decided to keep it.

Her long white hair clung to her nightgown as she shook her head in disbelief. When the bag of kibble emptied, she turned it upside down and gave it a few shakes.

"That's it. I have no more for you little beasts," she said. Then Auntie smiled as they rubbed up against her bare legs. As if saying, "Thanks for the food."

Auntie gathered the bottom of her nightgown together and watched the sweet babies as they kept circling her feet.

She couldn't help it, as her heart filled with joy. She loved them all, even if she couldn't name each one.

Her favorite cat sat waiting back at the house. Taking a gentle step back. The greedy little fur balls didn't notice her anymore as they moved toward the food. Smiling, she turned and went back inside the house to the kitchen.

Auntie walked to the cabinet, where she reserved the best kibble for her darling companion. She took a cup of food over to his bowl, then noticed his bowl was left uneaten. Worrying over her cherished cat, she walked over to the window ledge, where he sat, looking out over the backyard.

A magnificent gray and white long-haired Maine Coon cat sat, like a proud king, on the ledge. On his perch, he looked upon the cluster of cats scurrying for their last bit of food. His attention turned to Auntie when she sat down on a kitchen chair next to the ledge.

"Mr. Grimm, we need to have a talk. This is the third day you haven't eaten, and I'm beginning to worry about you," she said with her hands folded in her lap. Then she crooked her finger and lifted his chin to get his attention.

Mr. Grimm gave her a disapproving look through glowing hazel eyes, but then relented and purred.

With a frown, she ran her hand along his fluffy coat. He meowed at her as if he understood what she was saying, so he hopped down and walked over to his kibble.

She slapped her knees and smiled. "That's my boy."

CHAPTER 9

CAMPING AND SPOOKY TALES

Billy and the boys watched as the fire burned low. Full from eating roasted hotdogs, flaming hot chips, and cookies, they sat dazed around the fire pit. They were mesmerized by the glowing red lines which snaked through the hot ash. A small breeze made the hot coals brighten and flicker as it danced with the wind, but the fuel from the wood was spent.

Now bored, they climbed into the tent and hung one lantern to set the mood. They rolled out their sleeping bags and settled down as Billy prepared to tell his story.

"Alright, y'all ready to hear a scary story?" Billy asked.

"Let's hear it," said Dean as he sat crossed legged on top of his sleeping bag. He grabbed his pillow, wrapped his arms around it, and rested his chin.

Everyone grew quiet, and Billy told his tale:

There once was a football player named Brody, and he asked this blonde-haired girl named Jessica out on a date. Brody liked her a lot. So, he took her to the local diner, where they had burgers and shakes with no onions. Often, that was a good sign they were going to be kissing later.

"Because onions give you stank breath," said Billy, as he pinned a look at his friends. "Girls don't like stank breath." The boys chuckled, then smiled, and eventually nodded.

Then back to the story he went:

Brody took her to the football field at the high school. He placed a blanket on the ground, where he made the final touchdown to win the last game of the season. But she wasn't impressed. Girls are weird like that, you know.

They sat chatting about a history class they took together and agreed that neither of them liked the teacher. Mr. Brooks was a real stickler for talking out loud, and he gave a pop quiz anytime he pleased. While relaxing on the blanket, they heard something in the woods.

Brody stood up and looked across the field when something caught his eye. He gazed deep into the shadows of the forest, behind the empty bleachers, when something dark and hulking moved. A glint of something small reflected off of the school's security lights. But the brightness and angle of the lights dissipated into the night, leaving it all to his imagination. One lonely streetlight stood next to the concessions building, and it kept the field from being blanketed in complete darkness.

Brody took a few steps toward the dark shadow, to get a better look. And he saw the glimmer of white again! Then the shadow stepped forward, and he saw what the light was struggling to capture. It was drool sliding down a massive set of huge canine teeth. The sharp teeth were larger than anything he had ever seen—

"Holy shit!" said Dean. His eyes grew wide as he hugged his pillow tight.

"Screw that! I'd take off like lightning!" said Butch.

"No! He needs to face it, while looking as big as possible, and then scream at it to scare it away! Wait! Does he have a weapon?" asked Troy.

"No, no, listen," said Billy:

Brody crept backwards while still facing the massive animal. But the menacing creature put its head down and took a step forward. Stalking them.

Without breaking eye contact with the beast, he quietly told Jessica, 'We have to get out of here, now!'

Jessica's blood turned ice cold when a set of glowing yellow eyes looked her way.

'Get up slowly,' Brody instructed.

Panicked, she couldn't seem to catch her breath, as she stood up and shivered.

While Brody faced the creature, he formed a plan. 'On the count of three, run for the car. Nod if you understand.'

Afraid to move, Jessica nodded slightly, as the creature took another careful step forward.

'Okay, here we go! One, two, three!'

Jessica turned and ran, and Brody snagged the blanket, thinking he could use it to throw at the beast. Then he took off like a shot!

By then, the beast's head was down, as it quickly made a beeline for them.

As it gained on them, they ran for their lives, toward the safety of Brody's sedan.

Brody sprinted around the car, as he pulled out the key fob. The horn blared as he hit the panic button, hoping to scare the creature away. Frightened, he didn't look back, as he hit the unlock button and jumped inside of his vehicle. That's when he noticed. Jessica had never made it into the car!

Scared and running for her life, she felt the hot breath of the beast on her neck. Jessica knew she would not survive the attack, and she screamed as she was taken down.

Brody was blinded. The automatic interior lights made it impossible to see anything outside of the vehicle. But he felt each jolt as the car rocked violently back and forth from the force of the attack.

Billy lowered his voice to a whisper. Silently, he looked at each of his friends before finishing the story:

The lights lowered, then shut off, and the vicious attack seemed to end at the same time. Jessica no longer made a sound.

Darkness surrounded him momentarily until his eyes adjusted to the night. He was scared out of his mind. The quiet was deafening. The only thing he heard was his own heartbeat as it drummed like a racehorse in his chest. He anxiously crept over to the passenger side window, terrified of what he would see. He was afraid the beast was still out there … waiting… to pounce!

Even though everything within him screamed to stop. He put his face closer to the glass to see if she was still there.

"WHAM!" Billy yelled, causing everyone to jump! "Her bloody palm slapped the window!"

As if the monster itself jumped on top of them! The tent caved in on both sides with a loud WHACK!

Frightened, the boys screamed and jumped on top of each other, trying to escape the tent.

Billy, being closest to the entrance, got out first as the rest of them came tumbling out behind him, knocking him down.

"Ha, ha! We got you; you bunch of Cricker-Hicks!" Max laughed.

While they were piled on top of each other, one of the boys let one rip.

Max and Jeff were bent over, rolling with laughter.

"Which one of you just landed an air biscuit?" Max laughed, "Congrats! Your butt just sounded like an old squeaky door!"

"Hey, that is the song of my people," Butch replied.

Max didn't know which one said it, but he heard their retort, and he laughed harder.

Billy stood up with clenched fists and yelled, "Dammit, Max, you're such a shithead!"

Max moved swiftly as he growled. "Come here, you little twerp!" He grabbed Billy and put him into a headlock.

Billy grabbed Max's arm and struggled to free himself as Max gave him a massive noogie, scraping his knuckles across Billy's scalp.

The pain was instant, as Billy yelled, "Let go of me!"

Max let go as he laughed and strutted over to his fishing pole and backpack. Which were leaning up against a tree next to the tent.

Jeff turned on a flashlight and placed it under his chin. The light lit up his face from underneath, making his features look morbid. Then he smiled a monstrous grin, and said, "Boo!"

As Billy caught his breath. Max and Jeff walked down the dirt path into the forest. They'd planned to hike down to the river for some night fishing.

Billy felt his anger boil over like red hot lava as he yelled, "Your breath is the reason for climate change!" Red faced and sweaty, he tried not to cry as he shrieked, "Max, you can kick rocks!"

The boys felt bad for Billy as they gathered around him.

Troy, being a sensitive soul, placed his hand on Billy's shoulder.

Billy took a deep breath. Then shook his head and looked him in the eye as he said, "I'm okay."

Troy asked, "You want to know something?"

"What?"

Troy grinned like a wicked clown, and said, "He really is a turd-muncher."

The boys chimed in as they laughed.

"No! He's a butt-muncher!" Butch grinned.

"An Asshat!" Troy supplied.

"Ha, Ass-Monkey!" Dean yelled.

They laughed, and the insults flew out of their mouths faster and faster.

"Shit bird!"

"Dipshit!"

"Bozo!"

"Wanker!"

"Butt-wipe!"

"Douche nozzle!"

Everyone yelled out their best insults. But when the ultimate insult, "Pig fart sniffer!" echoed out of Dean's mouth. It suddenly grew quiet.

Dean looked at the others with a shy, goofy grin.

The boys looked at each other, wondering what each person thought.

Billy cracked a smile and said, "That's a good one, Dean!" Then busted out laughing.

They were all laughing now, and the amusement grew into huge belly laughs. A few grabbed their stomachs, and others bent over to catch their breath. Then they laughed again, because now it was contagious.

CHAPTER 10

THE PUB

Mia took a sip of her amaretto sour and grimaced at the potent taste of alcohol on her tongue. It had been a long day filled with complaints from angry people throughout the town, and stress was a key factor as to why she was now sitting there in the bar.

She had gone home to shower and change out of her uniform after work. But the stress of the day clung to her as she brushed her hair. Mia looked around her living room, trying to feel the happiness she once felt when she first decorated her home. But the tension in her shoulders would not relent.

The small house with its open floor plan was airy, simple, and comfortable.

She loved it, right down to the small vase of flowers, which complimented each color of the room.

Mia looked into the mirror and parted her light brown hair down the middle. Then she slipped her long bangs behind each ear and called it good enough.

As she took a few deep cleansing breaths, she tried to let the stress go. But it didn't work. Since she was single and living alone, she broke the monotony and left the house. It was time for a change.

Normally, Mia wouldn't even think about going to 'The Buzz Pub,' with its boisterous music and lively crowd. Usually, she would opt for a run instead. But being alone right now didn't suit her. So, she sat on the yellow and black vinyl cushioned bar stool and rolled her slight shoulders to loosen up. Mia picked up the tiny white straw to stir her mixed drink, then took another careful sip.

Listening to the conversations behind her was difficult with the loud music. But she noticed the staccato in their voices and found the residents were on edge as well.

Since she grew up in this small town, she knew everyone in the bar by name. But when she became a sheriff, at twenty years old, everyone treated her as if she had the plague. Which was fine with her, even though it felt a little lonely sometimes.

When she heard a loud voice from the back of the bar yell, "Hey Coop, how the heck are ya?" Mia felt her shoulders shoot straight up to her ears.

"So much for relaxing," she grumbled to herself, as she dropped her head and turned her attention to the front entrance of the bar. Cooper's six-foot-tall frame was standing there as he smiled like an idiot. Annoyed, she turned back to her drink.

She had dealt with him once already today and once was enough. Sure, it was a small town, and the odds were high that they were going to run into each other from time to time. But tonight, she didn't have the patience for his irritating country boy charm. The guy's presence irked her, and she was off the clock.

Maybe it was because he had stolen her purse back in high school. She had something important in her purse. Something that was special, and irreplaceable, and she had cried for days when she had lost it.

Mia's temper flared as he walked up to the bar. His hands slid past her peripheral vision and landed on top of the polished wood, right next to her, as he sat down. She immediately tossed back the last swallow of her drink, and with too much force, slapped it down. Hence creating a loud echoing 'knock!'

She immediately cringed at the attention the blunder drew to her, as she looked inside of her purse to pay for her drink.

"Hold up there Mia, I want to talk to you."

The bartender looked at Coop and nodded a friendly hello as he waited for his order.

"I'll have a beer and whatever she's having." Coop smiled his thanks.

The bartender placed two cardboard coasters down in front of them and sat a bottle of beer in front of Coop. He swiped her empty glass and created another mixed drink.

Mia felt miserable as she clenched her teeth and pasted a polite smile onto her face. Then she stared at the numerous bottles of alcohol gathered on the shelf against the mirrored wall behind the bar. She saw a glimpse of her reflection in between two half-emptied bottles and realized that she looked somewhat deranged. So, she unscrewed her face and tried for a genuine smile, as she said, "Thanks, but I was getting ready to leave."

"If you have a minute, I wanted to ask you a few questions," Coop said, as he took a swig of his beer.

An excuse formed on the tip of her tongue as a fresh drink was placed neatly in front of her. A few cherries floated to the top, and she sighed in defeat. She really liked cherries. She picked up the glass and took a sip. Then replied, "Ask away."

"Does Sheriff Halsey know who tore up my truck?"

"He's looking into a few people. Let me ask you a question. Have you recently made anyone mad?" she asked, raising her eyebrows.

"I don't think so. The only person I've had any problems with lately is my neighbor Lyle. He likes to party, and last night at one in the morning, I had to go knock on his door to ask him to turn the music down. Because I had to get up early today. But his car looked as bad as my truck."

Mia took a sip of her drink and wondered if another neighbor took their anger out on Lyle, but got Coop's truck by mistake. "Do you possibly know when the vandalism occurred?"

"It probably happened between 1 am to 5 am." Frustrated, Coop put his fists on the bar. "I wish I would've heard someone breaking my windshield, but I was wearing earplugs so I could sleep. Lyle's bass speakers were actually vibrating my bed, and that's why I went over there."

"What about another neighbor? Maybe they got sick of hearing the racket."

"The house across the street is vacant and my other neighbor is out of town, on vacation. Besides, most people know what my truck looks like, since I use it for work around town."

"You're right. 'Hic,' everyone knows your truck." Mia wasn't much of a drinker and had already downed most of her second glass.

Coop was quiet for a moment as he took another swallow of beer.

"I have one more question, and then I will leave you alone," said Coop.

Embolden by the alcohol and the numb feeling which came with it. She pointed finger guns at Coop and said, "Shoot."

"Why do you hate me?"

Mia wobbled in her seat and put her hand on the bar to catch herself as she turned to face him. She hadn't been this close to him in a long time.

His youthful appearance was almost gone, making way for a lean, tanned face. His sun-bleached hair differed from the way he had kept it in high school, and it only added to his good looks.

She looked into his sad green eyes and saw the question hanging there.

His bright white smile, which he flashed with skill at every pretty girl back in the day, was replaced by a dejected frown.

Her emotions warred inside of her like a tornado with flashing signs. Mia felt sad for him at first, but then she knew he was conniving, which created cynicism. But ultimately, she remembered the hurt he had caused, and her anger erupted like a volcano.

"You stole my purse!" She yelled, as she hopped from the barstool and poked him in the chest. Mia stood toe to toe with him and asked, "How exactly am I supposed to feel, huh?"

Thrown off guard by this spitfire confrontation, Coop gritted his teeth and took her by the elbow.

"Put it on my tab," he said to the bartender, without breaking eye contact with her.

Which confused Mia. She wasn't expecting a mean retort, as she exclaimed, "Why you son of a—"

"Come with me," he growled as he interrupted her and spun her toward the front door.

Mia grabbed her purse and muttered, "Not again."

He walked her out into the humid night air and then let her go.

Embarrassed, she stepped farther away to calm herself. She'd already been in a lousy mood and failed to keep her temper in check.

Mia stood there for a moment with her arms crossed.

Even though the hour late, it was luminescent outside as Mia looked toward the glowing moon. It was almost full; she noticed as she dropped her arms to her sides and took a deep breath.

She tried for a decorum of calm and turned toward him. Nonchalant, he stood leaning against the building, and it made her want to put her fingers around his neck and squeeze. She took a step forward, then stopped when he moved one step toward her with lightning speed.

"Look, I took nothing from you. I've never done anything to you," said Coop.

"You were there that night. You were sitting behind me at the ball game and my purse was right next to me on the bench. Then it was gone."

She could tell he wanted to say more, but he remained silent. Was he lying to her?

When they were teenagers; he was in trouble a lot. Coop spent plenty of time in detention, because he was always pulling stunts and pranking his friends.

"Maybe you should talk to your best friend, Carry," said Coop.

"Why do I need to talk to Carry? I haven't seen her in years, and she wasn't my best friend. We only hung out twice."

"That explains a lot," said Coop, as he understood why Carry would do such a thing.

"What do you mean?" Mia asked, frustrated. "Please explain to me what happened to my purse. I had something in there and it meant a lot to me."

Coop moved closer to her and explained, "One night we had a party, and the entire gang was there. They invited some girls out, and Carry showed up with them. She was laughing while digging through a purse. Carry took items out of it and put them into her bag. Then she chucked the purse right into the river. Never did like her much after that night. When I realized she must've stolen it. I never thought the purse belonged to you because I assumed she was your friend."

Full of remorse, Coop looked at Mia. "I knew you didn't like me, but I never understood why." He stepped closer and stopped when he could see the amber flecks in her eyes. "If I had known it was yours, I would've taken it from her." He shook his head. "I'm sorry I didn't know," he said with sadness in his voice.

Mia felt deflated. She had disliked this guy for so long because of something he had never done. It made her question her abilities as a sheriff. But more importantly, what kind of person did it make her?

She believed him, because she remembered an incident with Carry and her sticky fingers at the local gas station. After that little stunt, she decided Carry was no longer someone with whom she wanted to be associated with.

"No, I need to apologize. I feel terrible for not coming to you, to ask you about it. Then I continued to harbor ill feelings toward you this whole time, and I'm sorry."

"Will you do me a favor, and please go back inside with me?" asked Coop. Then he felt the need to explain. "Every gossip in town will be spreading rumors about me tomorrow. I know I was a mischief-maker back in the day, but I'm growing a business, and I could use as much help as I can get," he said with an extended hand.

"Come on, I'll even buy you a drink." He offered with a genuine smile.

Mia wobbled a bit and said with a grin, "How about a water instead?"

CHAPTER 11

THE CURSE

Later on, after the boys straightened the poles and fixed the tent. They climbed back inside and settled into their sleeping bags.

Then Billy asked, "Does anyone have a scary story to tell?"

"I have one," answered Troy, as he reached into his backpack.

"I brought an old book from home. It was found in an old dusty trunk, which was hidden underneath some junk in the attic," said Troy, as he pulled it out.

The golden leaflet on the cover winked as it caught the light, and the worn brown cover was threadbare at the corners, where soft board poked through.

"It's called, 'Centuries Old, Myths, and Legends,'" said Troy.

Billy turned on a battery-powered lantern to generate more light as Troy searched for the story he wanted to tell.

When he opened the book, the musty smell of the old yellowing pages hit the air.

"So, this one is about a curse. I thought it would be a good story, since you have a crazy cat lady living next door," Troy said. Then he found the page and read aloud:

'The Curse of the Vandalow,'

There were people which roamed the land for over a thousand years. They wandered into small towns and made money selling elixirs, medicines, and items to ward off evil spirits. The people told stories, sang songs, and danced. They even gave readings to the desperate people of the town. Then, a few days later, they would vanish.

As legend would go, if you mistreated the travelers, or made them mad. They would put a hex on you!

One morning, an old farmer named Bidlow came into town for supplies. He saw the colorful, wooden carved caravan of vardos, or wagons, and was angered. The townsfolk surmised that he had been duped by an earlier caravan.

Boldy, he walked up to the group and shouted at them. He told them they were not welcome there and they must leave at once!

The leader of the caravan was an elderly man with black and silver-streaked hair. He wore an old top hat with a matching black vest. When he approached the angry man; he muttered with a decorum of calm, and he lifted his hands, palms up, in a pleading gesture. The headman informed him they only needed supplies and soon they will be on their way.

The next morning, the angry man, Bidlow, showed up again. He brought a few friends this time, and they rode into town on horseback. The leader, yet again, came out and spoke to them. They had ordered their supplies and were waiting for their purchases to be delivered. But not to worry. They would be gone by the next day.

The third day dawned, and Bidlow came early. He brought even more men with him to chase them right out of town. The men were angry, and the travelers were frightened by them. They packed everything up as hastily as they could.

A young gypsy girl seen playing several feet away from the caravan was accidentally run over by a horse and rider. A young woman screamed and cried as she ran to her daughter. She scooped her up and ran back to the safety of the caravan.

An old crone heard the screams and stepped outside from the back of a brush vardo. Using an old, crooked, walking stick, she took care as she stepped down the stairs attached to the back of the wagon. She leaned her walking stick against the wooden vardo, then walked toward the angry man. The old woman's white hair was covered by a black scarf, and her beaded necklaces and bracelets glimmered in the morning sun. Her face was bronzed and wrinkled from traveling in the harsh elements, and her hands were knobby and twisted from age.

Unafraid, she walked up to the angry man and yelled, 'You! You are the leader, so you must pay!'

She spoke in a foreign language, none of the townsfolk had ever heard before, as she made a wide circular motion with her hands and threw tiny seeds at him from her pockets. A great wind blew as seed and dust circled into the air around them.

At the end of her invocation, she pointed an old, crooked finger at him. The horses became spooked as they whinnied and shied away from the old crone, and the men grew fearful as they rode out of town.

Years later, the man became old and frail. Widowed and alone, he moved into town. His wife had passed away in a tragic accident.

One day, the horses came loose from her buggy as she drove from town with supplies. She had stated to the storekeeper the farm was overrun with cats, and she needed to be rid of them.

When the farmer moved to town, the townsfolk began to have troubles and tribulations. There were vandalisms and thefts. Objects worked one minute and were broken the next.

But what was most troubling were the cats! They showed up one day and the count grew more and more.

The old man, frail and weak, soon died. But the town continued to have problems.

On a bright full moon night, the mercantile owner was brutally attacked. He was found in the morning bitten and bloody, while sitting on the wooden floor leaning against the wall. The shop owner had taken a brand-new shotgun from behind the counter, and a box of spilled shells laid next to him as he sat shaken and exhausted.

The people were frightened by the story he told. Fond of cats, the store owner was delighted to see a calico wandering around the back of the mercantile. Enchanted by the little lady. He allowed her to enter the store to hunt. Expecting to get rid of a few mice he had observed earlier that day. He doted on the cat, and served her a small saucer of fresh cream, then went to the backroom to do inventory for an hour.

Suddenly, he heard a commotion at the front of the store. Instantly regretting his decision to allow the cat inside, he walked out of the back room. He was certain the cat had knocked a lantern over and shattered it.

But the cat was no longer there. What he saw chilled him to the bone. He felt his eyes were deceiving him at first, so he swung the lantern farther out in front of him to get a better look.

Standing in the front window, backlit by the full moonlight, was a wet looking, gray-skinned creature. It stood two feet high on its back legs, had claws at the end of its little gnarled hands, and big pointy ears. It bared its pointed white teeth as it growled at him and hunched its tiny back. Then it sprang and ran at him!

He grabbed the closest weapon next to him, which was a broom, as he ran to the back door. He swung the wooden door open as the creature reached him, and he gave it a whack out onto the porch.

But when he opened the door, more creatures were waiting. They growled and sprang at him. He fought them off with a broom and sprang back inside, then barricaded the door shut!

Of course, the town folk didn't believe him. But he limped over to the backdoor and showed them proof. The door was scarred deep with scratches about 3 feet high. The store owner swore the cat had transformed into what they now called a *Vandalow*.

Since the wild creatures vandalized everything, they touched, and the old man named William Bidlow brought them there. They named it, in part, after him.

The story spread like wildfire throughout the town. Families, which were already hit hard by the Vandalow, pulled up stakes and left. Mothers and children were sent to stay with family elsewhere.

Then the men of the town acted. They fought the Vandalow until every one of them was gone.

They learned a hard lesson that summer, long ago. Never mess with the travelers.

We believe we found the curse! It was hand-written in an old book of curses and recipes. We are certain it belonged to the very woman that cursed Mr. Bidlow.

Happily, we interpreted the invocation to English.

Troy created an atmosphere as he changed his voice. Now, with shaky breaths, he moved the pitch of his voice up an octave, to sound like an old crone as he read:

Upon a certain age, when death is near, the slow death takes place, and the curse appears. A wisping of creatures, escape from the breast, when the soul is absent during the little death. It

will manifest in darkness and hide at night.
Hidden in form until sacrificed to the full
moon's light …

"Oh, that was a creepy story," Dean said, while hugging his pillow close.

"It makes me wonder about the old lady and the cats next door," said Billy, as he leaned back on his pillow and laced his fingers behind his head. He stared at the shadows playing across the top of the tent.

"I think it's strange that you had to work on your brand-new bike already," said Butch as he leaned forward.

"You know something? I think you're right. I rode it home from the store yesterday, and I didn't have any problems with it." Billy thought about the chain and how it hung loosely on his bike. "There's no way it just popped off like that. Not all by itself."

Troy put the book back into his bag and said, "You probably didn't notice the chain was loose when you bought it." He shrugged, then opened his sleeping bag and climbed inside to relax.

CHAPTER 12

THE NIGHT RIDE

Sheriff Halsey worked a few quick night shifts. He implemented a plan to watch over the town while the residents were safely tucked into their beds.

He wanted to apprehend the person or persons who vandalized the vehicles and bring them to justice. With deft hands he guided the cruiser as he drove west, then took the curve north, toward the center of town.

Upon entering the plaza, he slowed down and scanned each of the stores. He drove past the church with its bright white facade, easily observing if any miscreants were lurking about. Moonlight fell upon the landscape, creating an ethereal scene in the center of town, as he saw the dark, luscious garden, and the grand gazebo.

The Sheriff made a complete loop around the block of businesses, seeing nothing suspicious. So, he drove through the neighborhoods, beginning with where Jeff Trowbridge lived.

The boys were going to suffer the consequences if they didn't accomplish what they were instructed to do. The next step for them would be community service, and Halsey had decided they would help the elders of the town. For now, it was a wait and see type of situation.

Halsey smiled as he drove passed the Trowbridge's place. Jeff did a great job taking care of the lawn. He even edged the driveway, which made the property look sharp.

"I might have to pay that kid to work on my lawn." Halsey spoke aloud to the empty car. Then he grinned as he coasted on down the road. Maybe he was making a difference after all. Even if it was a slight one.

CHAPTER 13

NOSEY NEIGHBORS

It was growing late into the evening, and the air had cooled outside, so the boys settled down to unwind.

Relaxed, Billy sunk into his pillow with his hands cupped behind his head. Deep in thought, he stared at the stars through the netting at the top of the tent.

Butch sat cross-legged on his sleeping bag, busily searching for his own story to tell at the next sleepover.

He looked up when Billy asked, "What time is it?"

"It's almost midnight."

It was quiet in the rest of the tent since Troy and Dean had fallen asleep.

"You know what?" Billy asked.

"What?"

"I've been thinking about Troy's story, and how the old lady next door has had more and more cats show up this last week."

Butch put his phone down and the tent grew dark, as he asked, "Are you serious?"

"How else can it be explained? I mean, my bike worked perfectly yesterday. And before you say it's just my imagination, I really looked it over before spending money on it."

"How can we tell if it's these Vanda-thingies?" asked Butch.

"It's Vandalow." Billy corrected.

"Okay, Vandalow. How are we supposed to find out if they're real?"

"Let's go check it out." Billy said, as he sat up to gauge Butch's expression.

"That's not a good idea. We might accidentally scare the old lady, and I really don't want to get grounded again."

"Come on, we'll only be over there for a minute, and then we'll come straight back." Billy grew eager with the idea as he begged. "And if something happens, I'll take the blame. We won't be over there long. Just a skip over, and then a hop back. I promise," said Billy as he waited for an answer.

"Fine! But if we get caught, you're on your own." Butch relented and fumbled for his sneakers. Then grabbed a lantern and turned it on to its lowest setting.

Billy stood up, completely dressed.

"Seriously?" asked Butch as he rolled his eyes.

Billy shrugged as he replied, "Apparently, you forget who my brother is."

A few minutes later, they snuck to the doorway, unzipped the canvas tent, and slipped out into the darkness.

An old privacy fence sat between the adjoining properties, so they walked to the street and crept in from the front. A lamp post sat along the street. But the tree next to it swallowed the light, leaving everything in shadow.

Butch held the lantern while Billy fiddled with the old, rusted latch on the gate. When it finally let loose, he pushed it open. But immediately stopped as the bottom corner of the gate made a loud scraping noise across the sidewalk.

Butch whispered, "Wait! You need to lift the gate to keep it from making noise."

Billy nodded, then lifted the gate up and swung it open.

Surprised that the hinges didn't squeak and give them away, they crept through the entrance.

Butch switched his phone to flashlight mode and handed it to Billy. Then Billy pointed the light to the left of the house, as they both looked at each other and nodded.

Once they were at the side of the house, Billy shut the flashlight off.

"Turn it back on," whispered Butch.

Billy shook his head, whispering, "We need to let our eyes adjust to the darkness. Otherwise, we are going to get caught."

They stood still for a moment to let their eyes adjust, and it didn't take long since the moon was glowing a spectral light all over the yard.

Billy asked quietly, "Ready?"

Butch replied, "Ready."

Together, they walked up to the first window and looked inside.

The soft yellow light originated from a single petite lamp with a shade so heavy it diminished the light in the room. It was placed next to an old television. Across the tiny room sat a solitary, yellow cushioned chair, with a matching ottoman placed next to it.

Billy had never visited his neighbor's house, and it made him sad to see one lonely chair in the living room.

"Let's go," Butch whispered.

Through the tall weeds, they made their way to the next window and looked inside. To the right of the room, on the far wall, there was a doorway that led into the kitchen. A bed was placed with its headboard to the left against the wall, and the covered mattress took up the middle of the room. They saw a light filtering in from the kitchen somewhere, and it created a muted atmosphere.

The silhouette of a small woman rested on the bed with her back to them. Then, from the form, something moved.

Shocked, the boys jumped back and looked at each other.

"What was that?" Butch whispered.

Billy fought the ghoulish images that whirled into his mind as he stepped forward and slowly peeked inside. He squinted his eyes to get a better look, and said, "It's a huge cat!"

Butch asked, "Really?" As he looked for himself.

Then the old woman rolled onto her back, with her face pointed toward the ceiling, as the huge cat sat on the far side of her body and stared at her.

What happened next took Billy's breath away. He could hear his heartbeat, rapid fire, in his throat.

The bodice of her nightgown began to glow.

It started small, with a bright, bluish white radiance coming from her chest. The cat moved closer to the illumination, and they saw the swirling of light in the cat's eyes as it seemed mesmerized by the movement.

Suddenly, a small ball of light came out of her chest. It streamed up with a comet-like tail and shot up toward the ceiling. It bounced along the ceiling and slipped out through the top of the doorway into the kitchen. Then up popped another.

The giant cat grabbed it with its huge paws and gobbled it up with lightning speed. While the cat was busy eating the tiny globe, two more popped out and floated and bounced in the same direction as the first. They watched in disbelief while the cat grabbed another Wisp as it escaped from her body.

"The cat is killing them," said Billy.

Then more came out of her chest with such speed that their tails of light seemed attached to the next globe. It looked like a beam of constant light. There were so many orbs that the ceiling became bright with them, and the room glowed an ethereal bluish white.

A few floated by the window, searching for a way to escape. One bounced along the glass, then it hung motionless right in front of their faces.

Billy put his face close to the window to get a better look, but Butch backed away. The globe morphed into a wicked looking, light gray, wooden faced creature with an enormous head and a tiny body.

It made no sound as it opened its mouth in a silent, angry scream. Billy yelped and jumped back. He turned toward Butch and said, "Run!"

But Butch had already turned toward the front of the house and was two strides into a sprint. Billy felt so scared that he didn't even give the situation another thought. He just ran.

CHAPTER 14

AFTER MIDNIGHT

When he turned the car swiftly around the corner, Midnight knew he was closing in on them. His headlights beamed the truth of the situation straight to his brain. They're here, he thought, while shadows danced around the car.

The count grew as he rolled along the darkened street. They silently ran back and forth across the road while he made his way closer to the epicenter. Their glowing yellow eyes gave them away when they looked at the oncoming headlights. They hid behind cars and underneath bushes as he drove by.

Midnight gripped the steering wheel tighter, while the hairs rose on the back of his neck. He was close.

Midnight drove past a gray house with black trim and several cats were sitting like statues in the front yard.

The next house looked overtaken by movement, as little shadowy figures moved in a constant state of unease. This had to be the place of the portico. Midnight kept the rental safe, as he drove around the corner and parked the car. From there, he would walk back to investigate the anomaly.

He popped the trunk open to inspect the cache of his trade as he palmed a long, heavy silver flashlight and a few other devices for protection. Discreetly, he shut the trunk with a click and made his way back to the point of contact.

The aggravating limp would not relent from the injury to his foot as Midnight stretched his legs. The doctors said, 'it will heal in time.'

Unfortunately, he didn't have the luxury of time and this town didn't have the luxury either.

Midnight turned the corner and noted two shadowy figures moving in front of the house. Quietly, he crept back into the shadows, observing the two individuals as they entered the front yard. He continued forward when they walked out of sight, past the corner of the home. Camouflaged by the cover of several bushes, Midnight remained hidden and watched closely.

Curiosity got the best of him, when he saw two youthful faces step to the first window of the home. Their expressions were lit up by a yellow light coming from the room, and by their height and appearance, he realized they were just boys. He watched and waited while they proceeded along the house, disappearing into the night.

But then he saw their faces again, as they stood motionless, gazing into the next window. Their faces glowed with a pallor of blue, as one boy backed away, and the other drew closer to the light. The boy, who stepped

87

away, turned, and ran toward the front of the house while the other boy jumped back from the window.

Midnight heard one of them say, "Run!" as he gripped the flashlight and readied himself for action. He watched as they ran out of the gate, down the sidewalk, and around the privacy fence to the house next door. Then the boys sprinted down the driveway and disappeared.

Primed to see what frightened the boys, he snuck across the street and made his way to the second window. Midnight looked beyond the glass, and for the first time, he believed the legend was true. The curse was real! He hadn't seen it firsthand for himself and thought, like many other myths; the story was fake.

Midnight took in the scene, as he watched a beam of light stream from the tiny woman. It swirled, then broke apart, and bounced around the top of the room. He saw a huge cat swipe at the ray of light with its massive paw and pop a globe into its mouth. The cat chewed once, then swallowed. Her mighty protector was doing the best he could at keeping the Wisps from entering this realm.

Midnight stared, hypnotized by the globes, while they flowed like a river toward the ceiling. Then he noticed her shoulders were lifting from the bed as the glowing orbs pulled from her chest. She was limp as her upper torso floated up with the draw of the escaping Wisps. It was as if they knew their entrance to this realm was closing soon, and they were rushing the gate. He had to act fast. They were going to kill her if he didn't stop them.

With his foot screaming in pain, Midnight leaped away from the window and ran toward the front entrance of the house. He pulled open the wooden screen door and jiggled the handle, but it was securely locked. The next course of action needed was to use his shoulder to breach the door, and when he took a step back to gain momentum; he was stopped short by a deep male voice.

"Stop, right there!" Sheriff Halsey shouted.

Midnight froze.

"Now, slowly, step away from the door," Halsey commanded.

A blinding light lit up the front of the house, and his dark silhouette was the lone offender. He raised his hands and backed slowly away from the entrance. He knew how it looked and it looked dishonorable. Midnight used caution, as he calmly turned and walked toward the blinding light.

The Sheriff called him over to the car as he exited the vehicle and met him at the small wooden gate.

"Do you have any weapons on you?" asked Halsey as he placed Midnight against the cruiser.

"I have a few," Midnight answered.

"Please, put your hands on the car."

Midnight knew he needed to help the old woman, but rushing an officer of the law would only escalate his circumstances. He had tangled with the police before, and he knew his way around every procedure that fell his way. But rushing an officer in the middle of the night, when he was alone, could make for a dangerous situation.

"Do you have anything in your pockets that might poke me if I search you?" asked Halsey.

"No," answered Midnight, as he felt the unnecessary frisk. The Sheriff confiscated his weapons and flashlight, then set them on top of his cruiser. Midnight was thankful he'd left his 9mm handgun locked in his gun case inside the trunk of the car.

Sheriff Halsey spoke with authority, "I'm going to place handcuffs on you for your protection, as well as for mine. The cuffs will come off when everything gets settled, and you've explained to me why you were breaking into that house."

Midnight felt the metal handcuff wrap around his wrist, and with a few clicks, it tightened. His free hand was brusquely taken from the car and promptly placed behind his back and secured within seconds.

"Now, why are you breaking into Ms. DeLeon's house?" Halsey asked, as he stood there looking big and intimidating. Which wasn't difficult for him to do.

"I believe the woman inside the house may be in danger right this second. Will you please go check on her?" asked Midnight.

Midnight could tell by the look in the Sheriff's eye that he believed him. But he was no fool.

"If you'll sit in the back of my cruiser. Then I will do a welfare check on her," said Halsey.

Midnight nodded and waited for the officer to open the door. He quickly sat down and slipped his feet inside the car, as the Sheriff stooped to look him in the eye.

"I have a question before I go check on her. Are you here alone?" asked Halsey.

Midnight thought of the issue at hand and the boys from earlier, as he replied, "That is a troublesome question to answer. I came here alone, but you may not be alone out there. So, please be careful."

Halsey furrowed his brow at the man and promptly shut the door in his face. Then stood up, shaking his head and faced the house, mumbling, "What kind of answer was that?" Then he fished his hand into his pocket and pulled out his keys.

Halsey was suspicious of him, and he wasn't sure if the man had an accomplice. So, he held his key fob eye level to the stranger's face, and as he looked him square in the eye, he pushed the button. The locks on the doors made an audible click as they rolled into place.

Halsey turned around, walked up to the front door, and knocked. Then, after a few moments, he knocked again. Since he heard nothing and saw no movement. He walked around the corner of the house and followed the driveway to the backyard. A cat yowled when he accidentally stepped on its tail as several more cats ran past the illumination from his flashlight.

"My God! How many cats did this old woman have?" Halsey asked aloud, as he walked to the back door and banged on it. He inspected the kitchen through the square window, but a white gauze curtain blocked his view. With his nose pressed to the glass, he squinted his eyes, watching for any movement. Then he checked the doorknob, and it came open with half a turn. The Sheriff stepped inside and spoke loudly with a firm voice. "Hello Ms. DeLeon! This is the Pope County Sheriff's Department!"

But nobody answered, as Halsey checked the first door to his right. It was an empty bathroom. Turning around, he could see through the empty hallway to the front of the house. There were no sounds alerting him of another intruder, so he peered into the next open doorway.

Laying there on the bed was the old woman he had talked to that very day at Luther's hardware store. She was busy buying WD-40 for the squeaky hinges on her cabinet door and was asking around for a handyman to help with the upkeep on her house.

"Ms. DeLeon, it's me Jake Halsey."

She didn't move.

"I'm stepping into your room, and I don't want to alarm you," he said as he moved forward.

Still, there was no movement.

Halsey walked in and bent over her. He didn't know if she was breathing, so he checked for a pulse. But it wasn't there.

He took the blanket from the foot of her bed, and with great care, Halsey covered her body with it. Jake stood for a moment, thinking about Ms. DeLeon and what a shame it was to see her now deceased.

Then he walked back into the kitchen and studied the room. A window had been left open, so he stepped across the small kitchen to close it as he glanced outside.

It was a dark night indeed, he thought, as he felt despondent. Halsey had lost someone under his protection. Auntie had depended on him to keep her safe, and he had failed her.

At first, he felt sad, then guilty, but now he was working on mad as his enormous hands balled into massive fists. He knew what kind of damage they could do if he lost his temper, so he took a minute to calm himself. The anger he felt consumed him for a few moments as Halsey let it rage and run its course so it would dissipate. Then he popped his knuckles and took a few deep breaths, because he knew his anger could cloud his judgement. Movement and action would help clear his head, because he needed to do his job and do it well.

Walking through Auntie's home, he checked every room and window throughout the rest of the house.

While he was in a secure location, he took out his phone and made a call.

"Pope County Coroner's, Angel speaking." He saw the irony in her name when he had to call her, but never for one second thought it funny.

"Angel it's Sheriff Halsey. I need a deceased person picked up over here in Sugar Bee." He glanced at an envelope to confirm the house address and as he recited the information. "The address is 1313 Black Willow Lane. It's Ms. Auntie DeLeon."

"Do we need an autopsy performed?" Angel asked, clear and concise, with a hint of a southern drawl.

"Yes, but I believe she may have passed away peacefully. I just need to make sure," Halsey replied.

They said their goodbyes, and he slipped his phone back into his pocket.

He opened the back door and was at once taken aback. Astounded by the wave of yellow eyes that glowered at him from the darkness. Realization then hit him! They were cats! But the number of cats was astounding, as the light shining from the kitchen reflected in their eyes before they scurried away. Halsey made a mental note to have Mia make some calls about this issue in the morning.

Then he went out the back door, being careful not to step on them as they crossed his path. A few of those fuzzballs made their presence known with a yowl as Halsey walked into the night.

Midnight knew, when he saw the sheriff's face as he walked back to the cruiser, that it was going to be a long night.

* * *

Billy and Butch sprinted up the driveway to the backyard. When they reached the tent, their hands shook, so much that they fumbled with the zipper. They couldn't get it open fast enough. Then, as it opened, they both dove inside and frantically zipped it closed.

"Guys! Guys! Wake up!" Billy yelled; he needed his buddies alert.

Butch shook them and yelled, "Come on, wake up guys, it's an emergency!"

Troy and Dean roused sleepily.

"Throw in a word like emergency, and it did the trick," said Butch.

Troy sat up first and stifled a yawn. "What's happening? Is it still dark? It's still the middle of the night," he finished flatly. He gave in to his next yawn and stretched for a second. Then he realized, "Did somebody say it was an emergency or was I dreaming?"

Dean sat straight up, which made Billy flinch. He didn't even have his eyes open as he asked, "What?"

Billy looked at Troy and back at Dean, and said, "You guys will not believe what we just saw!"

"What!" Dean said, with his eyes still closed. He wasn't even awake and looked as if he planned on falling backwards at any moment and going back to sleep.

"The old lady next door! She has the curse!" Billy whispered, fearing what might happen if he said it too loudly.

With that bit of useless information, Dean flopped back onto his pillow, and with a groan, he said, "Billy, I'm tired. Let me sleep."

Butch's voice shook as he said, "I saw it with my very own eyes. These glowing lights that resembled orbs were coming out of her."

"If this is a joke. I'm not laughing," Troy scowled.

"Does this look like a joke?" asked Billy. In the excitement, Billy had clutched Butch's phone and somehow hit the record button. Billy handed it over to Butch to show him what he'd done.

Dean sat up, and everyone gathered around the phone as Butch hit play.

Their faces lit up from the light of the screen as they gathered around it and watched everything unfold. The screen was showing only darkness, but you could hear their gasps of surprise. Billy's words echoed out of the speaker when he said, "The cat is killing them."

While watching the screen, Billy realized at that exact moment he was going to change their perception of the world.

In the video, he shot his hands out forward and Billy yelled, "Right there!"

A floating, blurry, blue-white light came onto the screen. Butch paused the phone and backed it up a few frames. It was hazy. But there it sat frozen, morphed into an angry looking, night light bobble head.

The face was made from a light blue shadow. It looked identical to a chubby, round-faced baby created out of wood. It had tiny, gray vertical lines which looked like the bark of a young hickory tree, and the top of its head was jagged. Just like a broken tree limb. It glowed bright white, blurry, and floated in the air.

Butch let it continue to play, and Billy whispered loudly, "Run!" The phone screen jostled with movement and the video ended with Butch turning on the lantern, and a yellow glow could be seen as they got inside the tent to safety.

It grew quiet in the tent. Not a word was uttered until Troy broke the silence and whispered, "It's the curse!"

Everyone was silent again as their brains tried to wrap around the very thought of the myth being real.

Then a loud banging from next door made everyone jump!

Troy and Dean scrambled to put their shoes on, and each one grabbed a light source and climbed out of the tent.

Billy was leading the way as he crept to the corner of the house. After seeing what he had already been privy to, he wasn't sure what else he was going to find. Then a thought popped into his head, as Billy halted and thought about the storekeeper. The man had been attacked by a Vandalow in the story. He didn't have to think twice as he turned around and looked at his friends and said, "We need weapons."

Everyone nodded in agreement. Billy led the way as they snuck over to the shed. He opened the door and looked around with his flashlight as he handed an old wooden baseball bat to Troy. Next, he found another one, which Max had altered with nails hammered through it. The nails were sticking out everywhere as he carefully handed it to Butch. He needed two more weapons as he continued to look around the dusty shed.

At some point, Max, accidentally, or on purpose, broke a wooden rake handle and Billy found it leaning in the far corner of the shed. He pulled it out and handed it to Dean.

"Sweet, I get a spear!" Dean smiled as stuck it into the ground.

Billy discovered a small, handled axe hanging on the wall, resting on two rusted nails. As he pulled it from the wall, he noticed the heft of the axe, and it felt good in his hands. He turned around with a look of determination and asked, "Ready?"

They cued up their weapons and signaled with a nod.

The boys snuck over to the corner of Billy's house next to the driveway. They looked toward the street and saw the end of the sheriff's car with its hazard lights flashing.

Billy eyed the privacy fence with apprehension because they stood straight across from the bedroom window. He almost jumped when a glaring light from the cruiser shot across the property. It brightly illuminated the house and tall weeds in the yard to a faded white and threw everything else into a dark shadow.

Billy noticed the light was on in her bedroom and braced himself for what might happen next. But he realized the illumination was different. It was a warm and inviting light that filled the window. Inquisitively, he walked over to the privacy fence and peered through it. He saw Sheriff Halsey standing in Auntie's bedroom right beside her bed. The Sheriff was talking to her as he bent over, probably to check on her. But then he straightened and just stood there for a few minutes.

The boys watched as he picked up a blanket and spread it over her.

Butch asked, "Is she dead?"

Billy couldn't believe what happened to the old woman, and he felt guilty, as he said, "It looks like it."

They watched while Halsey shut the light off and walked into the other room.

Billy snuck along the driveway toward the street. He saw the car and noticed there was a shadow in the shape of a person, sitting in the back seat as the boys gathered behind him.

"Who is it?" Butch asked under his breath.

"I don't know." Billy stared.

They watched as Halsey walked to the car and opened the driver's side door. The lights came on, and they saw the man with dark hair sitting in the back. His expression was grave as he gazed at Halsey.

They overheard Halsey tell him she was deceased, and they were waiting for backup.

The man leaned forward in the seat and said something to the sheriff, but they couldn't hear him. But they heard the Sheriff's reply, as he stood with his head ducked down, looking at him.

He said, "What blue light? The only thing I saw out there were way too many cats. I don't know about the town being in big trouble, but I am certain of one thing right now. I found you here with a deceased woman, and that doesn't look good for you."

The boys waited and watched while a white van with no windows parked in front of the neighbor's house. On the side of it, in generic writing, it read, "POPE COUNTY CORONER." They watched two men with a gurney, as well as Halsey, go inside to convey the body.

Then, a few minutes later, they came back outside with her. A black zippered tarp blanketed her slender form as they transferred her to the van.

It felt terrible to see the little old lady being hauled off with no one to mourn her. By now, a few porch lights had popped on and a few nosey neighbors were standing along the sidewalk across the street.

Billy didn't want to see anymore. "Let's go back to the tent and look at that story again. But first, let's get our stuff and go inside the house."

The boys agreed as they turned and walked to the tent. They quickly grabbed their sleeping bags and backpacks, then waited for each other in the yard.

Butch and Dean each grabbed a handle on the end of the cooler and hefted it up into the air while the group walked toward the safety of the house.

Since Billy's mom was busy working a twelve-hour shift, she wouldn't be home for several hours. Which worked out perfectly. They wouldn't be bothering her as she slept.

The boys were yawning when they dragged themselves into the living room. They were tired from the frightful events of the evening and the lack of sleep. After one crazy night, they all agreed to look at the book in the morning and passed out.

CHAPTER 15

MIDNIGHT GOES TO JAIL

First, Halsey pulled into the department's garage and let the automatic door roll shut. Next, he walked to the trunk to retrieve the black evidence bag. Then he walked around to the passenger door and opened it.

Midnight put his feet on the ground and slid out.

Halsey said, "Let's go," as he pointed toward the door.

Halsey watched as Midnight walked with a limp, but he also noticed the man looked formidable, which kept him on guard while he transported the prisoner.

Midnight stopped and waited while the sheriff entered the key code to unlock the steel door and open it for him.

Recycled, cool air hit them as they went into the interior of the building. Halsey led a handcuffed Midnight into the hallway and said, "Turn to the left."

Midnight turned and entered a white, sterile looking room.

Halsey took one metal cuff from the man's wrist and watched while he stretched and brought his hands forward, as if he'd done this before. Then the man waited for him to place the cuffs back on in front of him.

"Sit, right there." Halsey nodded to a brown metal chair.

Midnight pulled the chair out and took a seat. On the wall opposite of his chair, there was a small, mirrored window. This was a setback. A hiccup in his plans.

Halsey left the room and came back a few moments later, carrying Midnight's wallet. He opened the black leather square, took out Midnight's driver's license, and studied it for a moment. The man's smug expression was captured perfectly on the card. He flipped it over and tested the corner for sturdiness by bending it a few times.

"Oh, it's real," said Midnight. The handcuffs clinked as he placed his elbows on top of the table and clasped his hands together.

Halsey read aloud, "Midnight Javez Leõn."

"My name is pronounced, Midnight Havez, the 'J' is silent, Lee-own. But you may call me Midnight."

"Forty-one years old, brown hair, blue eyes. It says here that you're from Filigree, Louisiana." Halsey noticed Midnight's hair was shorter in the photo.

"Yes, that's me."

"Well Midnight, I need to know why you were at Auntie DeLeon's house."

Midnight paused for a moment. This is where things got tricky when dealing with law enforcement. It was always best to have them talk to a higher power. Sometimes he got lucky, and they would believe every word he uttered, but unfortunately, he ran into Halsey prematurely.

"Will you please do me a favor and pull out the black card?" asked Midnight.

Halsey searched his wallet and pulled the card free.

"Yes, that's the one. Please call the number on the card," said Midnight.

The only thing written on the card was a phone number printed in gold. Halsey flipped it over and the number glinted at him again.

He looked up at Midnight and said, "So, you will answer none of my questions." It wasn't a question, but more of a statement.

"I'm sorry, but no," replied Midnight. He spread his hands as far as his restraints would allow.

Aggravated, Halsey stood up, making the chair shoot back, as he barked, "If you think I am going to…" Then he stopped mid-sentence. He would not call a number where someone on the other end of the line would tell him to let this guy go free. So, he bit his tongue and kept it to himself.

Giving no more away, Halsey lowered his voice and grumbled, "I'll be back." Then he turned around and stepped out of the room. He needed to get away from this guy, because his anger was getting the best of him.

That calm, polite demeanor either meant he was working in a field higher than his pay grade, or he was a psychopath. Either way, Mr. Ponytail wasn't going anywhere for a while.

Midnight knew there was a possibility that he could be held for up to 24 hours. He had hoped the Sheriff would make the call to set him free. Unfortunately, how this was playing out, there was a likelihood he might be sitting in here for a while. So, Midnight leaned back in the chair and resigned himself as he patiently anticipated a jail cell.

Frustrated, Halsey walked to the front office. It was nearing dawn, and Mia's shift would be starting soon. In fact, she should be coming through the door any minute now. With his hands on his hips, he took a few deep, calming breaths. He wasn't going to let this guy walk out of his station without saying a damn word to him. He wanted answers. Why was he at Auntie's place? What happened while he was there? Why is he here, and what the hell was he talking about when he asked about the blue lights?

Mia breezed through the entrance and noticed Halsey's angry expression. "What's up?" she asked while hurriedly placing her purse and latte down on her desk.

"We had a death last night. Auntie DeLeon is at the coroner's office with Angel. The man in the processing room is who I caught at her house. I'm not sure if he was breaking in or walking out of her place when I rolled up to the scene."

Mia let out a breath she hadn't realized she'd been holding. She knew eventually things would happen in her sleepy town. But she still wasn't prepared for it.

She walked over to the small window to look in on the man who sat in the interrogation room. Then wondered if this guy was the stranger everyone noticed roaming around town.

"What do I need to do?" asked Mia.

"The first thing we need to do is put this guy in a cell. Next, we need to call someone to take care of the cat problem over at Auntie's place."

Mia nodded as she picked up a notepad and informed him. "John Parker recently called. He has a rodent problem out at the mill and was asking around for several cats."

"Good, but we may need to find a way to rehome the rest. Because there are a lot of them." Halsey walked over to the black bag sitting on the back row of filing cabinets. He pulled items out of the bag as Mia stood next to him, looking at the stranger through the small window.

As if he knew what she was thinking, he added, "His name's Midnight Javez Leõn. He's from Filigree Louisiana, and I'm sure this guy is the stranger that has been loitering around town. When I caught him, he told me the town was, 'in trouble.'

I'm not sure what he meant by that, but when I asked him questions, he clammed up and told me to call a number in his wallet."

Halsey pulled out a heavy silver flashlight, a black telescoping baton, and several color coded, four-ounce bottles. He held them up to the light and sat them down next to the weapon. But then Halsey saw one more item in the bag and pulled it out. The bag was filled with a white substance.

"What is that?" Mia eyed the bag.

"I'm not sure," replied Halsey, as he sat it on top of the cream-colored filing cabinet and opened it.

105

Mia's eyes grew wide, and her heart sputtered at what he did next. Because she wouldn't have been so bold.

Halsey gave it a slight sniff and stuck his thumb and forefinger inside of the bag. He pinched a small amount and rolled it between his fingers. Then he took the substance out and tasted it.

Mia's eyes grew wide as she watched him.

He looked at Mia and said, "It's salt."

"What the heck? Why carry salt in a sandwich baggie?" she asked.

"I don't know, but I'm going to find out."

Halsey picked up the small bag and walked around the corner. He opened the solid door and entered the small white room where Midnight sat waiting.

The Sheriff placed the bag down on the table and pointed.

"Explain to me why you carry around a bag of salt?" asked Halsey.

Midnight's lips grew thin, and with raised eyebrows he said, "I could explain it to you, but you wouldn't believe me."

"Try me," Halsey said, short-tempered. He stood up, using his full height to intimidate Midnight.

"Tell me, did you make the call?" Midnight asked. Even though he already knew the answer to the question, he wanted to gauge the Sheriff's reaction.

Halsey took a breath and leaned back, and with that tiny movement, Midnight had his answer.

"I asked you about the salt. Why do you have it?" asked Halsey.

Midnight relented. "The salt is for protection."

"Salt. For protection," replied Halsey, as he shook his head in disbelief. Then he asked, "Did you take this from Auntie's house?"

"No, I never went into her house." Midnight gazed at Halsey. "I know you won't believe me, but I was helping her. She was in the throes of death when I arrived."

Midnight noticed a change in his surroundings, and he stared at the small, mirrored window. A sensitive soul was standing there, and he could feel their eyes on him. Midnight had a way of knowing when a person was close to whom he could connect. Someone with empathetic capabilities.

He knew from experience that empaths had a gateway to more capabilities. These abilities are nothing like superpowers, but they are more connected and highly attuned to the emotions and energies around them. They can see more, and be more aware of things, than the average person. He felt the openness, and empathy, to the individual right now, and he sensed it was a woman.

Midnight grew hopeful. He wanted to be able to help these people, and the only way to do that was to grow a connection.

Gazing into the mirror, he lifted his cuffed hands, showing his inability to do any harm. He wanted to help with the problem at hand.

"If you'd call the number on the card, you'd understand that I'm not here to hurt anyone. I am here to help you protect the town," Midnight said.

Halsey saw Midnight staring toward Mia in the mirror and grabbed the salt as he left the room and slammed the door behind him.

Mia was scrutinizing the stranger, and she felt he was telling the truth. But then she jumped at the sound of the door slamming and stepped back as Halsey marched around the corner.

Irritated, Halsey looked at her.

He didn't have to say a word, because she knew he was about to explode with anger.

"We are holding him for 24 hours, and I'm moving him into a cell right now," Halsey growled through clenched teeth.

Mia felt drained. She shook the feeling away and bobbed her head.

"Do me a favor, call Cooper Daniels and have him go over to Auntie's. I want him to check the place over and pick up the strays."

"I'm on it," Mia replied, and hurried to her desk. She barely sat down, and the phone rang. Mia lifted the receiver and said, "Pope County Sheriff's Department, how may I help you?"

"Who is this?" Mia asked as she scribbled on the message pad.

"Let me get your number too." Mia continued to jot down the information.

The phone's second line lit up while she was still talking to the first caller. "Please hold for a second," she said. Then answered the second call. It wasn't an emergency, but another complaint.

Halsey was busy moving the prisoner when he heard the phone ring, then another line rang, and another. What the heck was happening? He thought to himself; they were never this busy.

As if Midnight knew what he was thinking, he said, "It will only get worse."

Then Halsey walked him across the hall and into a room with two cells. Midnight stepped into the first cell, turned around, and held out his hands.

Halsey took the cuffs off and backed slowly out of the unit. He shut the barred door and locked it with a smooth click. Then, with a smug expression, Halsey said, "Let me handle it. You stay right here."

Midnight stood in the middle of the chamber as Halsey left the room. He could smell the stench of the antiseptic which did little to mask the stink of anxiety and body odor. The floors were white tiled, and the walls were painted gray, as if to remind the detainee their future looked bleak. He tested the door, and it was solid. Midnight limped to the bed and sat down to the smell of bleach as it wafted up around him. He had been in worse places, Midnight thought, as he leaned back against the wall and closed his eyes.

CHAPTER 16

MUSIC MOVES THE SOUL

John Parker drove in off the dark, deserted highway as he took exit 22 toward Sugar Bee. He had driven this road so many times that he could almost do it with his eyes closed. With every curve and hill, his truck glided like it was on autopilot.

It felt warm outside, but he rolled down the windows and smelled the sweet blossoms from the magnolia trees as he took the main road towards town. JP was listening to the radio play a magical guitar riff from a 70s song, as his excitement grew. He automatically tapped his brakes as he drove past the Fire Department and the Sheriff's station.

Then, John made the slight jog to the left to go down to the mill. The books needed to be checked for orders, and requisitions had to be signed. Moving into the new house would consume a significant amount of time, and he wanted to get the move-in done without too many interruptions from the mill.

As he drove up to the office, his headlights caught movement along the wood piles. Those dang rats were becoming a problem, he thought, as he coasted up to the office building and stopped. Then he placed his hand on the gearshift and threw it into park before he cut the engine. Already in work mode, he left his cell phone charging on the bench seat of his pickup truck.

JP walked into the office and turned on the radio. He was used to the noise from the mill and the office chatter, and with everyone gone, it was downright spooky. After turning on the radio, he walked over to his enormous desk and sat down.

Now settled in his chair, he wiggled the mouse back and forth, and waited for the computer screen to light up from sleep mode. John scooted forward to tackle the issues at hand.

Focused on the piles of paperwork, time flew by. When he checked his watch; it read past five thirty in the morning. As John leaned back in his leather chair, he groaned. Stiff from being slumped over his desk, he stood up and stretched. The paperwork was caught up for now and he was exhausted. John decided he needed a pick me up, so he turned on the coffeemaker and made a cup of joe for the road.

Memories filled his mind when he smelled the hot coffee while it filled the cup. The aroma made him feel a moment of nostalgia as he leaned against the small counter. His father had owned the mill, and he had worked here since he was a young boy.

His dad taught him everything he knew about running the lumber and sawmill, and he felt fortunate to keep the legacy going. From looking at the books, it was still doing well, and it made him proud to have such a wonderful crew working for him. Soon he would be able to give out raises to reward their diligence. The machine sputtered to a stop and hot steam rose from the filled cup.

With a smile on his lips, he picked it up and took a sip. It tasted just the way he liked it. Hot and strong. He hit the power button to shut off the small black coffee maker.

John walked out of the office and saw a few lights had been left on in the main building. He was surprised he hadn't noticed it before when he pulled into the lot, but he chalked it up to brain-drain.

The lights were supposed to be shut off at night, but a few glowing windows hung on the side of the darkened building. Bleary-eyed and bushed, he felt grumpy, as he uttered a few choice words, and walked across the wide graveled lot to the heavy steel door.

In a hurry to get home, he unlocked the door and walked inside the huge shop. A radio was playing far off in the back corner, along with the noise of a conveyor belt. The guys liked to listen to the radio as they used large push brooms and swept the floors of the massive warehouse at the end of their shift.

While shaking his head in frustration, he sat his coffee cup down on a small table filled with pamphlets for safety, employment, and insurance.

Now, feeling more irritated, John pursed his lips and stomped toward the offending noise. He was going to have a talk with his foreman about leaving lights and unnecessary equipment on when they leave the building.

As he ground his teeth, John inhaled the smell of musty sawdust and marched around the massive machine. He pushed the button to shut it off and realized something didn't feel right as the radio went up in volume.

John stopped, cocked his head, and listened. Was it his imagination, or did the radio grow louder? Was it the lack of noise from the conveyor belt which gave the music center stage in the massive building?

Then the radio changed stations every few seconds. JP ducked down as he realized someone must be in there with him. He quietly reached over and picked up a short piece of lumber. It was generally used for pushing the last portion of a wooden plank through a cutting machine, but now it was going to be used for self-defense.

He kept watch as his sneakers silently padded across the floor, while using the massive machines for cover. As he approached the area where he believed the intruder was located, he hunkered down. His shoulders flexed as he lifted the piece of heavy wood like a baseball bat.

John was on the opposite side of the machine now, and his whole body felt like a coiled spring. Poised in position, he placed his hand on top of the metal corner of the machine to glance around it. But his hand met with something wet and slimy. As he pulled his hand away, a drooping string of clear slime came with it. JP studied the offending liquid sitting on his palm when he heard a low, guttural growl. He looked up, and his entire body froze from fright.

In a wide-legged stance above him stood a small gray creature with shiny, razor-sharp teeth protruding from its mouth. Its muscular shoulders were hunched as it looked down at him. The arms were strapping and long, and it had three fingers. The middle finger, being the longest, looked vicious with its black, pointed tip. Its face looked to be all teeth, with a small, distorted nose and yellow eyes.

It sported a gray, brown, and green leaf-like mask. But the mask was actually part of its face and protruded from its bone structure. In between the brow line, it dipped in the middle and looked like the stems of two leaves smoothly glued together. The saw-like edge of the leaves continued out to the side of its head. Then ended with curled, crispy, pointed ears. The creature had a tuft of hair. Although it wasn't hair. It was purple and green, and spiky like a Tillandsia Ionantha, an air plant. The chest, which heaved with each breath, and torso of the creature looked smooth and whitish gray. The sickly color looked like the underbelly of a snake.

The teeth ultimately seized John's complete attention. They were wet with drool and jumbled altogether in tiny pinpoints. The creature's purplish black, fat upper lip curled back and quivered as it snarled. Then its toothy mouth creaked open.

John jumped back as it lunged toward him with claws out. But it landed in a collapsed heap on the ground. He took the moment and swung the piece of wood at its head and connected with an icky thump. It fell over with the force of the blow and laid still. John stepped forward and poked at it with his weapon. It didn't move. He stepped back, freaked out by the encounter, and saw something move out of the corner of his eye.

Shadows danced along the back wall as one appeared, and then another. Machines turned on and noise filled the room. John then realized that he was in danger of being surrounded. He turned around and a few more gray, green, and brown creatures jumped up on top of the machinery. Now, he counted at least five of them. Three were now standing where the first one had stood before.

He decided retreat was his only choice, so he turned to run. He made it ten strides when one of them grabbed his leg. Something sharp sunk into his calf and he screamed and kicked his leg backwards, trying to shake it off as he hopped forward on one free leg.

The weight of the creature was making it difficult to run as it was clawing and biting him. He took the end of the stick and poked the creature in the head. It stopped and turned its leering yellow eyes on him and looked him dead in the eye. He watched his own red blood dripping from the ends of its jagged teeth, and something clicked in John's brain. It was a feeling he had never felt before, and it raged and felt primal. It was kill or be killed, and he wasn't going out like this. He was a force to be reckoned with, a fighter. The adrenaline that kicked into high gear through his veins made him feel unstoppable.

These little monsters were going to keep coming and he wouldn't be able to fight off a horde of them. He took the stick and jabbed it into the creature's cruel smile. It let go and rolled away. Freed, he ran again. Although the lights were now flickering off and on, John wasn't worried, because he could make his way outside by memory. But it was difficult to see how many creatures were chasing him.

John ran around another machine and slipped on something dark and wet. He fell to his knees and popped his head up to check his surroundings. He thought for sure there was a dead person nearby. But when he lifted his hand from the dark, slick fluid, he suddenly realized it was oil, not blood. Relieved, he uttered, "Thank God!"

JP slid as he tried to gain traction out of the pool of oil and glanced at a pile of sawdust, which had been missed by an employee, under a saw. He stuck his hands and shoes in it and instantly the sawdust clung to him and soaked up the inky grease.

John peered around and hoped the little beasts had lost sight of him. He heard a growl from somewhere to the right, and it was the only answer he needed.

John shot up and forward and tried to keep balance as the sawdust stuck to the bottom of his shoes, making it slick on the dried concrete. Soon, he was moving at a good pace. His wooden stick and clothes were blackened by oil, and it made him look like a rather deranged person.

JP could see the door now as he made it to the hallway. He could hear them behind him. They were growing closer and closer. His breath came fast as his mind raced. If he stopped to swing open the door, they'd be on top of him. He had to do it as quick as possible. John shoved the crossbar handle with such force it swung open and got away from him. He grabbed at it as two of the creatures escaped outside with him. John reached out and put his hand on the door and slammed it shut.

JP saw the creatures look at each other as if they were forming a plan, as they communicated without a word. In unison, they turned to look at him with their morbid smiles attached to their faces. He shook his head in determination and gripped the stick harder as he growled back two words. "BRING IT!"

CHAPTER 17

THE NIGHT SHIFT

Max and Jeff followed the moonlit path down to the river. The luminescent moon reflected off the dry packed earth, forming a white line to their destination. Light from the moon bounced off the top of the shiny leaves of the bushes and trees and left the bottom half in shadow.

The river had the appearance of roiling black liquid and flowed along the west side of Sugar Bee. Then it snaked east to run along the south side of town. It flowed past the mill and continued under the highway bridge, then turned south again.

"Hey, did you see Shelby Fontaine yesterday?" asked Max as they strolled down the hill.

"Is she the one that wore those super short cutoff jeans with a red bikini top?" asked Jeff.

"Oh man, did she ever she is mighty F-I-N-E, fine!"

"Yeah, but she looks like trouble."

"Oh, she can give me trouble anytime she wants to," said Max.

They both chuckled as they continued along the narrow path to the old stone bridge, where they planned to sit on the ledge and drop their fishing lines into the river.

Upon reaching the bridge, they walked to the middle, and Max sat his lantern on the ground. After sitting down, he reached into his backpack and pulled out a white styrofoam box. "That old sheriff is a pain in the ass," Max said as he lifted the lid and shook the box filled with worms and dirt, looking for the best one to use.

"Yeah, he is, but when I mowed the lawn, mom gave me twenty bucks for doing it," Jeff grinned. "So, I bought us a slice of pepperoni from the gas station." He pulled out the food from his knapsack and handed Max a cardboard package in the shape of a pizza slice.

"Sweet!" said Max, as he quickly put the lid on the box and sat the worms on the ground. While his mouth drooled from the smell of greasy pepperoni, cheese, and tomato sauce. He flipped the lid open on the package and took a greedy bite. After he smacked his lips, Max gave a sigh. "Mm, man! That is good," he murmured with a full mouth.

Jeff brought his hand out from behind his back and waved it back and forth in front of Max's eyes.

"Bro! You brought beer!" Max smiled a toothy grin while looking up at the can.

"Courtesy of a d-bag named Chuck. You know, the one that my mom's been dating," said Jeff with a smirk.

With a full mouth, Max smiled and took the drink.

Jeff reached into the bag and pulled out a small, black, portable speaker and sat it on top of a small flat rock. He pulled his phone from his back jean pocket and set the music to heavy metal. Then he grabbed his own beer and pizza and sat next to Max.

They bobbed their heads to the heavy beat as they gobbled up their pizza and popped open the beer. The beer was still ice cold and the sweat on the aluminum can made their hands wet.

Max produced a hellacious burp as he wiped his hand down his pant leg. After he belched loud and proud, he reached for his box of worms and plucked out a long fat juicy wriggling one.

"Bro! That hit the spot," Max said. He belched again as he stood up to bait his hook, and since Jeff brought a surprise meal, Max took a worm and baited his hook, too.

"Yeah, it was pretty tasty," said Jeff, then he took a sip of his beer. "Hey thanks for baiting my hook. Did anyone ever tell you that you are a master," he paused for effect, "baiter?"

Tight-lipped, Max closed his eyes and shook his head.

Jeff smiled at his own joke as he mimicked playing the drums with sound effects. "Ba-dum-tss!"

After dropping their lines into the water, they relaxed and listened to some tunes. But after a while, with nothing taking the bait, they grew bored.

Max stood up and announced, "I've gotta take a leak." He walked to the far end of the bridge to relieve himself as Jeff sat fishing and listening to music.

Max finished quickly and walked back toward their fishing spot. The forest was a comforting place for him. It blanketed him with calm. Max was never told what to do out here, and he liked it that way. He was free to do anything he wanted.

When his dad was around, and became mean, Max knew he could grab his gear that he kept hidden in his closet and take off to the safety of the woods.

At his loneliest moment, Jeff appeared one day, and they became fast friends. They climbed and traversed this entire area of Big Leaf, while fishing and shooting stuff with BB guns. One time, they caught a rabbit, and they skinned it and ate it. Max smiled at the memory as he reached into his backpack and pulled out a bag.

"Want some cookies?" Max showed Jeff with a shake of the baggie.

"Sure," Jeff said, with a nod.

"I snuck them from my brother's stash of goodies," Max said as he handed half the stash to Jeff and popped a whole cookie into his mouth.

* * *

After an hour of fishing and catching nothing, they packed up their stuff to begin the trek back up the winding path to the house. Jeff shut off the music and grabbed his speaker.

The instant quiet gave way to something rustling around in the forest. They both were now standing side by side, with packs on their backs and poles in their hands as they looked in the general direction of the noise.

"I hope that it's not a bear," Jeff said.

Max's heart skipped a beat. "Nah, it can't be a bear. Sounds too small. It'd make more noise."

"It could be a bear cub," Jeff said, as he pointed his measly cell phone flashlight at the noise. The weak light did little to brighten the bushes.

Unfortunately, the rustling was at the same end of the bridge they had to pass through to get home.

"I suppose we could try to scare it away," said Max, as he tightened the straps on his backpack. "Do me a favor. Grab the flashlight out of the side pocket of my pack so you can see."

Jeff stepped back and slid the flashlight out of the mesh pocket. Then he turned it on and realized it was a super bright LED light. "Thanks. It's like the surface of the sun. It's way better than my crap, light." He pointed it at the bushes as they shook again. "Yeah, let's see if we can scare it away." Jeff felt emboldened by the heft of the flashlight.

"Are you ready?" asked Max.

"Yeah." Jeff hiked his knapsack up higher onto his shoulders.

"On the count of three," whispered Max as he took the lead. "One, two…"

They both jumped back as a raccoon leaped out of the bushes towards them. Then it stopped and looked at them and hissed! After that, it ran away from them along the path. The same path that they were going to travel.

Max laughed, bending at the waist, and said, "That little turd thought he was going to get us!"

Jeff said, "Admit it! You were skeered."

"Bro! I thought you were going to pee your pants and fall into the river!" Max laughed again and then switched gears. He had a great idea. "Hey, you wanna go see if Shelby is hanging out with the girls over by The Buzz Pub?"

"Let's do it!"

They decided not to follow the path and the raccoon. Instead, they hiked straight up the big hill to where it would come out closer to the south side of town. Because of the physical exertion it took to climb up the hillside, they didn't talk much.

Soon, they heard faint music coming from the bar as they walked up the last steps to the edge of town. They sat their gear down behind a tree and peeked out into the parking lot.

Max chuckled, "Look over there." As he pointed to a car that bounced a little in the back of the parking lot.

Jeff snickered too when he saw the gray car moving.

"Hey, I've got an idea. Hang on a second and I'll be right back," Max said, as he slipped back into the woods.

Jeff watched while Max's silhouette popped out on the other side of the gray sedan. He was crouching as he snuck over behind the bar to where the dumpsters were hidden, in the back, behind the building. Then Jeff laughed when he saw him half crouched as he ran back to the woods.

Max popped back out of the woods next to Jeff and grabbed something from his backpack hidden behind the tree.

"What are you doing?" Jeff asked.

"I picked up these cigarette butts from over there. Just watch," whispered Max, as he flicked the lighter and lit the ends. Then, when they were glowing red, he stepped back into the darkness and put them several inches apart. It looked like two menacing, glowing eyes.

"Oh, ha ha! You're gonna scare the sauce out of them!"

"We've just gotta time it right and, oh man! I can't wait. Let's go!"

They backed into the woods and snuck out closer to the car. The music was so loud inside the bar that the thumping of the bass and the muffled lyrics were easy to hear behind the vehicle.

Max made sure that the butts were lit well before they got there. But by the time they found a suitable spot, one of them had already snuffed out. Now they needed to use the lighter again, which could give them away.

They planned to hide behind a gigantic tree and huddle around the lighter as they lit the old acrid cigarette butt. A streetlight's luminescence struggled to reach through the thick forest and shot past both sides of the giant tree. Which made it feel as though they were walking through the forest with only a nightlight on. But they managed well enough to hide in the shadow of it. Their faces lit up brightly, as the flame licked around the white paper, and the last of the tobacco caught fire and glowed.

Max took his thumb off the tab of the lighter, and with the lack of fuel to feed the flame, it went out. They were momentarily thrown into blackness.

Max smiled a wicked grin and looked at Jeff. Jeff stepped back and the dim afterglow from the streetlight lit up his expression. Max's image of joy turned to confusion as he saw Jeff's face.

He had never seen Jeff look the way he did right now, and the night blindness from the light of the flame made him feel like his eyes were playing tricks on him. Jeff looked scared.

"What?" asked Max, and then he realized Jeff wasn't looking at him. He was looking behind him. Max quickly turned. He wanted to see what horrified Jeff so badly that he made such a disturbing looking face, with wide eyes and jaw dropped, leaving his mouth hanging open from shock. But he saw nothing.

"What?" he repeated, and that is when it stepped out of the shadow. Just one weak stream of light shot across its face. It was a wet looking gray creature with huge spikey teeth. It had sunken beady eyes, and what looked almost like a snout, and wide, big, pointed ears that shot out from the sides of its head.

For this reason, Max expected it to be tall and massive. Was it crawling on the ground? He never heard of a werewolf story where they slithered on all fours like a snake. It was confusing to see. His brain went straight from numb to dumb.

Its lips vibrated with a low throaty growl as its mouth widened. Max did the only thing he could think of doing. After the fact, he honestly didn't know why he reacted the way he had. It was pure instinct, or was it just a bodily reaction to facing certain death? He didn't know, but without one perceivable thought, his foot shot out and he kicked the creature right in the face! The thing that happened next was totally unexpected. It flew back like a soccer ball into the dark forest.

"Run!" Max yelled, as he turned toward Jeff and shoved him. The choice was to either get Jeff out of the way or run him over. Either way, he wanted to get away from it. In case it came after them. All he knew was that he didn't want to be there if it came back!

They ran around the tree and up the hill into the parking lot. That is when Jeff decided to start screaming like a banshee, as they ran past the car with the foggy windows. Interrupting the couple and their make-out session.

Max never knew he could run that fast, nor that far. He didn't relent as they raced all the way to Jeff's house, clear on the other side of town. He didn't know when, but at some point, Jeff stopped screaming. Because he was winded from running, like a racehorse at the Kentucky Derby.

They got to Jeff's house and ran straight into, then through the backdoor. It was the only unlocked door, because his mom was working the night shift and Jeff was supposed to be at home in bed. Jeff grabbed the door and slammed it shut. Then he locked both locks, while Max grabbed a kitchen chair and shoved it under the doorknob for good measure.

Jeff walked over to the kitchen sink, flipped the faucet handle up, and the water shot out full blast. Without waiting, he stuck his entire head under the stream and let it wash over his head. Then he slurped water like a dying man.

Max saw him stick his head in the sink and he walked over to the fridge and grabbed another tallboy of beer and popped the tab with one hand. He was now a man, and he was going to have a man's drink. Especially since he just survived his first near death experience. With his sneakers spread wide, he leaned back and chugged as much beer as his windpipe would allow.

When he got his fill, he brought the can down and belched a loud, gnarly burp, then as he crushed the can, he yelled, "Man! I was thirsty!"

Max gave his head a shake and sweat sprayed off his brown, collar length hair. As the curls on his sweat-soaked head sprung up and clung to his skull in one direction.

Jeff shook his head like a dog after a bath, which made his black hair shoot out in every direction.

Max grinned as he watched Jeff and thought he really looked like Sid Vicious. Then he wobbled a little from drinking the alcohol so quickly as he asked, "What in the hell was that greasy looking bastard?"

Jeff shrugged and grabbed a red tea towel from the stainless-steel oven handle to wipe his face and said, "I don't know, but if I ever see it again, it will be too soon!"

"I thought it was a werewolf at first," said Max as he walked over to the kitchen sink. His sneakers squeaked as they hit the wet spots on the floor. Then he stuck his head under the faucet and turned it on cold, full blast. After cooling off, Max stood up and hit the handle. Jeff tossed him the small towel, and he quickly dried off and tossed it back.

Jeff shuffled over to a doorway with a cramped room containing a washer and dryer. Without a care, he chucked the towel on the floor in front of the laundry hamper. With a serious countenance, he faced Max. But as shock gave way to relief, his smile grew wide, and he chuckled. When he eyed Max's worried expression, he laughed.

Max shook his head, looking mystified as he watched Jeff act like a madman.

Jeff's laughter turned maniacal, while tears sprung to his eyes as he hooted. Then he calmed down for a second and looked at Max again.

Max smirked and asked, "Are you done?"

The look on Max's face sent him into a laughing fit again.

He struggled to spit the words out as the memory kept replaying in his mind. Finally, Jeff calmed down and said, "I can't believe you kicked that sucker! It blitzed through the air like a football splitting the uprights!"

CHAPTER 18

JOHN AND HIS WOODEN BAT

The deadly creatures stepped forward on two tiny legs with knobby little knees.

John decided he would not wait for them to attack, so he yelled and started swinging. He hit one, and it flew like a beach ball off to the side and bounced along the ground as it landed to a stop.

The other one reacted fast and jumped on John's hurt leg and sunk its teeth into him. He dropped the bat and grabbed it by the ears and rammed it into the solid steel door, knee first. It dropped lifelessly to the ground.

John heard the scratching sound from the creatures on the other side of the door as he quickly snatched up his stick and ran toward his office. But he slipped and fell. Spitting the dirt from his mouth, he jumped up and continued to run.

Halfway to the office, the warehouse door busted open, and a small pile of creatures came running and falling out.

John made it to his truck and dove inside, slamming the truck door closed while simultaneously throwing his wooden weapon onto the dashboard.

After hitting the lock button, he fished in his pocket for his keys. But he felt a gaping hole in the bottom of the empty pocket of his shredded pants. The keys were gone.

He was stuck, imprisoned, in the truck and the little monsters were almost there.

It chilled him to watch them. They looked as if they were hopping and dancing toward him in the shadows of the dimly lit parking lot. The frightening scene was surreal.

With his heart pounding, John looked down and felt around on the seat. JP placed his blood-stained palms flat onto the bench and moved them all over the seat cover. His phone had been sitting right there. He thought as he frantically searched the entire area, but it was gone.

John cringed as he heard one long squealing sound against the metal of his truck. He glanced through the windshield but dipped his head when he saw a little beast. It stood there looking at him, as drool slipped down its spikey teeth, and dropped to the hood of his truck. The creature tapped a clawed toenail as it clicked on the metal, and it had three toes in the shape of a gargoyle's foot.

Soon, two more jumped up and stood next to the first one. John covered his ears as the creatures made deep scratches on his truck. The noise was like fingernails on a chalkboard, except it was earsplitting and more disturbing.

The monsters jumped, scratched, and peeled the paint as John searched for a flashlight. Luckily, he found a small

LED light on the end of an emergency tactical knife that he had kept inside the console under the dash.

After flipping it on, he searched the floorboard for his phone, but it was nowhere to be found. A thought had entered his mind maybe one of those vicious demons had stolen it, and he gave up hope of ever finding it.

Next, he checked his deep painful wounds, as he ripped bandages from his destroyed pants and tore them into strips. After that, he placed the bandages over the gashes on his leg. The small puncture holes in the shape of a wide mouth were bleeding profusely. The oozing blood dripped onto his upholstery, but it didn't matter to him. A few stains were the least of his problems, and he was glad to be alive. Besides, the creatures were ruining his truck, as he heard a loud screeching noise scrape across the very top of the pickup. It was so jarring; he covered his ears.

Finally, JP finished bandaging his leg as he thought about counting the creatures. He turned around to look into the bed of his pickup. But it was gone, yet only a minute ago he could hear it in the back scratching around. He looked out each window, continuing to search for them, but he didn't see anything.

Daylight seemed to chase away the darkness and turn everything into a hazy, gray, smoke-filled color. He didn't see the creatures as he looked out over the hood.

"I've got to get help as soon as possible," he muttered to himself. But there was no way he was leaving his truck.

John sat and waited as the sun continued to rise. At some point, he nodded off from blood loss and exhaustion. By the time he awoke, it was mid-morning. Thirsty and hot, he needed to leave the truck before he baked from the bright, burning sun. Since today was Sunday, nobody was coming out to the mill.

Before opening the door, he searched again, but nothing was out there. He looked toward the warehouse and its metal door. Two of them should be lying dead on the ground, but there was no sign of what happened in the dark.

When he lifted himself above the seat to get a better view, his head touched the top of the cab. He looked everywhere as he whispered out loud, "Where did those little bastards go?"

After waiting another fifteen minutes, he unlocked the door and grabbed his trusted weapon from the dash. It grew hotter as he sat inside the truck, and he realized that this situation wouldn't work. He needed help now. He cringed as he pulled the handle to the door as it unlatched. Then he pushed it open and moved slowly and quietly as he slipped out of the truck. Instant pain screamed down his wounded leg from the weight of his body. JP wanted to make sure that he wasn't walking into a trap, so he stooped to make sure they weren't hiding underneath the pickup. But he saw neither hide nor hair of them.

John stood up and searched the parking lot, but they were gone. It took a few moments for him to decide to run to the office. But he didn't have his keys. He looked in the back of his truck bed and saw his old red rusted toolbox. It was by the tailgate. He hated to leave the safety of his cab, but it had to be done. JP hobbled to the tailgate, swiveling his neck as he went. He quietly unlatched the toolbox and flipped it open to find a long flathead screwdriver. Anxious, he looked around again, then limped his way to the door, and made quick work of the latch.

With a bump of his shoulder, the door swung open, and John flew inside, slamming the door behind him. He leaned against the door, and realized the radio was playing. Had he left it on by accident? The cold feeling of terror coursed through his body as he heard the happy lyrics of a song.

His heart dropped to his stomach as John whispered, "Not again." He slipped the flathead screwdriver into his back pocket and gripped his wooden stick. Waiting to be attacked at any second, his eyes darted around the room. He listened for the creatures that might spring at any moment.

The phone seemed so far away as he made a beeline for it. John put the receiver to his ear, but he heard no dial tone. He walked over to another phone on the secretary's desk, picked it up, and put it to his ear. No sound came from the receiver.

"Dammit!" He groaned, in a low raspy whisper as he fought the urge to slam the receiver back onto the offending phone bank. His tongue stuck to the inside of his mouth, and it felt like a desert as he inhaled through dry, parched lips, just to utter that one word.

Dehydration had set in from his exertions and blood loss. He needed a drink. Fearful of the open space of the room, he eyed the refrigerator, which sat in the back corner of the office. John was desperate for a bottle of ice-cold water to quench his thirst.

Silently, he made his way to the refrigerator and placed his hand on the door handle. He paused for a moment, wondering if a creature might be sitting inside, waiting to spring at him. Scared to even open the door, something he had done well over a thousand times, he grew frustrated, then angry. Even if he had to fight five of those slimy bastards, he was going to get that bottle of water. John readied himself and grappled with the handle. Then, with a steadied calm, he ripped open the door.

The light popped on and the condiment bottles shook in the door as it slammed against the wall.

"Whew! Sweet victory!" he rasped, unable to recognize his own voice. He tried to clear his throat while grabbing two bottles of water with one hand. Paranoid, he turned around and faced the room as he sat one bottle on the counter. Worried that if he let his guard down, he would be attacked. But everything looked normal, which was unsettling. While watching the room, he snaked a bottle from the counter and unscrewed the lid. With one breath, he drank the entire contents, draining it dry. When he caught his breath, he felt the water soak into his thirsty body. It felt like he was renewed, and his energy level increased. He nabbed the other bottle and took another sip, then put the cap back on, and shoved it into his empty back pocket opposite of the screwdriver.

"I have to get out of here," he whispered to the empty room as he limped back to his desk and slipped open the middle drawer. There, sitting on a silver ring, sat his extra set of keys. He now had access to every building, his new house, and his truck.

After grabbing the keys and leaving the radio playing a long ago hit song, he shuffled to the door and carefully opened it to make sure they were gone. They were nowhere to be seen. He looked toward his pickup and saw the damage from the onslaught earlier by the tiny beasts. It looked almost war torn. The scratches were deep, and the trim was either gone or bent up and scratched. He wouldn't have recognized it as his own vehicle, but the evidence was sitting right there before his very eyes.

"Come on John, you've got this!" He whispered as he swung the door open.

After slipping outside, he limped as fast as his leg would allow, and made it without incident to his truck. Quickly, he swung open the door, jumped inside, and hit the locks. Shocked by the bottle of water and screwdriver pressing into his backside, he grabbed the offending items and sat them next to him on the seat.

Adrenaline soaring, as fear gripped him. He fumbled with the set of keys. After he was able to get his fingers to work, John found the one for his truck on the silver ring. Finally, he picked it out and slid it into the ignition. After turning the key, it made no sound. The truck was dead.

Dani Denali

CHAPTER 19

BABY BRO

The morning light lit upon the window and filtered through the thin gauze curtains illuminating the small, gray living room. Inside the brown carpeted room sat a cream sagging couch, and a blue cushioned swivel rocking chair. A few pictures of Billy and Max hung on the wall, and the entertainment center held a rather average sized tv and a gaming console.

The room was usually kept tidy, but this morning, it looked more like a warzone. Slumbering bodies in army-green, black, and navy-blue sleeping bags were spread across the floor.

It was serene as the morning light appeared and the birds arose to tweet and whistle to kick-start the day.

But Billy slept fitfully, as a constant nightmare of flipping pictures flashed before his eyes. The frames flicked from one to another like a stop motion cartoon. The old woman is lying in repose with blue light beaming out of her chest and little glowing monsters are chasing him throughout the house.

He startled awake and sat straight up on the couch. Then, after realizing that he was safe and sound inside his home and surrounded by friends. He took a deep breath and got up. As he stretched his body, he went to the kitchen and grabbed a drink of water.

The rest of the boys started to move around when he walked into the room and flopped onto the couch.

Troy sat up and reached into his bag. He fished out the old brown book with its tattered corners and handed it to Billy. "I bookmarked it last night before I fell asleep." He said with a yawn and walked out of the room toward the bathroom.

Billy ran his fingers across the front title of the hardback. The sensitive tips of his fingers felt the dips and bumps of the pressed golden letters.

'Centuries Old, Myths, and Legends,' was written in Old English lettering down the front of the book. Billy noted the bookmark and held the top of it as he let the book fall open. The musty smell of the old pages hit his offended nostrils, and he opened his mouth to take a breath.

"Yuck! This book is so old that it smells," said Billy, as he pinched his nose.

The boys gathered around him to look at the book.

"Gross, it stinks," Dean agreed.

Billy read the words out loud to everyone:

The Curse,

Upon a certain age, when death is near, the slow death takes place, and the curse appears. A wisping of creatures, escape from the breast, when the soul is absent during the little death. It will manifest in darkness and hide at night. Hidden in form until sacrificed to the full moon's light.

Billy looked up from the words on the page and wondered. "What do you guys think? I mean, well, my neighbor was old, and she died. Do you think the curse killed her?"

"It's possible," said Troy with a shrug.

"But it says, 'at a certain age, when death is near.' Maybe she was going to die, anyway," said Butch as he pointed at the page.

"Okay, Butch is probably right. I bet the slow death and the curse, is what was happening while she slept. Those little blue monster balls were creep-y." Billy stifled a shiver.

"Did those things actually come out of her chest?" asked Dean.

"They sure did, and they came out so fast that it looked similar to a lightsaber glowing straight up to her bedroom ceiling. But then they bounced around like tiny helium balloons." Butch said.

"Hey Butch, did you notice they were going toward the other room?" asked Billy.

"No, I was paying more attention to that poor old lady."

They grew quiet for a moment.

Then Troy broke the silence and asked, "Why didn't we ever see those blue glowing balls? I mean, y'all said there were a lot of them."

Billy looked down at the page and said, "I'm pretty sure they called the creatures, *'Wisps,'* when they are blue and floating. It says that 'they hide at night.'"

Then Billy read the next line aloud. "'It will manifest in darkness.'"

Troy was an avid reader and said, "Manifest means 'clear or obvious to the eye or mind'. What is obvious to the eye over there?"

They were quiet for a moment, then Troy said it for them. "The cats!"

"You're right! There are so many cats over there. Way more cats than there were a few weeks ago," Billy agreed.

"So, they turn into cats?" asked Dean.

Billy and Troy nodded in unison.

"Oh man! Does it mean that if the cats kill and eat some-thing on a full moon, they change again?" Dean asked.

The boys were surprised by Dean's statement. The look of shock was apparent as they gauged each other's expressions.

Troy looked at Billy and nodded, as he said, "Read it."

Billy skimmed the words on the page, then read the last sentence aloud, "'Hidden in form until sacrificed to the full moon's light.'" He looked at everyone. "Guys, I'm sure Dean is right."

Butch's head shot up from his cell phone. His eyes were wide with alarm as he said, "If he is right, then we are going to have a real problem. Because tonight is the full moon!"

Butch turned his phone and showed them the picture of a blue screen with a closeup of the moon in its fullest phase. Written in black across it was today's date.

Billy looked at the page of the book again. "Isn't there a way to reverse the curse?" he asked as he flipped the page.

Troy helped study the book with him, and something caught his eye. "Wait! Turn it back to the next page!"

Billy obliged, as they both inspected the book.

"There's a page missing!" said Billy. He saw the visible remnants of the torn page sticking out close to the spine.

"Great! Now what do we do?" asked Dean.

Billy thought about it for a moment and said, "We need to go see the stranger."

"Billy, do you think he's still in jail?" asked Butch.

"I don't know. But we need to find out."

Butch rolled up his sleeping bag and soon everyone followed suit. As they were busy picking up their belongings and filling their backpacks, the backdoor slammed.

Max came walking into the living room, followed by Jeff. He was wearing sunglasses and looked like he had partied all night, as he flopped onto the blue swivel rocker. Jeff quietly took a spot at the end of the couch.

Since Max was around, the boys grew tense and watched in uneasy silence as they waited for the fallout that inevitably ensued.

Max shot forward and put his sunglasses up onto his head. He took both hands and rubbed his eyes with his fingers, then slapped his hands on his kneecaps and said, "Man, you won't believe what we saw last night!"

The boys started talking over each other, all at once about the old lady that died next door and the curse.

"We have proof. Show them, Butch!" Billy said.

Butch took out his phone and played the video. Earlier, he had taken a snapshot of the little floating monster and coolly shared the image.

Then they grew quiet as Max told them about the greasy gray monster he had dropped kicked into the woods.

They were stunned into silence by his story.

Billy spoke up first as he said, "There's a guy in jail right now that we think knows what is happening. We were thinking about going there to talk to him, because he might know something about the curse."

Then Billy showed him the book and pointed to the page and told him they had just realized that the next page was missing.

The boys waited to see what Max was going to say as he finished reading the page in the book.

"I don't think they come out in daylight. When we walked through town, we didn't see anything."

Impatient, Billy asked, "Hey Max, what do you think about talking to the guy? You know the guy that got arrested?"

"It might be a good idea." Max nodded. "But you aren't going anywhere without me. Those little monsters have huge teeth and look deadly." Then he sat back and slipped his sunglasses down onto his nose and shut his eyes.

The boys took it as a sign to leave him alone. Billy heard a truck pull up next door, and he peeked out the window.

"Who is it?" Max asked without moving.

Billy watched as the truck idled a few moments. He had no clue who it could be, so he waited until a tall blonde man got out.

"It's Coop. It looks like he is walking over to the old lady's house with a few pet carriers."

"We think that the blue wisps turn into cats at night. Then on the full moon, if they kill something, they turn into a Vandalow, and the full moon is tonight." Billy stated. The word Vandalow felt strange on his tongue. Like saying it out loud made it a reality.

"This can't be real," Billy said under his breath.

"Oh, it's real alright Baby Bro, the Vandalow are here," Max said, as he leaned his head back on the chair. "I need some shuteye. We stayed up all night."

Billy looked over at Jeff, who was already sleeping with his head leaning on the arm of the old couch. He had put his feet up as soon as Billy had moved.

Billy looked at his friends and nodded to the backdoor. Then, one by one, they snuck out of the living room. Without making a peep, they tiptoed down the hallway and exited through the back door.

Billy walked over to the privacy fence and peeked through the small gap to see Coop catching the cats.

"Holy cow!" Billy exclaimed. "I bet there's at least a hundred cats over there!"

The rest of the boys stepped up to the fence and looked through the gaps and empty knotholes.

"Do you think they are all Vandalow?" asked Butch.

"I hope not! But we better prepare for the worst. I don't think we should wait for Max. We need to go see the stranger as soon as possible. Who's with me?" asked Billy.

"I'll go. But I need to go check in at home first," Butch answered.

All of the boys needed to check in, so they agreed to meet back at Billy's in one hour.

CHAPTER 20

BILLY TAKES A STAND

Betty and Mable walked this morning's route, past Auntie DeLeon's house. They'd already heard through the town chatterbox that poor Auntie had passed away last night. Curiosity got the best of them, as they wondered what they were going to do with all of those cats.

They were huffing and puffing this morning, as they rounded the corner to Auntie's house to do a little snooping.

Surprised that someone was already there, Betty wheezed a smidge, as she asked, "Hey, isn't that Cooper Daniels' brand new pickup truck?"

"Looks like it." Mable blew out a quick breath.

"It's too bad that she passed on. It's a strange feelin' when someone passes right after you've seen 'em alive," Betty thought aloud, as they walked toward the house. "Bless her heart." Betty panted, out of breath.

Mable nodded as she repeated. "Bless her heart."

They walked up to Cooper Daniels' new truck, and Betty looked inside the cab. "Mable, would you look at how nice this truck is? I bet it must've cost a pretty penny."

"It's quite fancy, that's for sure. And now I know what a radiant red tint coat looks like on a pickup," Mable said as she eyed the side of the shiny pickup.

Coop walked around the front corner of the house wearing long sleeves and leather work gloves. He was busy carrying two pet carriers by their black plastic handles. A few growls came from the medium-sized containers, and the intermittent hissing and spitting set off as soon as he sat them on the ground together at his tailgate.

"Hello, how are y'all doing this fine morning?" He asked with a brief smile that didn't quite reach his eyes.

Betty and Mable walked to the end of his truck.

"Oh, we're out gettin' our mornin' exercise in while the air is still cool. But we just had to stop and admire your new truck. It sure is a beaut," said Betty.

"Thanks! I really like it!" He beamed with pride and placed his hand on the side of the truck.

He had one heck of a charismatic smile, Betty thought as she smiled back. What a real charmer. "Say, what are you goin' to do with all those cats?"

"Well, it depends on how many I can catch," he chuckled. Coop picked up one carrier at a time and sat them in the back of his pickup. Then closed the tailgate with a click of the latch.

"I'm taking a few of them out to JP's mill this morning. But I'm not sure what I'm going to do about the rest of them." He stood with his leather gloved hands on his hips, feeling frustrated at the prospect of catching so many wild cats.

"Don't you worry…it'll all come out in the wash. We saw 'em when we walked by here yesterday. I'd have to say there's doggone near fifty of 'em…and poor Auntie was out front feedin' the clowder. Bless her heart." Betty frowned.

There was a lull in the conversation and Betty said, "Well, we'd better let you go. It looks like you have your hands full. Come on, Mable, lets walk over to JP's new house and see if he's finished plantin' flowers in his front yard."

Betty took a few steps and then turned around, smiling. "When are you goin' to teach me how to grow those hydrangeas? We saw them puttin' on a show at the park, and they sure are stunning to look at."

Coop smiled. "I'll be at the park later this week. Then we can catch up, and I promise to tell you…my secret," he said with a wink. "Well, you ladies have a great day." He touched the brim of his hat, and Betty and Mable walked on up the street.

Coop wondered how he was going to catch all those cats. When he had walked around the house earlier, he couldn't believe his eyes. It was an inconceivable sight. The whole backyard was moving with a multitude of little fur bodies. He had never in his entire life seen so many of them. Every color of cat that you could imagine was roaming around in that backyard. Black, white, orange,

147

brown, gray, and every mixed-up color in between swarmed around each other. Pointy ears and perched tails were floating up to the sky as they moved in a chaotic rhythm.

He had to create a solution for this problem, because it wasn't going to be easy to catch them all. But for now, he was taking the few he had caught to the mill.

He heard voices and turned his head to see Billy Galloway with his buddies. They were standing and talking to each other at the end of his driveway. Then his friends hopped onto their bikes and started pedaling down the hill as Billy yelled, "See you in an hour!"

Billy eyed Coop standing at the end of his truck and ambled over to him. "Hey Coop!"

Coop was very busy this morning, but he liked the kid, so he waited. "What's happening, Billy?"

Billy had a few questions on his mind. "Did they say what happened to the old lady?"

"All I know is that she passed away in the middle of the night. Why? Did you see something?"

Boy did I, Billy thought. But he figured he better keep it to himself. If he told Coop what he saw last night, Coop would think he was crazy. The only way for someone to believe him is if they saw it happen on their own.

Even now, he struggled with the reality of it all. But the stranger was there, and Billy hoped the outsider had the answers they needed for it to all make sense.

"Not really. I saw a man in the back of the cop car and Sheriff Halsey was questioning him." Billy mimicked

Cooper's stance by putting his hands on his hips. He rocked back and forth from heel to toe and blurted out his question. "I was wondering about the big cat in the house. What's going to happen to it?"

Coop was surprised that there was yet another cat inside the house. He planned to eventually to check the house out, but the shock of seeing how many cats there were had made him forget all about it.

"Well, I've been told to take care of the cat problem. So, do you want the cat?" Coop asked, feeling hopeful.

Billy saw what the cat was doing last night. It was protecting the old lady. Hopefully, his mom wouldn't mind if he took the cat in, so he smiled and said, "Yes."

"I need to check the place out, anyway. Do you want to come with me?"

Billy felt immediate trepidation and his heart did a flip at the question. But the curse said that they hid at night.

"One more question. Are the cats outside acting strange? Are they mean?" asked Billy.

Coop wondered if the kid was afraid of cats. But dismissed the thought when a cat in the carrier yowled and hissed and Billy didn't react.

"I think most of the outside cats are wild and aren't used to being handled. But the house cat will be tame," said Coop.

"Okay," Billy said quietly. He figured since Coop had caught a few cats and hadn't come out screaming, then it was probably okay to go with him.

"Are you sure you want the cat?"

"Yes, I'm sure," Billy replied with a toothy grin. "Let's go."

"Alright, let's get you a cat!" Coop nodded and turned toward Auntie's house.

Billy followed Coop as they walked into Auntie's yard. His heart raced as he saw continuously more cats the farther back into the property they walked.

He noticed an old, rusted car at the end of the driveway, and it was covered by vines and shrubs. The cats were living inside the car as several jumped out of the window that hung halfway open. But none of the felines hissed or growled at them as they walked around the back of the home. "OH MY GOSH!"

Coop smiled when he heard Billy's reaction to seeing the unbelievable number of felines. He looked over to where Billy stood motionless with his mouth hanging open in shock! Coop couldn't help but chuckle. He was positive he made the same face when he first saw how many cats he was supposed to trap and rehome.

Billy noticed a privacy fence built along the back of the property. It was covered with green moss and weathered gray by the elements. He watched as the cats trotted and then leaped through a hole provided by a half piece of broken fence board. They kept hopping through the gap like an endless train and were gathering in the backyard as he stepped closer to Coop.

Coop picked up the key left under the doormat and unlocked the door. Then he stepped inside and looked around the kitchen. Billy followed close behind and shut the door.

It felt strange being inside the house. He felt creeped out by what had occurred only a few hours before. The thought of the grim reaper claiming her soul made Billy shiver. The tidy house smelled old and musty as he looked around the kitchen.

Coop walked up to a cotton knitted bag that hung on the kitchen wall and slipped it off the hook. Then he looked inside to make sure it was empty.

"Do you want to grab the cat bowls?" asked Coop.

Billy looked around the kitchen floor and saw the pair of blue matching bowls. They both had the name, "Mr. Grimm," hand painted on them in a metallic white. He carried the water bowl over to the sink and dumped it. The food bowl was half full. He looked over at Coop, wondering if he should ask for the cat food.

Coop understood the question without being asked. "Check the cabinets. I bet she has plenty of food for him and the horde."

Billy opened the cabinet doors until he happened upon a box of kibble. There was a huge cat head printed on it, and it stated that it had moist, tender centers. He dumped the dry contents from the bowl back into the box and stacked the bowls. Then he carried them over and placed them inside the waiting bag.

As if on cue, Mr. Grimm stepped into the kitchen. Billy figured he must have heard the kibble being poured. He sure hoped he was doing the right thing as they both stared at each other for a moment.

Coop handed the bag to Billy and explained, "I need to check the rest of the house before we leave."

Coop left Billy holding the bag, and looking quite nervous, as he went to check the bathroom. She had a leaky faucet, so he shut off the water valve.

With his heart thundering in his chest, Billy watched the huge cat. The cat haughtily looked him up and down as if he were judging his merit.

"Hey there, Mr. Grimm, if it's okay with you. You're going to come live with me." He stood perfectly still and watched the cat step slowly up to him. Then Mr. Grimm walked around and through his legs, making a figure eight. The cat stepped closer, nuzzling his furry body as he passed against Billy's legs. Then he purred.

The loud purring eased Billy's misgivings as he petted the humongous cat on top of his head. Billy kneeled and let Mr. Grimm slink under his hand, from the top of his head to the tip of his tail. Billy's anxieties over taking the cat diminished as he watched Coop step back into the kitchen.

"Well, do you think he will let you pick him up?"

"I guess we'll see," said Billy, as he put the strap of the bag onto his shoulder and kneeled to embrace the cat and lift him up.

Coop smiled when the cat stayed put in Billy's arms. "He sure is a huge cat."

Billy grinned and said, "He's light as a feather. I think he's all fur."

They both chuckled.

Then Billy asked, "Did you happen to see a pet carrier somewhere?"

"I did. Let me go get it." Coop stepped into the old woman's bedroom.

While Billy stayed right where he was. There was no way he was going in there.

Then Coop walked out with a nice sized cat carrier and sat it on the floor. Billy opened the latch on the metal door and placed Mr. Grimm inside, and said, "Don't worry. I'll let you out as soon as we get home."

Mr. Grim meowed as if he were answering, "Okay."

Coop stepped out the backdoor first.

The moving cluster of cats halted and then stiffened. In unison, they turned their curious eyes toward Billy and the pet carrier as he maneuvered it through the doorway and outside to the stoop.

Coop looked out among the throng of fur and thought, what a strange reaction to seeing the big cat.

Billy braced himself as panic kicked in. He realized he was partly correct. He had wondered if the cats outside would remember their first enemy as they escaped the woman.

Fear crept like ice through his veins as he watched every cat look at him, and he wondered what was going to happen next.

At the same time, the cats lowered their heads, flattened their ears, and one growled, as their tails twitched. Then, the hairs on their backs raised as several more cats started to screech, hiss, and yowl.

Billy was fixing to turn and retreat into the house when the carrier shook violently, and he almost dropped it! Billy gripped the handle tighter as Mr. Grim hissed a long guttural hiss!

A few cats slinked forward; their bodies low to the ground, as if they were stalking their prey.

Suddenly! A thunderous, bone chilling growl emanated from the pet carrier and Billy was frightened! It was primal and shocking! It sounded as if a demon from hell, mixed with multiple cats, roared in unison from Mr. Grimm.

The hairs on both Coop and Billy's neck raised as they stood frozen in place. They had stepped straight into a nightmare. Over one hundred cats were staring at them while hissing and spitting, with their backs raised in the air.

Coop was sure they were going to be attacked any second now, as he stepped closer to Billy. He was ready to push him back inside to the safety of the house if the cats came any closer. This could get ugly fast, he thought.

Again Mr. Grimm growled louder, and the cats froze, then he roared as the pet carrier shook! The cats panicked and scattered in a streak of jumbled color. The crazy cats were running every which way to escape the yard and the proximity of Coop, Billy, and Mr. Grimm.

They disappeared all at once! The yard was now empty, except for the lingering fur which floated on the air and fell to the ground.

Coop shook his head in disbelief. "What in the heck just happened?"

Billy knew, but he wasn't going to say a word. There were no words, except for one. Protector.

CHAPTER 21

MABLE GETS A DELIVERY

Betty and Mable finished walking their route after stopping by JP's house. They were disappointed he hadn't added to his yard yet. Nothing had changed.

Mable left Betty at her house with a wave and said, "I'll talk to you later." Then she continued the short walk to her house.

As she walked around the lilac bush growing in the corner of her front yard. She saw the big box sitting on the ground right before the eight steps that led up to the front porch. She was instantly on fire!

Mad as a wet hen, she grumbled, "I'm fixin' to pitch a fit, and the next time I see that hifalutin delivery man, he's goin' to get an earful!" She huffed. "Great, just great. How in Sam Hill am I supposed to get this microwave up them steps and into the kitchen?" As she often did, she was talking to herself out loud.

Mable thought about her dilemma as she tried to lift the heavy box. "Well, that ain't gonna do," she said, feeling frustrated.

"Aha, I have an idea," she smiled to herself, "and it just might work."

Mable had a small hand cart she used for moving groceries.

She stepped through the front door into her living room. Then walked through her pristine little house to the kitchen. Inside the living room, tiny glass Knick knacks sat everywhere. The cute little figurines were carefully collected through a lifetime of travel and adventure.

She walked into her kitchen and took a gander. The walls were lined with vintage, porcelain state collector plates, and it made her smile and think of her late husband. It was a comforting, yet colorful menagerie of collectibles, and she was proud of her collection and spent many hours cleaning them. Not one speck of dust settled in her house for long.

She sought the two-wheeled cart, and it was right where she had last left it. The flimsy little thing was folded up and leaning in between the refrigerator, covered in magnetic flowers, and the cabinet. Mable smiled as she opened a drawer and pulled out a spool of ribbon and slipped it into her pocket.

As she planned her next move, she slid open the sliding glass door, stepped out onto the brick patio, and opened the gate of the wooden planked privacy fence.

"There, now to get the cart and get that dadgum thing inside the house!"

Mable wheeled the dolly out the front door and wobbled it down the steps. She unfolded it and sat it next to the box. Lifting the big box and sliding it over onto the two-wheeler was a cumbersome chore. Mable pulled out the spool of thick yellow ribbon and tied the box to the dolly.

Determined, she pushed the box against the step. If she could get it lifted on the heavy end, to use the fulcrum, she'd be in business. Working the box up the step until one side sat on top of it made the dolly slant at an awkward angle. Mable placed her foot at the back of the dolly and pulled back on the handle.

"Somebody call the president. We have liftoff," she huffed.

Mable pushed it along the sidewalk until it met up with the concrete driveway, then turned toward the back of the house. Sweating, she walked under the shade of the carport that was built long ago with the home. Then came upon the entrance to the gate and was surprised as it went through without a hitch. The brick pavers jostled the microwave and slowed her progress, but she made it to the opened sliding glass door. Wiggling one wheel at a time, it bumped over the low threshold, and she sat it on the kitchen floor with a '*Thunk*!'

"There! Land sakes, I never thought I'd get you in here!"

Mable pushed the box across the floor, over to the open spot on the counter. Then opened it up with a pair of scissors. As Mable pulled the packaging out, she added a cut down the side of the box. Next, she pulled out the styrofoam on the corners that held the microwave.

"It's time to rest for a spell." Mable poured herself a tall glass of sweet tea and sat on a cushioned kitchen chair. She pinched the front collar of her shirt and fanned herself with it. "Whew! That was a workout!"

Mable thought she was talking to her Lil' Mama cat and her three babies. But as she looked around, they were nowhere to be seen.

"Here, Lil' Mama," she called, "Trixie, Merl, Dolly! Where did you go?"

Mable looked at the door and said, "Oh Shoot! Please tell me you little beggars didn't escape out the back door!"

She slid the glass door open and stepped outside onto her patio. The momma cat was busy licking her paws as the three small fuzzballs were curled up together, sleeping in the sunshine. Mable smiled at how cute they looked, all cuddled together.

It made her think of how she came by Lil' Mama. She was walking in the square one afternoon around four or five months ago, and the sweetest little girl had walked up to her, crying. She was carrying Lil' Mama as she asked, "Please, oh, please, could you take this cat?" She sniffed. "I sure love her, but my mommy won't let me have her."

That's all it took for Mable, because it just plain broke her heart to see that sweet little girl cry. She promised to take care of the cat, and that Lil' Mama would have a wonderful home. The little girl smiled her thanks, wiped her tears away, and off she went. Little did Mable know; the cat was pregnant.

"Come here, Lil' Mama," she said as she walked over and picked up the babies while they dozed in the grass next to their mother. Mable carried them back into the house and Lil' Mama followed her inside. She closed the door and turned to see that heavy thorn in her side, still sitting on the floor.

She made a call, and after a few rings, Betty answered, "Hello Mable."

"Betty, I'm gonna need a little help."

CHAPTER 22

JOHN PARKER

Angry, John Parker slammed his hands on the steering wheel several times. "What else can go wrong?" He shouted, feeling discouraged.

He looked around the outside of his truck, watching for any sign that he may still be in danger. But everything looked normal.

"Ha! Nothing is normal," he growled with frustration.

He popped the hood with a push of a button, grabbed his bat, and quietly slipped out of the cab. JP felt extremely paranoid as he limped to the front of his truck to unlatch the hood. Worried he might be attacked again; he slowly pushed the latch to the side. Carefully, he lifted the scratched hood and peeked inside the small gap. Nothing was out of the ordinary so, he lifted it up, until the springs caught and pulled it wide open.

The first thing he noticed upon viewing the engine was the battery cable. It had been disengaged from the battery. He reattached the cable and made sure it was secure, as he prayed that it was his only problem. Hastily, he staggered to the cab and turned the key. The motor coughed a few times and then started. It sounded rough, but it was a tiny victory.

Feeling hopeful, JP sighed. "I just might survive this yet."

He limped back to the hood and slammed it shut, then jumped back into the truck as fast as his injuries would allow. While locking the doors, he tossed the bat onto the dashboard.

JP threw it into gear, and peeled out, throwing gravel as he fishtailed out of the parking lot and onto the gravel road. He wasn't far from the Sheriff's station. Help was only a few miles away. But as soon as he finished that thought, his truck sputtered and then it hiccupped.

"Come on, baby, keep running!" JP begged as he repeatedly tapped the dash.

It didn't quit, but it was going to be a long drive. The engine continued to sputter as it bogged down. Then the truck lurched forward, coughing, and hiccupping along the graveled road.

CHAPTER 23

A BUSY DAY

Anxiety ramped up another notch as Mia finished yet another complaint call. She ended the conversation and dropped the phone into the receiver when something hit the front door with a loud *Bang!* Startled, she looked up to see Lyle Mayhew speedily walking through the entryway.

In a hurry, Lyle had to shoot out his hands to stop himself before running into the counter. He was inebriated and smelled to high heaven.

Mia stood up, because for a second, she thought he might jump over the divider onto her desk.

His eyes were wild, and his hair looked as if a firecracker had blown it in every direction. He looked like a madman.

"What's going on, Lyle?" she asked, as she took a step away from her desk chair.

"I am fixing to tell you something that you ain't gonna believe." He half chuckled. "I wouldn't believe it myself if

I hadn't seen it with my very own eyes." His hands were splayed on the edge of the counter as he leaned forward.

"I am not *crazy*. I might be a little *drunk*. But I am *sober* and *sane*!" His voice grew more emphatic with every punctuation of each sentence.

"H-how can I help you, Lyle?" Mia stammered. She hadn't dealt with Lyle before and was on edge by his antics. Mia knew he was quite the party animal and had dealt with several calls about him. He wasn't violent. He only listened to loud music and constantly disturbed the peace.

"I was taking out the trash last night, and I saw something! A lot of them. I don't know what to call them! But there were a lot of them!" Lyle exclaimed. He wasn't making any sense.

"Okay. Slow down, and take a few deep breaths for me," Mia said, as she walked over to the mini-fridge and produced a bottle of water. "Here, drink this." She slowly handed him the bottle.

He opened the plastic bottle and drank half of it.

Halsey stepped out of the cell room and directly into the commotion. "What's happening here?"

Mia looked at Lyle as she said, "Lyle saw something last night."

Eyes wide, Lyle's chin worked up and down as he said, "I'm telling the truth. There was something running around the neighborhood last night. I was taking out the trash and saw them. Creepy looking little boogers! I ran back into the house and locked the door. Then I shut off my music and looked out the window to watch for them. They are small and scary looking with big teeth!"

Halsey watched Lyle with concern. He thought maybe Lyle was having some kind of reaction to a mixture of drugs. He partied a little too hard sometimes.

Halsey, with a pretense of calm, spoke unhurriedly. "Lyle, I need you to answer me honestly. Are you on drugs?"

Lyle shook his head in frustration. "No! I am not on drugs. Yes, I drank last night, but I did not partake of anything illegal."

Halsey made a calming gesture with both hands. He was hoping to slow down the conversation and take it down a notch. Because Lyle was bugging out. "It's okay if you are, Lyle. I just need to make sure that you aren't overdosing on something."

Mia immediately saw the tiny reaction in Lyle's face. It was frustration, paranoia, and, above all, anger. While Lyle was paying attention to Halsey. She moved closer and tried to calm him by placing her hand gently on his forearm. To pacify him, Mia spoke in a soothing voice. "It's okay Lyle. I believe you."

Lyle looked down at the touch of her hand, and then he looked up, and as their eyes met, she asked, "Please tell me what you saw?"

"I saw several small gray creatures, and they were scary as hell! They had big pointy ears and huge teeth!" His voice shook.

165

While Lyle was looking at Mia, Halsey snuck up behind him and took Lyle's left hand. Halsey slipped it quickly behind Lyle's back and leaned in, pinning him against the front counter with an "Oof!"

Halsey spoke with a calm and calculating demeanor that depicted intensity. "Lyle, I want you to remain calm. I want to detain you here until I check out your house and the neighborhood surrounding it. Now, can you be calm?"

Lyle got the message. He wouldn't be a problem. "I'm calm. I won't be giving you any trouble, Sheriff."

Halsey took his cuffs out, for the second time today, and put them on Lyle.

"I will come back and release you as soon as I make sure that everyone is safe. But for now, I am placing you in lockup for your own protection, as well as for ours."

Mia frowned in confusion when she saw Lyle smile and nod happily.

"I'm completely fine with doing just as you say, Sheriff. Put me in the clink." Lyle grinned.

Halsey took Lyle to the jail cell and put him into the empty unit next to Midnight. He came out looking confused as he walked up to Mia. "Is it just me or was Lyle a little too happy about going to jail?" he asked.

Mia's eyebrows shot up as she leaned back in her office chair. She tilted her head as she answered, "I thought the same thing. He is, without a doubt, one strange character. How is our other detainee?"

"He was asleep, but I bet he won't be for long," Halsey said with a chuckle.

The phone rang again, but before Mia could answer it. Halsey said, "I'm going to check out Lyle's place. I'll be back soon."

Mia nodded and answered the phone. She put her hand over the mouthpiece and said, "I'm getting quite a list of complaints. But none of them are detrimental to a person's health."

Jake nodded and walked toward the garage.

* * *

Halsey felt dog-tired. He wasn't expecting to be out all night long. The initial plan was, to work four hours at night. Then go home to catch a few winks before going into work today. But it was a long night and with no sleep, he thought, today was going to be rough.

They needed to hire another deputy soon. Especially on days like this when he could use some shut eye. Jake pushed the button to open the automatic door and sat patiently, rubbing his eyes. He yawned noisily as the door finally slid up and stopped. Then, with one hand, he steered the car out of the garage and cruised around the building.

Halsey looked in both directions as he tapped his foot on the gas pedal and eased out onto the road. He decided to stop by the coffee shop on his way to Lyle's for a pick me up, since he left his coffee mug at the station.

The next thing he heard was the crunching sound of plastic breaking, the grating of metal, and the spider webbing of glass. He felt like a bullfighter being rammed

167

by a 2,000-pound bull, as his whole body was jerked to the left, then blackness settled over him.

He woke up not knowing how much time had passed. But he was still inside the cruiser.

"Sheriff Halsey, Oh my God! Are you okay?" John Parker yelled.

Unable to move, Halsey thought he heard JP's voice. He opened his eyes to see a fractured image of JP's face, and at first, it confused him. He didn't expect to see him at such an awkward angle, because John was looking down at him.

As his head cleared, Halsey then realized he was upside down in the car. His last thought was, I'm probably in the ditch.

* * *

Coop bought a cup of coffee for himself, a vanilla latte for Mia, and several pastries at the quaint little coffee shop from the center of town. They had the best coffee around. His plan was to take an offering to Mia and ask what to do about the strays that were feral. They would not make very good house pets.

But the scene, which unfolded before his eyes, made him physically cringe. His heart sputtered as he sped up to the accident.

"Oh my God, Mia!" The words slipped out from between his lips when he saw the vehicles collide.

He was driving south out-of-town, fixing to follow the curve to the left. When he watched in horror as he saw JP's truck catapult from the gravel road that led down to the mill. The truck slammed into the cruiser at such a high rate of speed that it shoved the car sideways off the road and flipped it upside down in the grass.

Coop pulled over and slammed on the brakes as his tires spit gravel and skidded to a stop. Then he threw it into park, jumped out, and sprinted to where JP was bent down looking into the wrecked car's driver's side window.

JP looked crazed. He was filthy, covered in black, and looked disheveled, with a shredded pant leg. A filthy makeshift bandage was wrapped around his calf where black and red colors caked to his skin.

"Hey JP, are you okay?" Coop asked as he dropped to his knees to see if Mia was still alive.

He saw Halsey instead. Mixed with emotions of guilt and relief, he looked the Sheriff over, checking for injuries. The Sheriff's eyes were closed, and he was bleeding profusely from a cut on his forehead.

JP had stepped back to give Coop some room. "I couldn't stop! The brakes went out on my truck!"

"Hey Halsey!" Coop yelled at Jake to get him to open his eyes, but he didn't move. Cooper snagged his phone from his back pocket and called Mia at the station.

Mia answered at once.

"Halsey has been in a wreck and is unconscious. John Parker is hurt too, and they need an ambulance here ASAP. We're right on the curve where the three roads meet close to the station."

Coop paused, and answered, "Yes, at the corner of Magnolia Road and Magnolia Lane." He shoved the phone back into his pocket and looked over at John.

In a state of shock, JP sat on the ground with a far-off look in his eyes. He slowly pulled up his knees and leaned his elbows on them. Then he placed his head in his hands.

Not knowing if Halsey might be in danger, Coop decided to remove him from the car. He grabbed the handle to wrench the door open, but it didn't budge. Coop sprinted to his truck, took a pry bar from the toolbox, and hotfooted it back.

On the driver's side door, the broken safety glass had spider webbed. It hung precariously, with an enormous gaping hole. He took the pry bar, placed it into the opening, and pulled. The window gave way, as broken glass scattered everywhere in small chunks. As he cleaned the tiny pieces from the window frame; he heard the Sheriff moan.

"Hang on Halsey! I've got to get the glass out of the way. Just hold still for a minute." Coop spoke to him as he ripped off his T-shirt and covered the top of the metal door frame and thick grass. He lowered his head to make sure Halsey was clear of any foreign objects. Then he noticed Halsey's seatbelt remained strapped tight around him as the deployed airbags drooped.

"Halsey! Can you unlatch your seatbelt?" Coop yelled.

Halsey moaned again, but he didn't move. Coop took out his pocketknife when, out of nowhere, a seatbelt cutter was being handed to him. He shoved the pocketknife back into his front pocket and looked up to see Mia standing there.

Coop reached out and took it. "Thanks!"

He slipped the cutter around the strap and pulled several times. The belt split in two and came loose from Halsey's shoulder. Next, he cut the lap belt. Coop threw the cutter to the side. Then reached around Halsey's shoulders at an awkward angle and pulled.

Halsey was not a small man, and the way the car buckled around him made it difficult to pull him out. But Cooper kept at it, and finally Halsey's head and shoulders slipped from the cocoon of the wreckage. Mia stepped up with a neck brace, and Coop held Halsey's head still while she applied it around his neck.

Coop put his boots up against the vehicle. Then he carefully tugged on Halsey's upper half until he had him mostly out of the car.

Mia helped by holding Jake so Cooper could slide out from underneath him. Then, while Halsey was leaning against Mia, Coop hugged him from behind and pulled him clear of the wreckage.

Mia opened a large red medical bag and reached inside. She pulled out a blanket and wrapped it around Jake. Next, she took out a med kit and put on gloves. Mia applied sterile gauze on Jake's wounds and added pressure to where she saw bleeding. She looked him over and was relieved to see him breathing fine now. Mia had worried about his ability to breathe easily, while crumpled up inside the car.

171

Thirsty and hot from the physical exertion, Coop walked over to the bag and picked up a bottle of water. He noticed Mia had already put a blanket around John Parker and he was already halfway through a water bottle.

John remained sitting on the ground. With a grim expression, he shook his head as he looked up at Coop with bloodshot eyes.

"Are you okay?" Coop asked, for the second time.

JP stared off in a daze again. "You wouldn't believe the night I've had," he drawled as he looked toward Coop.

"Tell me what happened," Coop encouraged him. "I mean clearly by the looks of you, you've had a horrible night."

JP cleared his throat and said, "I have lived through a nightmare." He flipped his torn pant leg open and untied the bandage wrapped around his shin. John took his bottle and poured water onto the blood-stained material which stuck to his wound. Then, in obvious pain, he hissed, as he peeled it away from the puncture holes.

"You see, I was attacked last night. I was bitten by a wild gray looking creature."

Coop stood up to get a better look. The puncture holes were lined up just like teeth, and the angry red skin which surrounded each hole looked puffy and raw.

"What in the hell got a hold of you?" asked Coop. He couldn't deny the fact that it most definitely looked like a bite.

"I don't know exactly, but there were a lot of them. I was out at the mill working on paperwork. After I finished with my reports, I walked over to the main building to shut some lights off. They were in the warehouse." JP looked down and seemed to realize how filthy he looked. "While getting away from them, I slipped in a puddle of oil."

That answered the question Coop had earlier when he first got a glimpse of him. Coop realized Mia was standing next to him as she handed him his shirt. Then she bent down on one knee and examined the bite.

"You saw my truck, right?" asked JP.

Coop looked over at the smashed front end. The headlight on the passenger's side was completely missing and fluid was leaking all over the road. It was scratched up, just like Coop's truck. But it looked way worse.

"I got it started, and it barely ran. Then it sped up and started going too fast. No, let me explain. I didn't push on the gas pedal. It sped up on its own!" JP's eyes grew wide. "I tapped on the brakes. But the pedal went straight to the floor. I couldn't stop!" JP looked over at Halsey.

"Is he?" worried about the Sheriff, JP couldn't finish the question.

Mia answered, "No, he's unconscious right now. But the ambulance will be here soon." Then she asked, "Hey Coop, will you monitor the Sheriff while I help JP clean his wounds and bandage them?"

Coop knew JP was in shock, and he needed care. So, he walked over to where the Sheriff was lying on the ground and checked on him. Then he took it upon himself to watch over all three of them.

Mia cleaned and medicated JP's leg. She couldn't believe how much damage the animal did. She also noted how tall it must have been by the height of the bite marks.

"Whatever did that to your leg was a vicious little thing. Those puncture wounds look deep," she said. She watched as blood mixed with plasma and water oozed from the holes in his leg.

A few minutes later, help arrived. The ambulance from the city of Ska Dale was there in record time.

Mia heard the ambulance, and as she turned to look, she whispered, "Thank God."

CHAPTER 24

PLEASE REPEAT THAT

While bouncing the back of her hand against her mouth, Lana Galloway stifled a yawn for the hundredth time. Working a double was the worst kind of torture known to man, or in this case, woman.

A strong and salty character was paramount to this sort of abuse, and the paychecks were banging. She had two growing boys that did only one thing. EAT!

Lana looked into the mirror and thought, 'Daaang, girl, you look mighty fine! Except for those puffy eyes, frown lines, and crazy pieces of hair that are escaping your scrunchie.'

She pulled the hair tie out of the fashionable, high, messy bun and tossed her hair over her head as she bent forward. The five second hairdo was the only energy she could muster for the moment, and soon she needed to get it trimmed. But for now, the mess was going to be tucked up and pulled out of her face.

She took one last glimpse of herself as she washed her hands again and shook the excess water from them. Lana felt sublime as she sported a pair of comfy white tennis shoes and a soft, thin, white cardigan. She snagged a paper towel and placed it on the handle of the heavy wooden door. Then she pulled the door open and threw the wadded paper into the trash bin as she breezed out into the hallway. Hospitals were a disgusting place, and she didn't have any time to get sick.

She had a plan. A goal. She was going to move up the ladder and get out of the ER. But for now, she would learn everything she could to expand her knowledge of medicine and healthcare. Besides, someone has got to do it, and she was taking her lumps.

As she walked back into the sterile environment of the Emergency Room, she noted the two new patients coming in. While they were being actively admitted, Lana picked up her stethoscope and went to work. She walked up to the first patient, which was unconscious and grew instantly worried as she recognized Sheriff Jake Halsey.

"Oh man, I know this guy," Lana said as she grabbed his wrist and checked his pulse. She really liked Jake. He'd helped her get rid of that worthless husband of hers. God, what a difficult time that was. But Sheriff Halsey was always at her doorstep whenever she needed him. He was a caring man and proved it by his patience and actions.

The doctor overheard Lana and stepped quickly up to the patient to treat him while asking, "You know this guy?"

"Yes, he's the Sheriff in my hometown," she said with concern.

"You should look at the other patient that came in with him. I've got this one."

Lana nodded and reluctantly walked away. But she turned back and asked, "Will you keep me updated?"

The doctor nodded, "Sure. I'll let you know as soon as I find out his diagnosis."

Lana took one last look at Halsey and said a brief prayer. Then she walked over to the next exam room.

John Parker was sitting on a pristine white gurney. He was filthy, bloody, and disheveled. Lana had seen the gentleman around town but wanted to make sure that she got his name right. She looked at the computer screen and read his information.

Lana asked, "John Parker, right?"

John looked at her with exhausted eyes and bobbed his head once. He had a day's growth of scruff on his face, and his hair was matted with something black. She almost didn't recognize him because of the dried, bloody eyebrow and swollen eye. His clothes were covered with some form of black goo, and bits of dirt and dust stuck to it. She noted his fingernails were outlined with the same blackened gunk.

"I'm Lana Galloway. I think we've met in passing at one of the football games there in Sugar Bee."

Burned-out, he mumbled, "I thought I recognized you. I also go by JP."

Lana spoke in a calming, competent manner which always put her patients at ease, as she grabbed a new pair of gloves.

"Let's see about fixing you up and getting you better. What hurts worse?" she asked, as she collected sterile gauze and medical supplies.

JP half groaned and then chuckled as he said, "Everything."

"I see you've had a little care already. What happened to your leg?" she asked, as she moved the round rolling stool and a tray of supplies closer to him.

"I was attacked and bitten on the leg. Then I got into a wreck," said JP.

"Sounds like you've had one rough morning. Let's look at your leg first." Lana took a pair of scissors and asked, "Do you mind if I cut your pant leg off so we can get you taken care of?"

JP grinned, "Go for it. I don't think I will ever wear these pants again."

Lana cut away the filthy shredded cloth and removed the tape and gauze. Whilst working in the ER for quite a long time, she had seen a lot of dog bites, snake bites, and practically everything in between. But this? This was different. "What got ahold of you, JP?"

"You wouldn't believe me if I told you," JP said, with a grave look on his face.

"I can tell you right now that I've never seen this shape or size of bite before, and I have been doing this for a long time. You should know that you are going to need a round of rabies shots and antibiotics. I think a few of these are going to need stitches too," Lana said as she studied and cleaned the oozing bloody wound.

"I was attacked by something that I have never seen before," said JP. He paused as if to decide whether to tell her the entire story or leave out the insane parts.

"Spill it JP. I have two boys who roam all over that town, and I'd like to know that they are safe. Do I need to call them and tell them to get to the house and stay there?"

"Yes! You should definitely call them!"

Then he settled down and spoke with a calm voice. "I want you to know that I am of sound mind. I am not insane, and what I am going to tell you will sound like something out of a horror story. But it happened." He paused and looked her dead in the eye. "It really happened."

Lana gave him her full attention and spoke words of encouragement. "Start from the beginning and tell me everything."

"Okay." JP took a long breath as she used antiseptic on his wound. "Whew! Damn it, that feels like fire!"

"It will feel better soon. I promise." Lana gave him a shot to numb the pain while she worked on the larger tears in his skin.

"I was attacked and bitten by a gray looking little creature with big, pointed teeth."

Lana questioned what she had just heard. She tilted her head and looked him straight in the eye and asked, "Please repeat that?"

JP took another breath. "Let me start from the beginning."

CHAPTER 25

WHO'S THE BOSS?

Coop followed Mia back into the Sheriff's department. She switched the phone over to receive calls through the station once again and stood with her hands on her hips and then scratched her head.

"Give me a moment," she said. Then walked over and grabbed the keys to check on the prisoners. Mia wasn't quite ready for this kind of responsibility. At least not yet. But procedures had to be followed and things had to get done. She opened the door to the cell unit and stepped inside the room.

Coop was right behind her, but he only caught a glance inside the room as the door closed. He recognized Lyle, but Mia was blocking his view of the other cell.

Two sets of eyes looked toward her as she asked, "Are you guys doing good for now? I'll bring you a snack and something to drink soon."

They both nodded, but Midnight stood up and walked to the cell door. He placed his fingers around the bars and asked again, "Did you call the number on the card?"

With everything that had just occurred, it wasn't even a thought that she had processed yet. She had left those decisions up to Halsey. It was time to accept the role that she had thought would take her years to step into. But it was time to make the leap. She was the boss.

"I will make the phone call soon," Mia said with an authority she didn't quite feel. Then she nodded and quickly turned and left the room.

After she shut the door, she leaned on it for a moment.

Coop gave her a second to collect herself, then ambled slowly up to her. "I saw Lyle in there, but who's the other guy?"

"That's the man that was picked up entering Auntie DeLeon's house when Halsey caught him. Coop, I need help.
I could deputize you, and then I can bring you in on everything that is happening. Otherwise, it's an ongoing investigation and I can't legally say a word," said Mia.

Coop saw the pleading in her eyes. He was a sucker for Mia's eyes.

"Okay," he nodded, "Deputize me."

Coop followed Mia over to her desk and waited as she printed out a card and several pieces of paperwork, then handed it to him. He read the paperwork carefully, and she gave him a pen. Without a second thought, Coop signed it.

Mia stood and faced Coop with a solemn expression. "Let's make this official. Raise your right hand and read this sheet of paper aloud."

He took the paper and raised his right hand.

"I, Cooper Daniels, do solemnly swear, and affirm, to support and defend the Constitution of the United States of America, so help me God." He took the oath to heart, and Mia knew it by the vibrato in his voice and the look on his face.

She handed him a card, which stated that he was appointed to be a Deputy Sheriff and it held an end date of three months to the day.

"I appoint you to act on behalf of the Pope County Sheriff's Department. Congratulations," said Mia as she smiled and shook his hand.

Cooper smiled one of his million-watt smiles. Never in a million years did he think he would ever stand right here, in the Sheriff's office, being deputized by Mia Romero.

"Thank you, Coop. Now, let's get down to the business at hand," said Mia, as she took a sip of her cold latte, and then caught him up on the stranger. "His name is Midnight Javez Leõn."

Mia told Coop about the weird things that were on his person when he was detained.

"I think I met Midnight. He stopped by, out at Cartwright's farm, and helped me work on a tractor. I'm not sure, but the tractor looked like it was vandalized." Coop thought about it, and it made sense. "You don't forget a name like Midnight."

Mia was half listening to him as she thought about all of the strange activity going on. Then she thought about Lyle, as she said, "Lyle showed up at the office, and he was acting crazy, and claiming that he saw gray creatures with big teeth. The strangest thing happened when Halsey put Lyle in a cell before he left to go check it out. Lyle smiled when Halsey put him in cuffs. Not to mention JP and his entire ordeal with these gray creatures."

It grew quiet for a moment, as it donned on them both how seriously the situation was growing. They already had one deceased woman. An open attack on JP, and now Halsey was hurt and in the hospital. Something was happening in their community, and now it was up to Mia and Coop to figure it out.

Coop listened as she explained about the complaints she had received from the community. It ran the gamut from vandalism to theft. Neighbors complaining about neighbors and property being broken and stolen. To plain old dumpster dumping and scratching cars. As she spoke, he could see the stress of the situation written across her face.

"What do we need to do next?" asked Coop.

"We need to feed the detainees. I want to talk to Lyle and Midnight again, but first I need to make a phone call." She walked over to the black bag and pulled out Midnight's wallet and found the black card with the gold phone number. She only hoped that she was making the right decision.

"I'll go get snacks and breakfast for them. Do you need anything?" asked Coop.

"Another latte, please. I think it's going to be a long day. I need to call the coroner's office first before I make the call on this card. When you come back, we'll take them, one at a time, into the interrogation room, and have a talk." Mia sat down at her desk, opened the drawer, and pulled out a credit card. She handed it to Coop and said, "Please get receipts."

Coop said, "I'll be right back," and headed for the door.

CHAPTER 26

RIDING TO MIDNIGHT

Billy quickly carried Mr. Grimm inside the house. He slammed the backdoor door shut as fast as he could and flipped the deadbolt. The house phone hanging on the wall next to the door rang, and Billy almost jumped out of his skin. He put his hand to his chest where he could feel his heart beating a rat-a-tat-tat, like a drum roll on a snare drum. His other hand shot out, and he picked up the receiver.

"Hello?" Billy answered it quickly so Max wouldn't wake up.

"Billy, it's your mother," Lana said, feeling exasperated.

"I'm working a double shift, and I want you boys to stay inside the house. Something strange is going on, and I want you and Max to stay home and lock the door."

How did his mom already know that something strange was happening in the town?

"Umm, Mom, I wanted to ask you a question. You know the old lady next door? Well, she died last night, and I wanted to know if it's okay if I could have her big house cat?" Billy crossed his fingers as he listened for her answer.

"Oh no, Auntie passed away? That is just so sad. If you promise to take care of the cat. Then yes, you can have it. I know she also had several outside cats over there, and maybe it wouldn't hurt to have a few outside. But only two of them! I want only two," Lana repeated.

Billy physically squirmed at the thought of bringing over a Vandalow. "I promise I'll take care of him. He's a friendly cat, but the rest of the cats are already being moved somewhere else."

"Oh, okay. Please promise me you and your brother will stay home."

Billy crossed his fingers again. "I promise, mom." The lie didn't count if you crossed your fingers.

"I love you, Billy, and I'll be home later this evening." Lana gushed to her baby boy.

"Okay, I love you too," Billy replied and hung up the phone.

While still hoping that he'd made the right decision by rescuing the huge cat, he quietly snuck the large plastic carrier into his bedroom and shut the door. Then he took the water bowl and filled it in the kitchen. "Dang it, I forgot the kitty litter and a litter box," Billy whispered to himself. Then decided to get it later. After feeding the cat, he went outside to wait for his buddies.

* * *

The boys finally showed up together. Billy sat waiting on the front step as he watched them come up the road. He was ready to go. His bike was sitting in the front yard, and his backpack was already filled with a water bottle and a few snacks. Thick as thieves, they stuck together like glue, as they stayed in a tight-knit group riding along the street.

Billy stood up and traipsed over to his bike as they approached.

"Are you guys ready? I want to leave before Max wakes up, and starts in on me," Billy said, as he straddled his bike.

"Yeah, let's go," Butch replied, as he rode in a circle on the black pavement in front of the house.

Billy rolled out into the street, and they followed along as he pedaled down the hill. The ride was going to be easy getting to the Sheriff's station south of town, because it went downhill. Pedaling back was going to suck, but Billy felt the trip was going to be worth it.

The morning breeze was refreshing, except for the occasional smell of rotting garbage. It ruined the citrus; floral scent of the blossoming Magnolia trees as they coasted down Black Willow Lane.

Billy saw nothing amiss, except for a few dumpsters knocked over and trash all over the ground. They rode past the Buzz Pub before turning left and saw quite a few cars in the parking lot. It looked like they were abandoned, or maybe people were too drunk to drive. So, they left their vehicles to be picked up the next day. One had scratches all over it, just like Cooper's truck.

"Hey, look at that car," said Billy.

"Yeah, what are the odds of three automobiles looking like that?" asked Butch.

"Apparently, the odds are high," Billy said as he shook his head and pedaled on.

They breezed around the corner onto Magnolia Road, which was a straight shot to the Sheriff's department as they rode east across the south side of town.

They saw broken plastic and metal pieces swept to the side of the road as they passed the turnoff to the mill.

"Somebody got into a wreck here." Troy surmised.

They rolled up to the Sheriff's station and dropped their bikes. Except for Billy, who leaned his bike up against the wall of the building.

Dean stopped them in their tracks when he asked, "What are we going to say, so they'll let us in to see him?"

"I suppose I'll say that he's my uncle," Billy shrugged, "it should work."

"We don't even know his name, though," Troy said.

"We rode all this way, and I'm not leaving until we talk to him. Hopefully, they'll let us in to see him," said Billy. In a hurry, he grabbed the door and swung it open. The cool air wafted outside as they entered the building.

Nervous, Billy stepped up to the counter as Mia sat talking on the phone. He overheard her say, "Yes, Midnight Javez Leõn," and then she stopped and looked up at him. She held up her pointer finger to let them know she saw them, as she listened intently to the other end of the line and covered the mouthpiece. "Give me a second and I'll be with you," she whispered, and turned her chair away from them.

Billy smiled. He had his name.

Coop walked in with bags of food and coffee cups on a carrying tray. The boys turned to see who was coming into the office, and he was surprised to see Billy standing there.

"Hey Billy, what's up?" he asked, as he walked around the corner of the counter and sat the supplies on top of a desk.

"I need to talk to my uncle." Billy lied.

Coop's eyebrows drew together. "Your uncle?"

"Yes, his name is Midnight," said Billy, nodding happily.

"Okay, uh, wait for Mia to get off the phone, because she has the final say," Coop said. He took two drinks and two styrofoam containers smelling of bacon and eggs to a room as he disappeared behind a heavy door.

Mia thanked the person on the other end of the line and hung up the phone.

She had a strange look on her face as she stared vacantly at the desk for a moment. Then she snapped out of the dazed expression and looked up at Billy.

She had seen this group of boys riding all over town and knew a few of their parents. They were a well-behaved group of kids.

"How can I help you?" Mia asked, as she gave a cursory smile and stood up from her chair and stretched.

Billy put on a rather pitiful me expression and said, "I need to talk to my uncle."

"Your uncle?" she asked.

"Yes, his name is Midnight, and I really need to see him," said Billy. He straightened his back to look taller and, hopefully, a little older.

Billy hoped she believed the lie that slipped out through his teeth. He didn't enjoy lying to anyone, and his mom told him to always tell the truth and make honest choices. She'd be disappointed if she saw him right now, but this was important.

Mia's eyebrows drew together as she put her hands on the counter. "I wasn't aware that he had relatives in this town."

"Oh, yes! He's my father's brother, and he has been here visiting," Billy said, hoping that she didn't see through the fib.

Coop came back out of the room and stood next to her, while Mia paused for a few seconds as she considered Billy's request to see Midnight.

"Normally, I would ask for an adult to be with you—" Mia was going to say more, but Billy interrupted her as he pointed out his conundrum.

"My mom is working a double shift, and I need to ask him a few questions for her. But I guess it can wait. If you can tell me when he's getting out of jail," Billy explained. The lie was growing bigger with every word he spoke.

Mia put her hands on her hips as she first looked at Coop, and then toward the boys. Then she thought, what would it hurt if she let them talk? Finally, she blew out a breath and asked, "Coop, will you take Lyle to the room across the hall?" Then she looked at the boys as she continued talking to Coop. "We will let the boys visit Midnight, but only for a few minutes."

Billy smiled, "Thanks, my mom will really appreciate it."

Coop went to get Lyle while Mia made another phone call. She had already called the number on the black card, but this time the call was to the coroner's office.

"Pope County Coroner's office, Angel speaking." Her voice rung like a bell in Mia's ear.

"Angel, it's Deputy Mia from Sugar Bee. I wanted to know if you could go over the case that involved Ms. Auntie DeLeon?"

"Yes, I did the autopsy, and it looks like she died from a myocardial infarction. I am ninety-nine percent sure that is the cause of death. She may have had sleep apnea for a very long time, and it stressed her body out to where her heart just couldn't take it anymore. In layman's terms, she died of a heart attack."

"Okay, I will continue to look for her next of kin today," Mia informed her. "Is there anything strange about the autopsy?" Mia asked before she ended the call.

Coop walked out of the interrogation room and said, "Come on, Billy, follow me."

Billy stood frozen for a moment. Then he stammered, "Uh, can my friends come in with me?"

"I don't see why not," Coop said, as he motioned with his hand for the group to follow him.

They slowly filed in line, and followed Coop like he was a momma duck, and they were his ducklings.

"You have a few visitors," said Coop, stepping into the room.

Midnight was laying down, but his interest was piqued when he heard he had visitors. He sat up on the bed, wondering who it could be.

Coop held the door open for the boys as they filed into the featureless gray room. A wide stripe of yellow paint ran parallel to the bars in front of the cells on the floor.

Billy rushed forward and spoke first. "Hello, Uncle Midnight," he said and gave a wink, as he tilted his head and rolled his eyes toward Coop. He hoped Midnight wouldn't give them away.

"Stay on this side of the yellow line. Do not cross it," Coop instructed, as he pointed to the yellow strip on the floor.

In unison, they looked down and back at Coop. Billy spoke up as the others nodded. "We won't, I promise."

Then Coop stepped out of the room.

CHAPTER 27

MIDNIGHT MEETS THE BOYS

The room was quiet as Midnight, and the boys stared at each other for a few seconds. Then Billy stepped forward, making sure not to go beyond the yellow line.

"Hello, my name is Billy," his voice quavered, "and we have several questions for you."

This was a first for Midnight, and he had a feeling these were the boys from last night. He leaned forward on the cot and said, "How can I help you?"

"We know you saw the same thing we saw last night, at the old lady's house next door." Billy blurted out the words as if they were stuck in his throat.

There was a pause in conversation, as Billy looked at Midnight. He wondered if he was making the right decision by being here. Was this guy trustworthy? He was a stranger, after all.

Midnight sat silent for a moment. He looked up at the cameras and back at the young men standing before him. What did he have to lose? He stood up slowly, as they seemed to shrink back, away from the cell. With his hands at his sides, he stood motionless as he spoke.

"Yes, I saw the Wisps, and if we don't do something about it soon, there will be more trouble than I can handle," he replied. Even though time was of the essence, he remained calm and unmoving in the center of the cell.

Billy knew it! This guy was here to help them, but he had one more question. No, make that two more questions.

"If you are here to help, then what are they called?" asked Billy.

Midnight looked Billy in the eye and spoke slowly, "They are called many things, goblin, elf, and demon, to name a few. They adopted the name Gremlin, back in World War II. But a very long time ago, they were known as the Vandalow."

There was an audible gasp when they heard the name echo around the room.

"That's what we know them by, the Vandalow." Billy's voice shook.

"There was an old gypsy woman. She put a curse on a man who angered her and hurt her family. Through the years, the curse has grown weaker and weaker, and then it skipped every other generation. Which made it more difficult to find your poor, un-suspecting neighbor.

"The old woman next door to you slipped through my purview. You see, she was adopted, and became very challenging to find.

"I was trying to save her, but the Sheriff caught me before I could get into her house. Sadly, I was too late, and she died."

With that last statement, Billy had the answer to his second question.

Troy stepped forward and said, "We read the legend of the Vandalow last night," he pointed to Billy and Butch, "and then these two guys snuck over to the old woman's house and saw the Wisps."

Midnight put his hands together behind his back, then turned and paced as he spoke. "Yes, they saw the Wisps escaping from the underworld. Next, they will turn into the one thing the person favors or loves. It can be any sort of animal that eats meat. What happens next is the Vandalow."

He stopped pacing and turned to the boys and said, "In its first animal form, if it kills another animal or even an insect on the day or night of the full moon. It is considered a sacrifice. Then, the theory is, before daylight; they turn into their true form. That is how they become a Vandalow."

"How can we kill them, or send them back?" Billy asked.

Midnight was deep in thought, as he placed his thumb and first two fingers on his chin and stroked downward on the stubble, which had grown in during the last few days. Then he said, "You can't send them back. Not the way they came here. It doesn't work that way, but" he held up his pointer finger, "you can change them back into the form of the thing they killed at the time of the full moon."

"So, if they killed a rat?" Billy asked.

Midnight's hands became animated. He used them to punctuate his words, so the boys could understand what he was trying to convey, as he said, "Then they become a rat, until they die, and in essence, they are sent back to the underworld.

"Any form of animal, or insect that they killed to become a Vandalow, they will turn back into that form. If they kill a bird, they will become a bird or a spider, or a butterfly, a skunk, a rabbit, so on and so forth."

The room became unnervingly quiet as Midnight continued to speak. "They can die by our hand, or by sunlight, but only in Vandalow form. I suspect cats are the issue?"

"Yes!" Dean said.

"They will have to be gathered up and contained. Just to make sure they aren't Vandalow," Midnight instructed.

"How are we going to do that?" Butch asked.

"Those cats are loose and running around the neighborhood, right next to my house," Billy's eyes grew wide with fright, "we have to do something."

"Do you know what the rest of the curse says?" Troy asked Midnight.

Then the door swung open. "Come on boys, your time is up," Coop announced, as he held the door open.

"Can we have two more minutes?" asked Billy.

"Two minutes, then you have to go. We need to talk to Mr. Leõn before he gets released." Coop was fair, but firm.

"Okay, thank you, Coop," said Billy, as he smiled politely, and looked like the very picture of innocence.

The boys watched as the heavy steel door closed, painfully slow. As soon as it latched with a click, their heads swiveled right back to Midnight.

"Yes, I know what to do. I have the rest of the curse right here," Midnight said as he pointed to his temple. "As soon as they let me out. I will make my way to the dearly departed one's house." Then he pointed at the group and said, "I will meet you there."

Billy wasn't thrilled with his reply as he frowned and asked, "What can we do to protect ourselves?"

"Get a container of salt and weapons," Midnight answered.

Then the door opened again.

"Salt?" asked Billy.

"We will talk soon," Midnight said, as he stared at Billy and waved to dismiss them.

"Come on guys, it's time," Coop interjected, as he held the door open.

Billy walked past Coop, through the doorway, and his friends followed close behind. He saw Mia sitting in a room with Lyle as they passed the opened door. He overheard Lyle say, "I am telling you, man! There are little monsters out there, and I'd like to stay right here, in jail, where I know I'm safe!" He pointed toward the floor.

Gently, Mia said, "Lyle, I need you to go home. For now, I will allow you to go back to the cell and make plans to leave town. But you can't stay here indefinitely."

Billy and the boys got on their bikes and pedaled back toward town.

Dean spoke first. "Oh my God! What are we going to do?" He pedaled faster, to stay caught up with the group, so he could hear them.

"We definitely need a plan," Troy said as he huffed and puffed, fighting gravity as they went up the hill.

"We need weapons!" Butch added.

Billy smiled and said, "I have an idea. We need salt and lots of it." He suddenly felt resilient with determination as he stood up and pedaled harder.

* * *

Mia was frustrated by the lack of sound as she watched the interaction between Midnight and the boys on the computer screen. The camera fed her the image of them standing there, talking to him.

The phone call she had made before letting them in to talk to Midnight left her with more questions.

Coop was handcuffing Midnight to the table, as Mia gathered her wits before dealing with him.

Midnight sat straight in the chair and watched her patiently as she walked into the room. "You made the phone call, I see," he said.

"Yes, I did," she cleared her throat, as she sat down across from him, "and I have questions."

Mia looked for any cues from him, but he gave nothing away. His expression was passive, except for one raised eyebrow, as he made no movement, and said, "Ask away."

Mia began by asking, "What is L&M, Incorporated?"

Good. She pulled no punches. She got right to the point, thought Midnight. "It's a company that I work for, and we go where we are needed, to help communities with," he paused, "odd situations," unruffled by the question, palms up, he slowly spread his hands as far as the metal cuffs would allow.

Coop had left the room momentarily, but came back and leaned on the steel frame of the doorjamb.

Midnight turned his head and saw Cooper Daniels standing there. He nodded at Coop and looked back at Mia.

Midnight tilted his head toward Coop and said, "Ask Mr. Daniels about me. We met before my confinement."

Mia looked at Coop with raised eyebrows.

"It's true. Remember earlier when I told you about possibly meeting him on Curtis's farm? He helped me with the tractor and," now realizing Midnight had been pumping him for information. He stared Midnight down, "he asked me a lot of questions about the town."

Mia watched Midnight and asked, "What did your nephew want?"

Midnight changed tactics as he asked, "How about we talk about what is happening with your town?"

"Alright, go ahead." She leaned back in her seat and let him talk.

"My cell mate is quite a talker. He was telling me about seeing 'little gray creatures' around his house." Midnight paused, then said, "Look, you won't trust me. Not until you see for yourself. Has anything else happened?" Midnight asked with concern.

Mia leaned forward as she spoke. "Sheriff Halsey was hurt in a wreck. The other man had no brakes, and he hit Halsey's cruiser in the side. He said he was 'attacked by a gray creature.'"

Coop said, "I went to check on Lyle's house and my place while I was out getting breakfast. But the only thing I saw were some scratches on his door and a few dumpsters knocked over."

"You wouldn't see anything else. They hide from the daylight and if any were killed, they turn into something natural," Midnight said.

"What do you mean by natural?" asked Mia.

"They turn into a bug or an animal. They don't lay dead for you to find them."

"How are we supposed to take you for your word?" asked Mia. She was skeptical of Midnight and frustrated by his lack of forthcoming.

"You made the call, correct?"

"Yes, but this all sounds unbelievable."

"All you can do is trust me...I am here to help," Midnight said as he tilted his head and looked at her with a hopeful expression on his face.

"Give me a moment and I'll be right back." She stood up and walked toward Coop as he stepped back out into the hallway.

"Follow me," she said and closed the door.

Coop followed her to the front office, where she stopped and spun back toward him.

"Mia, before I went to get the prisoner's food, I also went out to the mill and dropped off the cats. I saw scratches on the doors clear up to the door handles. But I didn't see anything else."

"I want to trust this guy. My heart says to trust him while my head says another thing. This can't be happening. It's all too strange, and I must admit...quite overwhelming." She gave an unladylike snort, shook her head, and tossed up her hands in exasperation as she said, "It's my first day of acting Head Sheriff, and I can't believe that nothing is going right!"

"What did L&M incorporated say on the phone?"

"I called and was immediately put on hold. There were a series of clicks, like I was being transferred somewhere else. Then a man answered, 'L&M Incorporated, how may I help you?'

"I asked him if Midnight worked for them, and he said 'yes.' He also mentioned that 'he was in the field'. I told him Midnight was sitting in my jail cell right now, being questioned about a woman's death. The guy stated that 'Midnight was in the town of Sugar Bee, and he was looking for a woman named Auntie DeLeon.' He asked about Auntie, and if she was the 'deceased person.' I told him yes. The guy said that was too bad. They were there to save her." Mia shook her head in exasperation.

Coop stepped forward and lightly placed his hand on Mia's shoulder. He dipped his head down, and looked her directly in the eyes and said, "Go with your gut."

She took a calming breath and nodded. "I'm going to release him."

Coop smiled thinly as he gave her shoulder a slight squeeze. "I'll watch him. I promise."

CHAPTER 28

PREPARE TO DIE

By the time Billy and the boys pedaled into town, they had slowed to a crawl.

"Could that hill be any bigger?" asked Billy.

"Yeah, it straight up sucked," said Butch. "Get it? It straight up…sucked?"

"Hardy har har," Billy answered, "dude, that was so lame."

They stopped at 'Luther's Hardware and Feed Store' and leaned their bikes up against the side of the building.

"Hey Billy, what are we doing here?" asked Dean, as he leaned his bike against the wall and walked toward Billy. His bike sat too close to the building, and it immediately fell over when he stepped away.

The boys chuckled at Dean's reacted, which was no reaction at all. He just kept walking. Because he was red faced and tired. The boys knew just how he felt, but it was still funny.

Billy smiled a mischievous grin and said, "I figured we could pick up the salt, and maybe a few other things."

They rambled past Luther's and walked into the Stop-N-Shop. It was akin to a grocery store, but tiny. After walking inside, they were grateful for the blessed cold air, as they stopped and let the refreshing cool air circulate around them for a moment. They grabbed cold drinks and looked for the salt. Naturally, they found the bags and small containers sitting together on a shelf amongst other seasonings.

Billy planned on only buying as much as he could carry. But after everyone picked up what they could transport, it left the store with one lonely container.

Billy picked it up with a shrug and said, "Might as well take the last one for good measure."

The group carried their haul to the cashier to pay for it.

Billy was surprised everyone coughed up the cash to pay for it all. They left the store and walked around the corner to sit their bags of salt beside their bikes. It was a small enough town they didn't have to worry about someone taking their stuff. Besides, who was going to steal salt?

"Hey, my dad has a tab at Luther's, so we can get whatever we want," said Troy proudly. "Plus, I don't think he will complain once he finds out we bought the stuff to protect the town."

Billy held the door open to Luther's store and let everyone walk inside. The climate-controlled building cooled their damp skin and red faces as they searched for anything that looked like a weapon.

Dean walked straight to the crowbars and picked one up. But he put it back and picked up a shorter one and gave it a swing. He raised it and said, "I'll take this one! It's just the right size."

Troy walked over to the only telescoping baton they sold in the store. He picked it up and swung it. With a smile, he said, "I've got mine. I like how I can hide it and when I need it." He flicked his wrist out and the baton shot to full length. "It's ready and deadly."

Butch walked over to the machetes and carefully picked one up. Then he gave it a swing. It was just the right length, and it wasn't too heavy.

He looked up from the blade and noticed everyone staring at him. "What?" he shrugged. "This is the one I want."

Billy went his own way and disappeared. While the boys were busy picking out their new weapons, he ambled around the corner. When they saw him, several mouths dropped in surprise!

Billy smiled a wicked grin and said, "Prepare to die!"

He wore two black straps crisscrossing across his chest, and two tomahawks were sticking out from each shoulder.

Dean's eyes grew wide as he whispered, "Holy shit!"

Butch nodded his approval and said, "That's badass."

Then Billy smiled and pulled out a box he had kept hidden behind his back. "What do you think of these?"

"I am getting me one of those!" Troy said excitedly.

"I want one!" Dean yelled.

"Me too! Where are they?" Butch asked as he walked toward Billy.

"Don't worry, they have plenty. I'll show you." Billy smiled and walked back around the corner.

They waited until the coast was clear and Luther was busy with a customer at the back of the store. Then they walked up to the counter.

The young goofy looking teenager rung them up with no questions asked. He didn't even stop to think why a group of kids would be buying this stuff.

Billy was smart. He had planned it out so they wouldn't be refused.

He'd said, "I mean, who's going to sell a machete, a crowbar, two tactical tomahawks, and a baton to a bunch of young boys?"

The group looked at Billy and smiled mischievously.

With the price tallied up, Troy stepped forward and said, "Please put it on my dad's account. His name is Mr. Travis Casey."

The teenager shrugged and asked for a phone number. Troy gave him his dad's cell number, and they walked out of the store, grinning from ear to ear.

CHAPTER 29

ALWAYS BE PREPARED

Midnight called a car service to get to his car, which seemed ironic. The Sheriff didn't offer him a ride, nor did they smile about setting him free. However, he had done nothing illegal. He was caught in the wrong place at the wrong time.

Mia handed him his confiscated items by begrudgingly setting them out onto the counter. Midnight affably picked them up one item at a time. He looked through his wallet and made sure everything was there before putting it back into his pocket. He didn't blame them for not being too ecstatic about letting him go. But the law was the law, and he felt fortunate that Mia was in charge. Halsey would have been a harder sell.

After being released, he walked, with a slight limp, out into the bright sunlight. The sun was so blinding, Midnight squinted and pulled out his dark sunglasses. As he put them on, he wondered how he was going to help this small, sleepy town. It was now a ticking time bomb.

Midnight waited patiently for his ride, as he leaned on the rough brick façade. He watched a small red vehicle pull up into the parking lot, then pushed off from the building. His foot was aching, and it made him stagger slightly while walking to the car.

The driver rolled down the window and smiled. "I take it you're Midnight," said the woman, behind the wheel. She wore large movie star sunglasses and had big curly blonde hair.

He nodded and said, "Yep, that's me."

She smiled and replied, "Well, come on and get in. I'm letting out the bought air."

Midnight gave her directions to his car as he put his seatbelt on in the back seat and perspired. He disliked riding with someone else, and it gave him pause. The wreck he'd been in before having a crushed foot was the driver's fault. Reportedly, others had said it was her lapse in judgment. Still, to his very core, he felt it was truly his fault.

He should've known that she wasn't up to the task, and it was a difficult judgement to make. Every decision he made could lead to a life-or-death situation. Midnight knew that, but in that critical moment, he needed his hands free to retaliate with deadly force.

At one point, they were in a tricky situation. He told her to drive on the left side of the road and to stay away from the right. Midnight knew IEDs were buried in the dirt on the barren desert road, and he had informed her of them.

Unfortunately, they came under enemy fire, and while escaping; they approached a blockade. It was set up by the enemy to ambush them. Ultimately, at the blockade, she went right instead of left.

As a result, the massive explosion lifted the heavily armored truck and blew a hole in the undercarriage, right where the driver sat.

For that reason, Midnight's heart palpitated with the flashback of the memory. He pushed the emotions back and reminded himself he wasn't there. He was here. Back in the States. Where driving is safe and IEDs are not placed roadside. Despite the evidence and because of the trauma, Sgt. Rosalyn Baker's face was a ghost he would never forget.

Midnight wiped his brow and forced himself to think of the present. The things that were happening right now. He looked outside the window of the car and watched as they drove past the town square. People were busy strolling about, walking in and out of the small businesses. On the left, he appreciated the plants and flowers of the park as they drove past.

He noted the pristine white church with its very tall steeple as they drove by and turned right, proceeding farther up the hill. They were now driving toward the High School and with a quick jog to the left; the driver pulled up to his car.

Midnight smiled when he saw the car was left undamaged. It sat right where he had left it. Thank God for small towns, and even smaller favors, he thought as he thanked the driver, and got out of the car. Paranoia kept him on his toes as he looked around and made sure no one was watching. Midnight pulled out the key fob and hit the button to unlock the doors.

Being extra cautious, he opened the door and hit the trunk and hood buttons. He wanted to make sure the vehicle wasn't tampered with before getting behind the wheel. After checking under the car, Midnight slipped the cell phone out of his pocket and made a call to HQ. They needed an update.

* * *

Now that Midnight finished his phone call. He decided he needed a large cup of coffee and a fresh change of clothes. Since he had no place to change and clean up, Midnight drove to the highway and turned toward Ska Dale. Listening to the tires hum against the highway, he thought about his circumstances and the situation at hand.

He didn't want to be responsible for the boys who came to visit him. But they were already involved and too close to the situation. It could be dangerous for them either way, and he was already dealing with the guilt over the loss of Sgt. Baker. But with everyone at the company busy dealing with their own issues out in the field. He needed to recruit them. Could he take a chance on these kids? His mind screamed No! Although at this very moment, what choice did he have?

Since he was so hyper focused on deciding what to do, he almost missed the first exit to a hotel. If it wasn't for the large commercial road sign, which had four gentlemen in white and black checkered suits standing together, with cool whipped hair. As they sang into a retro metal microphone, with a logo boasting, Scoobedy Scoobedy Ska Dale. He would have missed the exit.

After checking in and grabbing his bag out of the trunk, he stuck the key card into the lock above the door handle and entered a nice, clean room.

"It's an upgrade from my previous sleeping accommodations," he said as he grinned, and dropped his bag on the bed and turned on the shower.

He made quick work of showering and getting dressed. Midnight picked up the paper cup of coffee he'd made with the mini coffee maker and snapped the lid on. He took the bag from the bed and jumped back into the car. It was time to meet the boys.

As Midnight drove back to Sugar Bee, his thoughts turned to the plan. But with every plan that was processed in his mind, there were too many scenarios that couldn't be compensated for. Since he didn't know what the actual situation was yet, he needed to see it for himself. Then plan for the worst and hope for the best.

After driving through town, Midnight pulled up and parked next to the house which belonged to Auntie DeLeon. He felt pity for the woman, even though they had never met. He had hoped to find her in time to help her. But sadly, it was too late.

Shaking off the melancholy that took hold as he sat waiting, he turned on the radio. The song ended, and a commercial came on about a concert on the night of the full moon.

"Tonight only! Chet Brown will play at Sugar Bee, debuting his new song, 'Moonlight and Magnolia's'! Don't miss this, one of a time opportunity, to see him. Live on his 'Full Moon Tour!'" The commercial ended and Midnight shut off the radio.

"Great! Let's just add one more log to the fire, Sugar Bee!" Midnight grumbled out loud as he tapped his fingers on the steering wheel. Now he was feeling antsy.

The road sloped as he gazed down at Black Willow Lane. Soon he saw a boy on a bike. His body bobbed up and down as he stood up on the pedals and worked his legs. He watched the boys struggle to get up the hill and put his hand on the key to start the car. But then thought better of it as his hand fell away from the key. He needed to earn their trust and vice versa. Their energy was being wasted, but they would bounce back with some rest, he thought to himself.

When he was in training, it was a brutal onslaught of mind-numbing exhaustion and pain. The thought of those days made him smile because he was better for it. It taught him to think and react quickly. To use critical thinking and the concepts of it with precision to befit any situation. Also, to develop a method to become five steps ahead of everyone who trained with him. Midnight's smile grew as he thought back to those days when he was young and cocky. But with age came experience and a modest amount of humbling, as he helped the less fortunate around the world.

The boy named Billy was the first to drop his bike and bag in the front yard. While the rest sluggishly made it up the hill, Billy disappeared behind the house and came back out carrying bottled water. The boys were sitting on the ground in the shade of a tree as he tossed the bottles to them. Good, they had a leader, Midnight thought to himself.

Midnight got out and leaned on the front corner panel of the car. He crossed his arms and remained silent as he stood there, waiting for them to rest and get their second wind.

He noticed the brand-new duffel bags with white price tags on them, and a few full backpacks. Plus a few grocery bags of what he hoped was salt. The bulk of the two duffle bags had heft. He could only assume they had bought some weaponry. He was impressed. They needed to be prepared for anything.

"I see you made it out of the slammer," said Billy.

Midnight gave a nod. "Yeah, they had nothing on me." Except trying to break into your neighbor's house to help her, he thought to himself.

"So, what's the plan?" Billy asked, folding his arms across his chest.

"I need to check out the cat situation."

"Uh-oh," said Billy, a worried look creased his brow. "Earlier today, Cooper Daniels let me take Mr. Grimm.

214

Auntie's Maine Coon cat, out of her house. You should've seen how mean those cats were when I brought him outside in a pet carrier. They don't like Mr. Grimm, and he doesn't like them too much either. The cats started to hiss and spit at us, and I thought we were gonna to be attacked! Then Mr. Grimm let out the loudest growl I've ever heard, and the cats became scared and scattered out of the yard."

"Let's go see if any came back," said Midnight. He hit the key fob as he walked to the trunk of the car, and the lid popped open. He reached into a bag and grabbed his telescoping baton.

The boys knew what he was doing, and they grabbed their weapons.

Midnight shut the trunk and turned around to see the boys standing there with weapons in hand.

Billy saw Midnight's surprised expression as he held one of his tomahawks down to his side. He shrugged and said, "Always be prepared."

"Right now, we are only dealing with cats. The Vandalow will come out at night," Midnight explained.

"We figured that out, but you didn't see how those cats reacted and I'd feel safer if I had a weapon," Billy said.

"It's daylight and I don't want your neighbors calling the Sheriff. Do you have anything other than these weapons?" Midnight suggested, "Maybe some baseball bats?"

Billy nodded and handed his tomahawk to Dean as he said, "Put them up for now. I'll go grab our other stuff. Troy, keep your baton."

Billy strode into the house and came back out carrying the baseball bats. Midnight saw a broken handle to an old tool and one of the bats had nails all over it. He approved of the weapons.

Midnight looked up and down the street for any sign of people, or worse, the Sheriff sitting nearby. But the street was silent. He saw no movement, and nothing had changed since he had parked. "Alright, let's go."

They snuck over to the side of Auntie's house. Watching for any movement as they walked closer to the backyard. Quietly, they crept to the back corner of the house and peered around the corner.

The cats had vanished. They were scattered into the woods.

CHAPTER 30

GRAY CREATURES

As soon as Midnight left, Mia turned to the internet. She was savvy with cyber space and could find any sort of information about anyone.

She looked up, L&M Inc. and found only one blip online. "That's strange. There isn't any information about the company Mr. Leõn works for on here. The name is there, but that's it." She looked to the side of the monitor and saw Coop doing his own research on Halsey's computer.

Coop searched for 'small gray creatures with big teeth.' Rabbits, fish, and lemur images popped up across the screen. Frustrated, he put the words 'mythical small gray creatures with big teeth' into the search bar. After hitting the enter key, images popped up of gargoyles, yeti, and other gray monsters with big teeth. They were very menacing and grotesque looking.

As he scrolled; he found a wicked-looking creature which was small in stature. He leaned around the screen and looked at Mia. "I have an idea. Let's bring Lyle out and see if he can tell us what the creatures look like from these pictures."

"That's a great plan." Mia's countenance changed from discouraged to hopeful and then to eager. She pushed her chair away from the desk and went to get Lyle, as Coop kept scrolling through the images. At one point, he stopped and scrolled back to the top. Coop's head popped up when he heard movement coming from the cell room, and he saw Lyle dragging his feet.

"Hey Lyle, I wanted to see if you could recognize the creature here online," said Coop, while he slipped out of his office chair.

Lyle hesitated and said, "I don't want to see another one of those things. They were creepy."

Coop held the chair out for Lyle to sit down and he pushed him up to the desk.

With a gentle voice, Mia encouraged Lyle. "It will only take a minute, and then you can either choose to spend another night here or leave."

Lyle looked at her with pleading eyes as he said, "I'd rather stay here."

"Okay, it's fine with me if you stay another night."

Nervous, Lyle rolled his shoulders to release the tension, and turned his blood-shot eyes toward the screen.

He only scrolled down once.

"That's it!" Lyle sprang up from the desk and pointed at the image. He looked pale as he shrank away from the monitor. His reaction seemed unhinged, like he was paranoid the creature might jump through the screen. "That's what I saw!"

Coop looked at the screen and clicked on the picture to enlarge it. "You saw this right here?" he asked, as he pointed at it.

"Yes! Oh man, there were a lot of them, too. Then one of them stopped and looked at me! I'll never forget its ugly face; it totally freaked me out! It was dark, but by the light from the porch and the streetlight, I could see it. I'm telling you, man; it looked just like that. At first, I was horror-struck, but when those little hounds from hell started coming closer, I ran into the house. I didn't sleep a wink all night, and I hitched a ride straight down here as soon as it was daylight. After dawn I looked for them, but they had disappeared."

Lyle was visibly shaking. He kept putting his hand to his mouth. Then he crossed his arms and shook as if he were cold and couldn't get warm.

Mia took pity on Lyle and walked over to him. "Come on Lyle. Let's put you back in the cell and get you a blanket. I'll bring you some hot coffee here in a second." Mia touched his elbow and escorted him back to the unit. After she came out of the room. She walked over to the coffeemaker and poured him a cup of coffee.

Coop picked up the phone and made a call.

"We need a plan," she said, walking away carrying Lyle's coffee.

Down to business, Mia returned a few minutes later.

"I called the Car Service, and they told me they dropped off Midnight close to Auntie's house," said Coop.

Mia wrung her hands for a moment. "Send me the image and whatever information you've gathered on the creature."

"Maybe we need to talk to Midnight again," Coop said, as he sent a copy by email to Mia.

Mia opened the email and looked at the picture. It was grotesque looking, with gray wet skin, batwing like ears, and huge teeth.

"Maybe we do. But for now, let's do the research. I want to know everything about these little monsters."

The phone rang, and Mia snagged up the receiver without a second thought and said, "Pope County Sheriff's Department."

"Mia?" a woman's voice enquired.

"Yes," she'd heard the woman before, but couldn't place the name.

"This is Lana Galloway." Her voice sounded anxious.

Mia immediately grew worried and asked, "How is the Sheriff?"

"He is doing okay, but they are running more tests. He is awake now and talking, but he's in a lot of pain. Jake has a broken radius and, of course, they are giving him a brain MRI to make sure he has no damage there; he was unconscious for quite a while." There was a pause for a moment, then she spoke again. "I was wondering if you knew about the attack on JP?"

"Yes, we are aware," said Mia. She was instantly interested in what Lana had to say.

"Whatever did this," Lana paused, "It's not a normal bite. What I am saying is, if what he told me is true, then you need to get to the mill. Plus, I need someone to go check on my boys, because I told them to stay in the house. I just want to make sure they're safe."

Mia could hear the fear in Lana's voice as she told her. "I'll go check on them. Cooper is here helping me, while the Sheriff is out. He went to the mill this morning and checked it out, but he didn't see anything. If we find out anything else, we will let you know. I'll tell your boys to get home, and stay there, and to call you."

"Okay, thank you. I really appreciate it."

Mia hung up the phone and grabbed her keys from the desk as she stood up. "I'm going to check on Lana's boys, and since I will already be in the area, I'll look for Midnight. Do you mind monitoring Lyle and doing some research?" Antsy, she tapped her foot and waited for his answer.

"Go ahead. I'll be doing as much fact finding as I can."

"Do me a favor while I'm gone." Mia wrote on a piece of paper. "Call this number, ask for this name, and ask this question. Then shoot me a text."

Coop took the paper and glanced at it. His face showed disappointment as he said, "Gotcha."

CHAPTER 31

LIAR LIAR PANTS ON FIRE

Billy heard the phone ringing and said, "Hang on, I'll be right back!" He snatched the phone off the wall and answered, "Hello?"

"Billy! What the heck? Where have you been?"

Billy rolled his eyes. "Mom, I've been sitting here with my friends."

"Why didn't you answer the phone earlier?"

Lana was mad, and Billy knew it from the soprano in her voice. Every time she got mad, her voice went higher in pitch and grew louder.

"I must've missed your call when I was sitting out on the front porch." Billy crossed his fingers.

"I thought I told you to stay inside the house!" Lana yelled into his ear.

"Geez Mom, okay, I will stay in the house."

He could hear her take a deep breath and blow it out slowly. "Let me start over, okay? I had a case earlier and this patient lives in our town. This person was attacked by some kind of gray animal, and then while getting help, said patient got into a terrible wreck."

Billy thought of the broken glass and metal pieces on the big curve to the Sheriff's station.

"There's an animal running around with seriously big teeth, and that's why I want you to stay indoors!" Lana paused and said, "Please do as I ask for once!"

Billy felt bad. She was only trying to keep them safe. "I'm sorry, mom. I promise we'll stay indoors."

"Thank you, I need to go, son. It's been busy here today. I love you."

"I love you too, goodbye."

As Billy hung up the phone, he thought about his mom and knew she could throw a monkey wrench into their plans easily. Billy had to keep her safe, happy, and out of this town for as long as he could.

He walked back to the kitchen table, and as soon as he sat down, someone knocked on the front door.

"Good grief!" Billy rolled his eyes as he got up and said, "I'll be right back."

He hurried down the hallway and looked around the corner to where Max was still passed out asleep. Sneaking across the carpet, he opened the door.

He was surprised as he opened the screen door. "Hello, let me step out here, so I don't wake up my brother," he whispered, while stepping outside and gently closing the door.

"Hey, Billy, I just wanted to make sure you were going to the concert tonight," said Katie Daniels.

"Do you know when it starts?"

"I think it starts at 8 o'clock."

"I might be late, but I'll be there." Billy promised.

"Okay, see you then." She smiled and waved bashfully, then turned around and jogged to a parked car, which was idling against the curb.

Feeling thrilled, he smiled with excitement as he watched the car pull away. She was so pretty, and he couldn't believe she was standing at his front door asking to meet him at the concert.

After watching her car leave, he heard another vehicle coming from the other direction. The look of shock on his face had to be clear when the Sheriff's cruiser pulled up and came to a full stop right in front of his house.

"Oh crap," he mumbled under his breath. He marched toward the car as the passenger window rolled down. It was Deputy Mia.

"Hey Billy, is Max in the house?"

Billy wasn't even surprised. "Yeah, do you need to talk to him?"

"No, I was just dropping by to check on you guys. Your Mom was worried when nobody answered the phone, so she called me."

Billy acted nonchalant. "Max is sleeping, and I was out here on the front step when I must've missed her call. Except for this morning, I've been here the whole time."

Mia's phone jingled, and Billy watched as she looked down and read the text.

Unexpectedly, Mia looked him straight in the eye as she smirked. Then one eyebrow rose, and she said, "When you see your uncle, tell him 'Hi' for me." After that, she stared at him as she slowly rolled away, letting Billy know he was busted for lying.

Billy stood there and tapped his foot for a few seconds as she continued to roll, like a turtle, down the road. Then he ran around the house through the backdoor and walked into the kitchen. "Sorry, I had to take care of a few things. One of which was my mother calling deputy Mia. She just stopped by to make sure that we were home."

After shutting the door, he turned toward the table and saw everyone quietly watching him. Troy, Butch, Dean, and Midnight were sitting there waiting on him with the book laying open on the table.

"It's a good thing you parked your car in the backyard," said Billy as he walked over to a chair at the table and sat down to listen to what Midnight had to say.

"I have a secret email on my phone. I know I told you the rest of it was memorized. But I wasn't sure who was listening in on our conversation." Midnight looked down at his phone and read aloud:

The rest of the curse was found separate from the book created by an old gypsy woman named Eldorai.
Like the seeds of a dandelion, the beasts will appear. Bringing chaos and death to all who are near.

*Now, to reverse the curse…The tricksters can be
lured by a booming sound.
Ring salt in a circle all over the ground. When the
creature draws its final breath, they shift into the
form of the sacrificed death. They will boil and
bubble at the dawning of the day. The creatures
will live on, in earth's mortal clay.*

He paused for a moment and said, "Sound draws them. Salt will imprison them, and the daylight will turn them into their natural earthly form."

Immediately worried, Billy said, "First thing you need to know is that a big concert is playing tonight. It's at the park right in the middle of town," Billy's eyes were wide with fear, "and we don't know how many are going to turn tonight."

"They have to sacrifice an animal or insect today, throughout the day, or by dawn tomorrow morning to turn into a Vandalow," Midnight informed them.

Midnight saw the shocked faces surrounding the table and said, "The real question is, when did they last eat? Billy, did you see her feed them?"

"I think I remember seeing the old lady feeding them once in the morning, and once at night."

Butch chimed in, "Okay, so they were probably fed yesterday evening. That means they missed their morning meal."

Midnight presumed, "They will hunt for food. Which will be considered a sacrifice if they kill something."

Billy was upset as he said, "I don't think you get it. There are a lot of cats, and by a lot, I mean possibly two hundred or more."

"Aim higher. There's at least three hundred, easy," said Max as he strutted into the kitchen. He picked up a cup with one hand and turned on the faucet with the other.

Midnight observed the boys. They were silent as they watched this older kid take a drink, which he surmised was Billy's older brother.

Max glanced at Billy. He used his cup hand to point at Midnight, and it looked similar to toasting him with a drink, as he remarked, "Who's the old guy?"

Midnight almost chuckled out loud, as he saw Billy duck from embarrassment.

Completely red from feeling awkward, Billy said, "Uh, Max, meet Midnight. Midnight, this is my brother Max."

Max wore a tough expression, but the outer corners of his mouth lifted when he said, "Sup?"

Midnight saw the smirk and recognized the scar. It was only on one side, but he bet it hurt, nonetheless. The kid had a Glasgow smile. He'd seen a few of those savage scars during his career. But it was a vicious thing to receive at such a young age and he knew this kid had to be one tough operator.

"Hey Bruiser," Midnight tossed the nickname to Max. "How many cats do you think there are, total?"

Max smiled, which made him look smug, and took another long drink of his water as he thought about it. After he swallowed, he replied, "I bet there's around three hundred and fifty. I've watched them grow in number recently, out in the woods, behind our house. They're always out there hunting," Max replied as he leaned against the counter.

"Have you seen anything strange here in town or out in the woods?" Midnight asked, while giving nothing away.

"Yeah, last night my friend and I were over by the Pub. We were screwing around when this little gray creature with massive, jagged teeth came at us." Max looked at him and waited for his reaction.

Midnight was sure the kid probably thought the only grownup in the room wouldn't believe him. But with a sober look, Midnight threw a nod his way and asked, "What did you do?"

Jeff appeared right then, and as he walked to the sink, he said, "Max punted that little sucker in the head, like it was a football! It was the funniest thing I'd ever seen!" He chuckled, turned on the water, then cupped his hands together and took a swig.

Max's expression turned smug as he lifted his chin and crossed his arms. Like he was daring the old man to believe him.

Midnight busted out laughing. He laughed for a good long minute, and then his laughter died.

The boys continued to chuckle at Midnight for laughing so hard.

"That's great! I bet it wasn't expecting that!" he smiled. But then he settled down and stared at the kitchen table...silent for a few moments.

His demeanor turned serious. "You only tangled with one of them, and if you are correct, with your count. We need to set up one hell of a plan to catch them. They are attracted to noise, and the concert is tonight, so I hope right now, half of them are cats. What attracts cats?"

Dean chimed in, "Cat food."

"Good," Midnight agreed, "what else?"

Billy remembered what the old woman did when she fed her cats and said, "They came running when she shook the cat food bag, and they seemed to like it when she talked to them."

Max snickered, "Great! Are you going to talk like a little old lady?"

"Mimicry is a great idea," said Midnight as he ignored the sarcasm in his comment. Midnight knew that creating a plan was going to be difficult. So, he welcomed the ideas as he asked, "How do we catch the cats?"

"We need a good-sized cage," Troy said.

"Maybe something that doesn't quite look like a cage?" asked Butch.

"Camouflage, that's a great idea," said Midnight, as he kept an open mind to every notion. Because, truthfully, they were going to need a lot of luck.

Midnight asked, "What could we use for the cage?"

"They have live traps here in town. Ask Cooper Daniels," Max said, while he smirked at the memory of watching Coop as he took the traps out into the woods to let skunks and raccoons loose. He always enjoyed watching Coop as he dealt with the angry, wild animals.

"What does it say again about the salt?" asked Billy.

"To 'ring' it in a circle on the ground to catch them. They can't cross a line of salt," Midnight explained.

"Is that while they are cats or Vandalow?" asked Billy.

"Interesting. Maybe we should test that theory. We should test that same theory with noise as well." Midnight was thinking out loud.

Troy was looking at his phone and said, "They say that cats are more active at sunrise and sunset. They love cooked chicken and mackerel, and they know when and where their usual feeding time is." Troy looked at Billy. "We need to set up our trap in your neighbors' backyard."

Midnight was impressed. "We have already missed their morning feeding, but we can try for the evening meal. We will cut it pretty close to dark, but I don't see a choice right now."

He looked at the boys; they were hanging on every word. Midnight asked Max, "Do you mind testing the salt and noise theory?"

Max stood in the center of the kitchen, exuding confidence. He lifted his chin and said, "I'm on it."

Max nodded and looked at his sidekick and said, "Come on, Jeff, we need to make some noise." On a mission, he grabbed the salt container out of the cabinet and slammed it shut. Then Max and Jeff swaggered out the backdoor.

Billy went to check on Mr. Grimm. The huge cat was resting on his bed, snoozing, as Billy walked in and gave him a pat on the head.

"Hey Mr. Grimm. I'm glad you look happy. Get some rest, and I'll be back in a while." Mr. Grimm meowed, rolled over onto his back, and purred. Billy was glad he brought Mr. Grimm home to live with him, and he was growing attached already. He was such a cool-looking cat.

When Billy entered the kitchen, Midnight was getting up from the chair, as he said, "We need those traps and an enormous cage."

"I'll call Coop and see if we can use his traps," said Billy.

Troy grew excited as he hopped up from the kitchen chair and said, "Get laser pointers. Cats can't resist laser pointers!"

"That's an excellent idea, and I'll add them to my list." Midnight walked to the door and placed his hand on the knob. "One more thing, get some rest, boys. I have a feeling it's going to be a long night. I need to find a big box store and buy salt and look for a large trap while in Ska Dale. But I'll be back later."

Leaving the boys to wonder what else they could do; Midnight drove yet again to Ska Dale. He still had a nagging feeling of guilt. He had hoped for back up from his company, because he didn't want these kids to see the ugly side of war. But the plan was now in full swing and there was no way he could do it alone.

CHAPTER 32

BRING THE NOISE

Max and Jeff strutted out to the shed, and Max swung the door open wide. He found his bag of firecrackers and shoved the salt container inside the bag.

"I think we should go hunting out in the woods away from here. We don't want to scare them further away from the old lady's house," said Max, as he formed a plan. He pulled the lighter out of his pocket and flicked it a few times to make sure it still worked.

Jeff stood in the doorway listening to Max, then stepped back when Max was ready to leave. Together, they walked out of the backyard and down the dirt path. They saw nothing skittering around, so they continued to walk deeper into the woods. They walked well over a half a mile without seeing a cat.

Jeff stayed vigilant, but soon grew disappointed and said, "I can't believe we haven't seen a cat yet."

"Yeah, it's strange they aren't closer to where they know easy food is at the ready, unless." Max stopped and pointed his finger toward something moving in the woods. "They are already eating something."

The moggies were surrounding something on the ground. Their number was so great that the forest floor looked as if it was moving.

"Whoa," Jeff whispered, "how are we going to test the salt theory?"

Max pulled the salt container out of the bag and said, "Just watch me." Moving with stealth, he hid behind trees and crept up to where the cats were eating their meal. Then, when he was close enough, he climbed a tree and scooted out onto a long branch. While a white, long-haired cat sat happily, cleaning its paws after eating, Max surrounded it with salt. He kept the circle wide as to not alert the cat.

But the cat noticed and stopped licking its front paw and froze. Then its head swiveled as it looked for what alerted it. Max halted to see if it would continue with cleaning its paws so he could finish. When the cat continued with its primping, he finished the circle and waited.

Max could tell they were dining on a deer carcass and wondered if they took it down themselves.

Usually, he wouldn't wonder about such a thing. But these cats weren't normal. He had a thought. If these cats took down this deer, would they turn back into a deer after they become a Vandalow? That would be freaking cool, he thought to himself.

Tired of waiting, he threw the empty container to scare the cat. It landed next to it and the mouser skittered across the line of salt like it wasn't even there.

"Well, there goes that theory," Max mumbled to himself, as he shimmied backwards along the branch toward the trunk of the tree. As he climbed back down and hopped to the ground, a few of the cats saw him and froze. They watched him with suspicious little eyes until they became distracted by two angry cats. The cats were hissing and growling as they fought over their main course. Then the felines stopped and ran back to the carcass.

Max strolled back to Jeff, took the bag, and said, "Let's go to the far side of the group and see if they follow the noise."

Jeff agreed with a bob of his head.

They walked a wide berth around the fuzzballs, with their twitching tails, and the occasional hiss and growl, keeping quiet so as not to alarm them. When they decided they were far enough away, they looked for a spot with a good view of the cats. Since they wondered what the moggies were going to do when they set off a few fireworks, they found a clearing.

Max took a few regular sized firecrackers, which he had modified, and spliced the fuses together.

"These things are so loud," he chuckled, as he sat it on a patch of naked brown earth.

Jeff walked away as Max bent down and lit the fuse.

"Bring the noise!" He shouted as he walked away.

Then they looked through the forest of trees and watched.

BOOM! The homemade device exploded!

Every cat jumped! Several froze and swiveled their heads around. Quite a few looked their way, but most of them scattered in every direction. But none of them ran toward the noise.

Max and Jeff waited to see if it was a delayed reaction. Subsequently, for good measure, Max lit one more. After the explosion, the same thing happened, but none of the furballs walked their way.

Max said, "Hey, I just had a thought. If we're going to set traps with food. Then it won't work well if they are full of deer meat. Maybe we should bury the deer."

"Yeah, that's a good idea." They walked over to the deer and chased off the few remaining cats.

Then Max looked around for a trench or gully. He spotted a place where water had washed down the hill, creating a dip in the land and pointed. "Look over there. I see a decent spot."

They looked at the small deer and each grabbed a front leg to drag it to the new area.

As Max pulled on the leg, he was surprised. "It's not as heavy as I thought it would be."

"Yeah, it's just a small fry." Jeff tugged on the carcass.

They placed the deer in the gully and grabbed sticks and several rocks as they covered it with dirt.

When they were done, they stood over the shallow grave for a moment.

Jeff frowned as he said, "It's my first burial. Should we say something?"

Max grinned and then he grew serious. He picked up a handful of fresh dirt from the grave, then put his hands together in front of him and stood like a statue. It was a stance similar to a bouncer at a nightclub guarding the door.

Of course, Jeff did the same thing.

Then Max became serious and dropped his voice an octave as he prayed, "Ashes to ashes. Dust to dust. May Jeff find a girl with a really big bust."

Jeff's eyes were closed, and one eye popped open as he grinned wickedly at Max.

But Max wasn't finished yet. "May she be game for anything, and always be true. Never leaving Jeff in a state where he turns blue. As long as I'm asking and I know it's insane, I'd like to make out with Shelby Fontaine." Max smiled and finished his prayer with gusto. "Give us a warrior's strength, as we prepare to go. To kick the ass of the Vandalow…Oorah!"

"Oorah!" Jeff echoed.

They both tossed the dirt onto the top of the grave and grinned as they stepped away.

Looking around for the cats, Max grew disappointed and said, "What a bummer! I had hoped that at least one theory would have worked."

"Yeah, this sucks!" Bored, Jeff kicked a rock.

"Let's go to the house and see what else is going on." Max took his bag of firecrackers and swung it over his shoulder.

They trekked up the hill through the woods and into Max's back yard.

Max took the lead, as he bounded up the double steps to the backdoor and opened it. "What the hell!" he yelled. A huge furry body hit him with so much force, it knocked him back as it escaped out the door.

Max and Jeff jumped back even further, as the biggest long-haired cat they'd ever seen shot into the woods like a bullet.

Instantly infuriated, Max looked at Jeff and asked, "What in the hell was that thing doing in my house?" He was livid. Not so much about it being in the house, but because it scared him!

Jeff's eyes were bugging out as he stated facts. "Dude! That cat almost made me streak a brownie in my shorts."

Max was not in a laughing mood. He shook his head, grabbed the door, and hopped straight into the kitchen. Max was ready to wring Billy's neck!

"Billy! Where are you? I am going to kick your little ass!" he yelled.

In less than five seconds flat, he had walked through the entire house. Standing in their empty bedroom, he threw his hands up and said, "That little punk isn't even here!" Max wanted to hit something. He took one step and hauled off and struck the weighted punching bag that hung from the ceiling in the corner.

* * *

"Billy, I don't think we should be in here." Dean whispered.

"Why are you whispering?" Butch asked purposely being loud.

Billy's head was buried inside his deceased neighbor's closet, as he mumbled, "Ugh, it smells like old lady perfume in here." He reached up and tugged on a dress. "Come on guys," said Billy as he struggled with it, "we need to find something she used to wear so we can fool the cats."

Troy walked through the bedroom door sporting a gray, curly-haired wig and said, "Tell me, boys. Do I look sexy?" as he posed, while puckering his kisser.

Dean chuckled and replied, "I'd never kiss your dirty piehole."

Instantly, everyone started hooting and hollering.

Busy pulling a white and blue flowered dress from the closet, Billy saw Troy, and laughed so hard, tears sprung to his eyes.

"Hey, don't be hatin'," Troy said as he flipped his hair, making the big curls bounce. His new hairdo went well with his round, wire-rimmed glasses.

Butch laughed, "Dude, you really do look like an old lady.

Dean chuckled for a second, then went back to looking worried as he shook his head and said, "We really shouldn't be in here."

Billy had the dress in hand and started for the door. "Keep the wig. We can use it. Let's get out of here before we get caught." Then he remembered the litter box. He walked over, picked it up, and dumped it into the trash. Then he grabbed the bag of fresh kitty litter.

They snuck out the backdoor and waited while Billy locked it up and placed the key back under the doormat.

Max had calmed down, and was sitting on the swivel rocker, playing a video game, when Billy and the boys walked in through the front door.

"Billy, why would you have a huge cat in the house?" asked Max.

Billy forgot to tell him about Mr. Grimm, as he sat the cat supplies down and started toward the bedroom.

Max already knew where he was going and said, "The cat isn't there. When I opened the back door, it hit me in the side and ran into the woods. It's long gone."

Billy yelled, "Dang it Max! That cat was Mr. Grimm! He wasn't a Vandalow." His words started in anger, but in the end, he sounded heartbroken.

Max felt bad, but he didn't relent, as he squinted his eyes and asked, "How do you know for sure?"

Billy fretted and chewed on his lower lip with worry, as he said, "You should have seen how those cursed cats acted around him. I hope nothing happens to him."

Butch carried in the bag of goodies from the old woman's house. He dumped it onto the couch and said, "I just want to know who's going to be wearing this!"

Max leaned forward in the chair and said, "Not it!"

239

"Why don't we draw straws? And Max, I need you to go get the traps from Coop," said Billy.

"Okay, and how am I going to do that?"

"I don't know. Ask one of your truck driving friends." Billy retorted, then turned away and rolled his eyes.

Max looked over at his buddy and asked, "Hey Jeff, doesn't your mom's boyfriend have a truck?"

Jeff slowly looked up from the dress and wig. His facial expression had changed to a demented snarl, as he spoke in a villainous voice, and said, "Why yesss, I do believe that he does."

"Then let's go get it!"

Jeff lifted both of his hands together as if in a prayer. Then while his hands were together. He formed heavy metal signs with both hands and swung them up and wide to the ceiling as he yelled, "Let's rock and roll!"

Max smiled, jumped up, and they headed out the door.

Billy frowned as he thought about Mr. Grimm. He shuffled over to the swivel rocker and plopped down hard.

Troy and Dean were bummed about Billy's cat. So, they turned on his favorite video game and asked him if he wanted to play while Butch left the room. They wanted to cheer him up and keep moving forward with the plan.

Butch walked to the kitchen, grabbed a pair of scissors, and found two straws in the silverware drawer. He quickly cut them up and wrapped his fingers around the uneven side of the straws. Then he walked back into the living room and said, "Alright guys, I hope you're ready to draw straws. The shortest one is the granny."

Everyone got up as Butch stood in the center of the room, and Billy went first.

He pulled a single straw out of Butch's hand and held it up for them to see.

Troy went next as he pulled a straw and held it up.

Dean had a fifty-fifty chance. He carefully chose one and pulled it out, as Butch and Dean held theirs up alongside each other.

"Oh, man. This is going to suck," said Dean, with a high-pitched whine.

"You just keep practicing with that voice right there," Butch grinned.

"You should try on the dress and see how it looks," said Billy.

Dean whined a little and finally relented, as he grabbed the wig and the dress. "You guys owe me big time," he grumped as he walked to the bathroom.

* * *

Max and Jeff didn't bother to ask as they walked out the front door. They took two bikes from the boys and started down the hill to Jeff's house.

He didn't know who's bike he grabbed, but it was sick looking. It was all black with camo wheels, and it rode like a dream.

They cruised across town and made a stop at Jeff's house. Jeff ran inside and came back out smiling, as he held his hand up while jiggling the keys and said, "Let the shenanigans begin!"

They cruised quickly past the town square and rolled up to 'Chuck's Auto Mechanics.' It was an old white cinderblock building which was once a gas station a long time ago. Vehicles of all makes and models sat in the parking lot, waiting to be fixed, and Chuck's truck was located among them.

First, Jeff and Max took the bikes and slid them into the back of the truck. Next, Jeff opened the old driver's side door and put the key into the ignition. Then he turned it to unlock the steering column and slipped it into neutral. After that, Jeff looked at Max while he stood at the ready in front of the truck and nodded.

They pushed it backwards, away from the wooden fence, as Jeff turned the steering wheel. Finally, they got it backed up far enough to turn it toward the road and proceeded to push it forward.

The boys could hear music playing in the shop, and they hoped Chuck wouldn't hear them start it up as they pushed it out onto the road. It picked up momentum as the truck rolled down hill and Jeff jumped inside so it didn't get away from him. Max was pushing from behind and he started running to keep up with the truck. He laughed when the truck started rolling faster than he could run and hoped Jeff knew how to drive, otherwise the truck was going to roll down into a big ditch.

He saw Jeff jerk the wheel, and the truck lurched back onto the road as it coasted quietly another thirty feet. The brake lights lit up, and it slowly came to a stop. Max was smiling as he ran up to the truck and hopped into the passenger's side. He slammed the door shut and felt elated. His heart was pounding from the exertion, along with the fact that they had just committed grand theft auto, and it made him feel giddy.

Max was impressed. Jeff was an excellent driver. "I didn't know you could drive." Max observed, as he rolled down the window.

"I've been practicing driving with this truck. Chuck took me out a few times and taught me how to drive. I usually drive around country roads, and I've practiced once or twice at the high school parking lot," Jeff said as he watched the road.

"That's pretty cool of him, to take you out driving," said Max. At least he had a guy that wanted to connect with him. It was hard not to feel a pang of jealousy. But there was no way he would ever want to see his dad again.

Luckily, he didn't have to worry about him since he was in prison for beating a guy half to death.

Max shrugged off the thought. There were always dreadful emotions when he thought about his dad. His feelings were so twisted up inside he couldn't name them all. Anger was always at the top of the pile of the hurt—his dad had inflicted when he was in their lives. Max sat up straighter and puffed out his chest as he mumbled under his breath, "Good riddance."

Jeff knew his friend had suffered at the hands of a father that was extremely cruel to him and he wanted to make him feel better. So, he said, "Hey, let's get a drink. It's on me, and the next time I go out with Chuck, I will drive by and get you."

Max nodded with a tight-lipped grin. "That'd be cool."

"Maybe he'll teach you to drive too."

Jeff put his hand on the top of the wheel and turned into a parking space in front of the gas station. He bought them a drink and a slice, and they hopped back into the stolen truck.

* * *

Billy was sitting in the swivel rocker as Dean came out of the bathroom and stood in the middle of the living room.

"Well, what do you guys think? Besides the fact that it smells funny," said Dean, as he wrinkled up his nose in disgust. He wore the wig and dress, with his white socks and sneakers. One shoelace was untied, and the frock looked tight in the middle and too long. Dean spun around once and the boys tried not to laugh because the hem of the gown was uneven, where it snagged on the waistband of his shorts in the back. A little yellow flower was pinned to the wig. It was from Billy's mom's hair accessary container, which sat in the bathroom next to the sink.

Butch snickered, "What's with the flower?"

"I thought it looked pretty." Dean sheepishly pouted.

The boys rolled with laughter as Butch stepped up and yanked the back of the dress out of his shorts.

* * *

Max and Jeff were to meet Coop at the town's garage, behind the fire department. They pulled up to the garage door and Jeff threw it into park and killed the engine.

Both of their jaws dropped open when Coop lifted the garage door and stepped outside into the daylight.

"Oh, shit!" Jeff ducked his head.

Max lowered his voice and said, "I am going to kill Billy!"

Cooper Daniels stood there in full regalia, of a sheriff's uniform. He was looking a little confused as he waited for the boys to hop out of the truck.

Max bent his head down as he shook it and closed his eyes as he whispered, "Man! We are so busted!" Then he looked up and saw the confusion on Coop's face. "Just be cool," he whispered as he sat up and smiled. Max hopped out of the truck and said, "Hey Coop. We thought we would help with catching those cats."

Cooper nodded and watched as Jeff got out of the truck and walked up to them.

Max did his best to distract him, so he smiled and asked, "When did you become a cop?"

Coop replied, "Just this morning," he frowned, "Halsey was in an awful wreck and Mia needed the help."

"That's too bad about Halsey. He's a cool guy," said Jeff as he stood with his hands in his back pockets.

"Well, we aren't gonna catch anything by just standing here. Where are those box traps?" asked Max, cutting the conversation short.

"Follow me," said Coop.

245

They walked into the garage together, and it looked trashed.

"What happened in here?" asked Max, as he saw the disarray.

Cans of paint were knocked over and brooms and yard tools were laying all over the floor. Hand tools were pulled from the wall where their empty hand drawn outlines remained. It was a big mess.

Coop sighed as he shook his head. "I don't know, but it wasn't like this yesterday." He moved the paint cans aside and walked to the far corner of the garage. Coop lifted the cage from the stack of six traps in total, and handed it to Max, and in turn, Max handed it to Jeff. Max handed another one to Jeff and took the next two for himself. Coop carried the last two out and they loaded them into the back of the truck.

"Thanks Coop. We'll do our best to capture as many cats as we can for you," said Max. Then he slapped the side panel of the truck bed and pushed away. He turned toward the passenger side door and took two steps forward, and Jeff almost made it to the cab on the other side when Coop stopped them before they could skedaddle.

"Hey guys, wait a second," said Coop.

Rooted to the spot, Max's eyebrows shot straight up. His lips pressed together so hard they became thin and colorless. He held his breath and turned around, while he waited for the other shoe to drop.

With a concerned expression, Coop warned them. "Watch yourselves. Those cats are feral and unpredictable. I don't want to hear of any more attacks today."

Max tilted his head and asked, "What do you mean, any more attacks?"

Coop replied, "JP was attacked last night. He was bitten on the leg. And when Billy and I were picking up Mr. Grimm from Auntie's place, there were tons of cats in her yard. They started acting wild, and I thought they were gonna attack us. Until Mr. Grimm roared and scared all of them away.

"I've been wondering what kind of damage that cat could've done if it wouldn't have been caged. But there were so many wildcats and with those kinds of odds, I don't think that huge cat would've had a winning chance.

"What I'm really trying to say is to be careful and wear leather gloves when you handle them. Here, take these so I know you have at least one pair."

He handed Max a pair of heavy-duty leather gloves.

Max looked sincere, as he took them and said, "Thanks, Coop. I really appreciate it." He opened the door and jumped into the cab.

Jeff saw the cue that it was time to leave and hopped into the driver's seat.

With a poker-face, Coop leaned into the open window in front of Max and mean-mugged Jeff, as he spoke with gravitas. "I won't bother asking if you have your license yet. But I'll be asking for it the next time I see you driving." Coop stared him down with intensity, and then flipped the script, and smiled at Jeff's reaction.

Jeff's Adam's apple bobbed up and down as he stared wide-eyed at him.

Then Coop winked as he backed up and walked away.

CHAPTER 33

IMPLEMENTING THE PLAN

It was late afternoon, and the sun was already past its halfway mark in the sky. They had prepared themselves as much as possible while waiting for Midnight, but the boys were growing restless.

Feeling impatient, Billy kept watch at the front window. He was ready to jump out of his skin with energy and excitement.

A black truck pulling a matching trailer whipped smoothly around the corner and slowed to a stop in front of Auntie's house.

Billy swung the door open and yelled, "Hey guys! He's here!" as he ran out the door. Everyone hopped up and hightailed it outside.

Midnight waited for Billy as he rolled down the window and said, "I need to back this trailer into her driveway."

Billy nodded as he signaled for the boys to stop. "Hold up guys, he needs to back the trailer into the driveway next door."

Everyone stopped in their tracks and waited, except for Max. He jogged over to the neighbor's house to help him out. Max gave Midnight hand signals to assist him in maneuvering the large trailer into the narrow driveway. When they were done, Midnight exited the truck and asked, "Hey, are you guys hungry?"

Billy was surprised Midnight wanted to feed them and his mouth watered when he smelled the cooked food drifting from the cabin. "I know, I am," he smiled.

Ultimately, their response was a big "Yes," as they stepped forward, drooling.

"Here's the deal. I need a team effort to help set the trap, and afterwards, we can eat," explained Midnight.

"Sweet!" Billy grinned.

Midnight walked past the end of the enclosed trailer and stopped to survey the property. "I'm gonna need a set of eyes. We need to move the trailer deeper into the yard."

Max stepped up. "I can do it."

With Max's guidance, Midnight drove the trailer farther into the backyard and stopped. He unhitched the trailer and parked the truck in the driveway.

"We need to set it up like she did when she fed the cats," Midnight instructed.

"I saw how she did it. She started down there at the end of the sidewalk and walked backwards toward the house, pouring a line of food as she went," Billy explained.

"Good, then we'll place the end of the trailer close to the fence, but we'll leave a lot of room for them to roam around. Even though the escape door is on the other side, it will still be closer to the house," Midnight explained.

The boys, along with Midnight's help, pushed the trailer into place. Midnight pulled on a few latches and opened the double doors. The boys were excited when they looked inside and saw the supplies Midnight had bought for their plan to work.

There was a box of laser pointers. A giant camouflage burlap tarp, five large bags of cat food, and he also had five regular box traps.

"That isn't everything. Follow me," Midnight said, as he walked toward the truck. He stopped short of the cab and looked inside the truck bed.

The boys followed and looked into the back of the truck where forty, twenty-pound bags of salt were laying neatly stacked.

Max walked up and glanced inside as he said, "I wanted to let everyone know we tested both theories. I circled the salt around a cat, and I blew up a few loud firecrackers. The cat walked right across the salt, and the explosion made them jump and run away. None of it worked on the cats."

Midnight crossed his arms over his chest and thought for a moment. "That's okay. At least we learned something by testing those theories. We know they lean toward the more natural side of the cat than the Vandalow. Which is good. It will help with setting our trap. Come on, that isn't all I bought," he smiled, "let's go to the cab."

The boys followed him and could smell the food as soon as he opened the door.

"I bought ten roasted chickens, twenty cans of mackerel, and a few bags of chips," said Midnight.

Max smiled enthusiastically as he said, "This plan just might work."

"My plan is to hang the chickens up inside the front of the trailer. Well, except for the few we are going to eat," said Midnight with a grin.

"Then we'll open the mackerel and place lines of it on the floor of the trailer. The cat food will only be an enticement trail to get them to the good stuff, and the burlap tarp will cover the trailer," Midnight explained.

"What about the laser pointers?" asked Billy.

Midnight replied, "Everyone will get a few of them. Then we're going to figure out how to place several lasers on the inside of the trailer. To entice the cats, they need to move back and forth against the floor and the walls."

"Here, Max," Midnight said, as he handed two ghillie suits to him.

"I'm going to need the both of you, up on top of the trailer. You guys are going to be in control of the door." Midnight explained.

Max and Jeff eyed the top of the big box on wheels. It drew the eye, but it was well built. Constructed of plywood and metal, it appeared to be the perfect trap to seal the cats inside when they shut the doors.

Animated, Max asked, "Do we get to keep these?"

Midnight shrugged and said, "Sure, I bought them specifically for you guys."

Max's smile grew wicked at the thought of being completely camouflaged. "This is amazeballs!" he said as he held up the suit. His active brain was already coming up with future ideas for wearing the gear.

Excited, he gazed at Jeff and with a hand raised in the air, like he was cupping a small crystal ball in the palm of his hand, he said with a raspy voice, "There will be skullduggery!"

Jeff smiled mischievously as he nodded in slow motion. "Oh, yesss, there will be skullduggery! Let the games begin!"

Max instantly formed a plan. They were going to sneak out to where the high schoolers partied in the woods. Then mess with the dumb jocks while they drank and acted like idiots around the fire pit.

Midnight shook his head, while hiding a grin and said, "Let's set up most of the trap and then we'll chow down."

Midnight was in his element. He loved planning and instructing people, and the boys were no different. To entice them to help him, he bought food, and they were all too happy to comply. Midnight still felt guilty, but he was in a sticky situation. He could keep them safe as long as they listened to his orders.

Midnight directed the older boys first as he said, "I need you guys to set the box traps. We now have eleven of them. You need to pair up a few of them by sitting the traps together, or side by side. But make the openings at

253

opposite ends. So, when a cat circles the first trap, it will walk into the other trap."

"What about behind the back fence?" asked Max.

"I also want you to set a few of them outside of the perimeter," Midnight agreed.

Max and Jeff understood the job and went to work. They pulled the traps out of the trailer and carried them to specific locations that would give them an optimal chance of success. They walked to the front of Max's house and pulled the rest of the traps out of Chuck's pickup. Then sat them in the front yard.

Jeff was sitting the metal trap down when he had an idea. "I noticed that a few of my mom's handheld fans are inside the truck. I can plug a fan into my phone to make it work. Do you think we can tape the laser pointers to it and hang the fan inside the trailer?"

Max thought about it for a second. "I think it'll work. Grab a few and we'll try it out."

Jeff reached into the truck and pulled out two of the small plastic fans. One was pink and the other was yellow. He leaned the bench seat forward and searched around for a moment and came out with a half-used roll of duct tape. Then he sat everything on top of a trap.

Max figured they better not draw attention to themselves and said, "We should move Chuck's truck. Maybe you should park it behind my house."

"That's a good idea. Let's move it." They hopped into the truck and parked it in the backyard.

Then they walked over to the water hose and turned it on, and waited until the water grew ice cold. Max sprayed Jeff twice before he relinquished the nozzle to Jeff. Then ran away before getting too wet by retaliation.

"Come back, you Cricker-Hick!" Jeff yelled.

Max laughed as he ran around the corner of the house. "Don't forget to shut the water off Sid!" Max knew Jeff hated to be called Sid.

* * *

Midnight had the other boys pulling out the massive burlap tarp and tying it down over the trailer.

"First things first, do any of you know how to make a bowline knot, or a trucker's hitch knot?" asked Midnight, as he pulled out eight packs of camouflage paracord.

The boys gathered to watch as Midnight showed them how to make two perfect knots to hold down the tarp. Midnight finished tying the bowline knot and gave it a tug. Then he held it tight.

"You see how when I pull on it, it has no give? That is what we call the load. Now we'll make this knot at the start of the line, and we'll finish with a trucker's hitch knot," Midnight explained. He handed every boy a pack of cord so they could practice the bowline first. Then he showed them the trucker's hitch.

"We have no grommets on this tarp, so I want you boys to look around for several good-sized rocks that are about the size of your palm, and they need to be as smooth as possible. No sharp or jagged edges," said Midnight.

The boys finished practicing their knots and went in search of rocks.

Billy walked past the old car and remembered how the cats ran in and out of it.

"Hey, Midnight, a lot of those cats were climbing in and out of that old car. Maybe we could set up a trap there, too," said Billy.

Midnight walked over to the old rust bucket and saw the passenger side window left open. Heavy brush grew all around it. Then he made sure the rest of the windows were closed tight, and there were no rusted out holes in the floorboards.

"I think that's a great idea. We can roll up the window and leave the door open wide. Then entice them with a few cans of mackerel and just shut the door to lock them inside," said Midnight.

Billy walked up to the car door and pushed the button on the old door handle. He pulled it open and was surprised it opened easily. It only protested with a squeak. Billy cranked the handle to roll up the window. Then he pressed his hand to the glass and pulled down, but it didn't move.

Midnight heard the door make a noise and said, "There should be a spray can of WD-40 in the truck cab. It's in my black bag in the backseat."

Billy ran to the truck and found the bag. He saw all kinds of tools and weapons as he found a small spray can. He picked it up and read the label. "I got it!" He held it up and hopped out of the truck.

"Good! Now spray those hinges until they're wet." Midnight saw how dirty and rusted they were.

Billy bent down and sprayed the parts that needed lubricated. Then he closed and open the door a few times and smiled up at Midnight. "I did it!"

Midnight smiled and gave him a pat on the back. "Good job! Now spray a little on the button of the door handle and on the latch. We want it to work without a hitch."

Butch carried a grocery sack with rocks in it as the boys walked into the backyard.

He lifted the bag and said, "I don't know exactly what the plan is with a bunch of rocks, but we have them."

He carried them up to Midnight and handed it over. Midnight looked inside and said, "They're the perfect size. Come over here to the tarp and I'll show you."

He pulled out a good-sized rock and held it in the palm of his hand. Then he took the tarp and covered the rock. Next, he grabbed the fabric, gathering it around the base, so the rock was surrounded by the fabric. Then he held it out to Billy.

"Here, hold this while I tie a bowline knot around it." He picked up the paracord and tied the fabric together. When he pulled the rock out of Billy's hand by the cord, the burlap looked like a little bag with a stone in it.

The boys were captivated.

Billy grinned and said, "How cool is that? Let's get the tarp on so we can eat!"

"Let's do it!" Dean nodded as he grabbed his cord.

"Start by tying another rock down along this end, then we can attach a line and toss it over to the other side," Midnight instructed.

The boys got to work covering the trailer, while Midnight went to the cab of the truck. He picked up a bag of plastic wrapped paper plates, a few roasted chickens, and the chips.

"Don't forget, we need to create a ramp or a step for the cats. We want them to easily walk into the trailer and it can't impede the swinging doors," said Midnight, as he sat the food on the tailgate of the pickup truck.

Max and Jeff walked into Auntie's backyard carrying the traps. They were wet and in good spirits as they sat the traps on the ground. Jeff took the duct tape and the mini fans out of his pocket.

Max walked up to Midnight and said, "We have a plan on how to put the laser pointers inside the trailer. It was Jeff's idea."

They explained their scheme and Midnight agreed that it was a great course of action.

Max and Jeff walked inside the trailer to set up the contraption.

The boys finished tying down the tarp and started creating a ramp for the cats. Midnight handed a hammer and a few nails to Max. He asked him to hang up the cord for the chickens to hang in midair from the ceiling deep inside the trailer.

"Come on, boys! Let's eat!" said Midnight, and handed out paper plates as they gathered around the food.

Billy stepped forward and picked up a chicken leg and said, "Oh man, this smells so good!"

The rest of the boys filled their plates with chicken and a handful of chips.

Max and Jeff walked out of the trailer, and Max motioned to the boys.

"Hey guys! Come check this out!" said Max.

The boys walked over while busy eating and looked inside the trap.

"Cool! A laser light show!" Dean said in awe.

The red beams of light shot all over the floor and parts of the lower walls. As the lasers were attached to the mini fan, and the mini fan was plugged into Jeff's cell phone. Everything was duct taped to the ceiling.

"Hey, that looks great!" Billy supplied as he took another bite of his chicken leg.

Butch asked, "What are those cords for?"

Max nodded toward Midnight as he walked up to check out how things were looking and said, "It was Midnight's idea to hang the cooked chickens from the ceiling."

"That's a great concept," Troy said, while he analyzed the lasers and the cords. Then he suggested, "You better make sure your phone is charged before it gets too dark."

Jeff nodded and said, "Yeah, I'm fixing to take my phone back down and charge it, so it'll be ready."

Midnight was checking the paracord to make sure it was tight, and said, "You guys did a superb job. We'll rest and eat, then we'll finish by getting ourselves ready and bring out the food for the trap."

Dani Denali

CHAPTER 34

THE TRAP

The crowded trees of the forest were silhouetted by the last rays of the setting sun's dying light. Everyone was in place and the traps were filled with the aroma of roasted chicken and the malodorous smell of fish.

Earlier, Max and Jeff had walked into the backyard wearing their ghillie suits and the boys ran up to them.

"Holy sniper suit! Those are freaking cool!" said Dean.

Max stood there with a smirk on his face as the boys walked around them.

Jeff tugged on the collar of the suit and said, "They are surprisingly comfortable and thin, but I'm already sweating my balls off."

Midnight walked into the backyard, also wearing a ghillie suit, as he carried a small cooler filled with ice and water bottles.

"They will get hot. Stay hydrated," Midnight said, as he opened the cooler and grabbed a few bottles of water and tossed one to each of the boys. Then he picked up the cooler and took it to the truck.

After everything was double checked, Midnight pulled bags of salt from their horizontal position and stood them up against each other. Then he unsheathed a black tactical bayonet. The thick blade looked deadly as he cut one corner off from each bag. It was so sharp that it sliced like butter through the heavy plastic woven bags. While Midnight was busy cutting bags open, Billy walked up and stood next to him.

"What are you doing?" Billy asked as he watched Midnight.

"When I plan, I always hope for the best, but prepare for the worst. I'm setting up the salt, so we can trap them in a circle of it. Make no mistake, a lot of them are going to change when the sun goes down, and we need to act quickly to ensnare them. I'll be positioned next to the car, hiding in plain sight, so I can shut the door. Max and Jeff will shut the double doors on the trailer, and Dean will need to escape into the house," said Midnight.

Midnight grew serious and said, "This could get pretty violent, and I want you boys to hide in Auntie's house and get Dean inside quickly. Then lock the doors and watch for us if we need to get to cover. Gather your weapons and stay inside the house."

Billy nodded, then walked over to Max, Jeff, and his buddies.

"We are going to be staying in Auntie's house, so we can watch what's happening. Dean, you need to get dressed, and we need to get our weapons ready in case they change into the Vandalow. Midnight said it could turn bad quickly," Billy said.

* * *

The plan was set into motion. The cat food was placed in narrow lines outside of the fence and continued up to the trailer. Now, it was time to wait for the cats to show their furry faces.

Billy looked out the window and, by the dying light, he could see Midnight crouched down in his ghillie suit. He resembled a lump of grass sitting next to the hinge side of the door to the abandoned car. He looked up to where Max and Jeff were hiding. But they were laying so still; it was hard to differentiate where they started, and the forest ended as it grew darker by the second. "Those camouflage suits are mind-blowing," Billy said quietly.

Billy watched as Dean called the cats with his best impression of an old lady.

Dean started out a few yards from the trailer. The plan was for him to back up into the trailer and sneak out the front side door. He was to lock it and sneak into the house.

"Here kitty kitty, come and eat this yummy food," he said, as he shook the bag, and kept cooing as one appeared.

"I see a cat!" Billy whispered.

"I don't see it. Where's it at?" asked Troy. As he peered out the window next to Billy.

"It's at the hole in the fence!" Billy replied.

263

They watched as it stuck its furry little head through the hole in the fence and looked cautiously around the yard. Then it stepped through and snacked on the kibble. Then another one showed up, and another. Before Dean backed up, there were thirty cats in the yard.

Dean's voice shook as he did his best to stay calm and call the cats. But Billy could hear the fear in his voice. "Dean is scared. I should've dressed as the old woman."

Troy wiped the glass clean with his T-shirt and stuck his face up to the window again, as he said, "We drew straws, and Dean knew what he was doing when he made the choice to be a part of the plan."

"It doesn't matter," said Billy, as he turned his head and looked at Troy with worry in his eyes. "I should've stepped up and took his place."

Butch was looking out the kitchen door window, but the back of the trailer was blocking his view. So, he walked over and stuck his face in the window above Troy's head.

"Don't worry, Billy. Look, he's already stepping into the trailer. He's almost done with his part of the plan," Butch said.

Just in the few seconds Billy had looked away, the yard had filled with cats milling about and eating the food. From their vantage point, they couldn't really see how many cats were entering the trailer. But they watched as at least ten cats entered the old car. Enticed by the mackerel, they were all too happy to jump inside to eat.

Billy smiled and said, "My plan is working."

He continued to watch as several more hopped into the car. Then he looked to the left and saw Dean sneaking hurriedly to the back door. Quickly, Billy unlocked the door and Dean ran into the kitchen, out of breath. Billy locked it up tight and turned around to see Dean do a heebie-jeebies dance.

"I never want to be the bait again! Did you see how many cats were out there?" asked Dean.

"Is it working? Are they going into the trailer?" asked Billy.

"Yes, I bet there're at least sixty cats in there now, and more were entering when I left and locked the door," Dean said as he ripped the wig off and slipped the dress over his head. He wadded them up together and tossed them in Auntie's room on top of her bed.

"They were starting to fight over the chicken, and I slipped out. It sounded like demons from hell were coming out of them as I locked them inside," said Dean.

"Uh guys," Butch whispered, "it's dark."

They looked at the window and only saw darkness, Butch's mirrored expression, and the bright reflection of the kitchen light.

"Man your weapons, and get ready guys," said Billy, as he readied himself and looked back out the window.

Midnight made no movement, as he remained crouched. He watched the cats walk into the trailer in droves. Max and Jeff were doing a good job using the laser pointers and directing the cats into the back of the trailer. In fact, there were more going into the trailer than the car, so he crept to the door and shut it with a click. Then he leaned against the door for a moment and continued to watch. The sun had disappeared, and the light was fading fast as the cats became more shadow than color.

The wandering cats stopped moving about. It was as if they froze in place. Their faces were pointed in different directions, which meant nothing piqued their interest.

Midnight became hyper aware as a peculiar and unfamiliar feeling spread through him. He could feel a change in the air, and it felt...alien to him.

Something was happening. The cats shivered and then quaked. The shaking turned violent, as if a building pressure was coming from inside of them. A cat near Midnight violently popped open! It was as if the skin rolled down and flipped inside out and turned into the skin of a Vandalow. It was an unbelievable sight, as the Vandalow was bigger than the body of a cat. No blood poured in the transition. Just a clear, primordial ooze splattered at the birth of the little creature. It stood still as if it were getting its bearings. Suddenly, it shot its small arms out, slinging clear slimy liquid everywhere.

The Vandalow slapped its small chest, and at that very moment, it looked as if it had activated itself into being. It was now aware. Then the Vandalow...looked slowly around the yard.

Midnight shot up and yelled, "Shut the door!"

"Something's wrong guys!" said Billy as he cupped his hands to the window and pressed his face to it. "I can barely see, but it looks like the cats aren't moving! Something…is definitely happening!"

As if night turned into day, the whole yard lit up, because Dean had turned on the porch light. The boys stared out the window and saw a slimy Vandalow slap its chest and shield its eyes from the blinding lights. Then, as it acclimated to the brightness, it looked around the yard. A few more cats popped open as a clear, thick liquid shot out with each transformation. The boys were thunderstruck.

Max and Jeff were already closing the doors shut, but there was a problem. One door bounced open.

"It won't latch!" Max yelled.

Pain shot through Midnight's foot as he ran, but he didn't let it slow him down as he continued to dart between the cats to the trailer door. He was surrounded now, as the cats shivered and shook all around him. They were popping open to the left and the right of him as he ran past. He hit the door with the full force of his body, and grabbed the latch, and locked it. Then he yelled, "Run! Get the hell off the trailer and get to the house!"

Max and Jeff slid off the top of the trailer to the ramp and stepped around the corner as Midnight followed close behind. He almost ran into them when they abruptly stopped in their tracks. As he felt his heart drop…to the pit of his stomach, he saw why. The Vandalow were blocking their way to the safety of the house!

The Vandalow turned, when they heard them coming, and stared them down. Their slick gray shoulders were heaving, and they looked demented with wicked, big, toothed smiles, as they wrinkled their upper lips and growled.

Unexpectedly, the back door shot open, and Billy was leading the way!

He wore black bandoliers and had two wicked-looking tomahawks sticking out from each shoulder. In his hands, he held a gun. But not just any type of gun. The weapon looked like a sawed-off shotgun with pump action. It was camouflaged and when he fired at it the first Vandalow, it made only a slight popping noise. The Vandalow grabbed its shoulder, where it had been shot, and screeched in pain. It seemed to burn like acid.

"It's A-Salt gun! Get It!" Billy yelled, as he pumped it full of salt to take another shot.

The rest of the boys held their own guns, and spread out, as they shot at the Vandalow. The little gray creatures dispersed.

The cats kept popping open, while Midnight pushed Max and Jeff forward and said, "Go, go, go! Get to the truck! We need to be mobile!"

Billy, Troy, Butch, and Dean kept firing at the Vandalow as their number grew at an astonishing rate.

"Like seeds of the dandelion," Billy said, as he shot another one with salt. "Fall back! We need to make it to the truck!" he yelled, as they covered each other and backed away from the onslaught of the Vandalow.

"Grab a bag of salt!" Midnight yelled to Max and Jeff as they made it to the truck. Max and Jeff grabbed a bag and

Midnight did as well, as they jumped into the front of the truck.

Billy and Butch split away from Troy and Dean as they evaded in pairs to each side of the truck. Billy grabbed a handful of salt out of his pocket and launched it like a grenade at the advancing Vandalow. The Vandalow hissed and scattered.

The boys reached the passenger doors at the same time and opened them while they kept covering each other.

"There's just too many! Let's get out of here!" yelled Billy as he kept shooting.

Butch threw their big bag into the truck and jumped into the cab. Then he leaned out the door and fired as Billy climbed in behind him and slammed the door shut. The other boys threw in a bag of their own and jumped safely inside the cabin.

Shell-shocked, they stared at each other. Abruptly, the truck lurched forward as Midnight peeled out. It threw them back against the seat. Then they were thrown to the right as he jerked the wheel to the left. The tires squealed as the truck hit the road and took off around the corner!

It was quiet in the truck while Midnight zipped past the school at high speed. He went the entire length of the road until it ended and then turned right.

"We need to find a place to regroup," said Midnight as he let off the gas a little.

"My house isn't far from here. Mom and Chuck are at the concert. It was all she could talk about this past week," Jeff announced.

269

Dani Denali

CHAPTER 35

MABLE HAS A POTTY MOUTH

While the moon floated slowly toward the inky night sky, the silhouette of the trees appeared to reach for the huge pink orb as if to plead. Please don't go.

This was Mable's favorite time of the evening. A sigh escaped her lips, while she happily sat rocking, in her favorite brown rocker, outside on the front porch.

A slight breeze rustled the dead leaves of Mable's Mexican sunflowers, and the withered undergrowth made a disturbing noise. It sounded like old, dried skeleton bones rattling together. Which made Mable's heart skip a beat as she jumped and looked toward the unsettling clatter.

"Well, that's enough of that!" she remarked as she got up and opened the door.

Mable stepped inside to a dark living room. The only light left on was shining from the kitchen, and it stretched across the gloomy living room carpet.

Then something ran past the doorway in the kitchen, and its shadow shot across the floor.

"What in Sam Hill, was that?" Mable whispered. If she saw it right, it was too big to be her mama cat.

Warily, she walked toward the doorway without making a sound.

Crash!

Mable stopped abruptly and covered her mouth as she gasped. She could only assume it was a porcelain plate falling from the wall and breaking on the linoleum floor. Then another crashed to the floor. Mable was not expecting it to happen again, and she jumped a second time!

"What in tarnation is going on in there?" she whispered as she walked closer to the kitchen. Maybe someone was in her house! She looked around for a weapon, but the only thing in the living room was her knitting needles. Then Mable remembered the broom was sitting against the doorjamb, just inside the kitchen. Sneaking one hand around the corner, she found the handle to the broom and grabbed it.

Success! Mable thought, while her hands wrapped around the handle. She sat the handle lightly upon her shoulder and gripped it like a wooden bat.

Mable backed up slowly and snuck over to the cordless phone. Quietly, she picked it up to dial 911, but then she stopped. What if it was something silly happening in there? She didn't want to feel foolish if Lil' Mama had jumped up onto the counter and knocked off a few plates. So, she took a deep breath, and with determination, she slipped the phone into her nightdress and turned toward the kitchen.

Bang! Another plate fell, but it didn't break. The plate wobbled around and spun like a top, growing louder and louder. Then it made a rattling sound at its final crescendo and gave way to gravity as it settled into place. Now it was deadly quiet.

Mable's blood pressure was spiking, and her hands shook. But fear was giving way to anger, and she was growing madder by the second. Whoever it was, was going to get a beating with her dadgum broom!

She gripped the broom handle tighter and jumped into the kitchen as she yelled, "HAAA! Oh shit! What in the heck is that?" Then her voice died in her throat.

On top of the counter stood a slimy looking little creature, and in that moment, everything seemed to freeze, as Mable took stock of its appearance. Its wet skin looked gray and knobby, with brown and green bits which varied from the size of a small button to the size of a quarter. The claws at the end of its three long digits turned black and pointed at the ends. It had little wrinkles where its knees and elbow joints were, and its three toes were gnarled with short black claws. Since its back was facing her, as it reached up with long arms to grab another plate, she peeped a little gray fanny.

But when she yelled, it stopped and looked at her. Its eyes glowered yellow and were cat shaped with a dark orange tinge at the edges. The eyes looked as if they were covered by an elongated mask. The mask was gray with portions that were green and brown with tiny flecks of gold. It looked like the veins of a leaf were imprinted on it, and it continued out to the side and ended with crusty looking pointed ears. At the top of its head grew several brown and tan, plant like vines. The vines were plump and hung down its back, past its shoulders.

Mable snapped out of her revery, as its big, green upper lip quivered with a growl. Then its mouth opened to show massive pointed, long, crowded teeth.

She turned to run back into the living room. But three little miniature versions with unimportant differences were blocking her way. They were bouncing up and down right in front of her. Two were looking at her, and the other was turned around, looking in the opposite direction. She took the broom and gave them a whack, in a sweeping motion, and they rolled away like tumbleweeds. After she swept them aside, she ran through the dark hall to her bedroom.

Mable turned to shut the door, with one last look. She saw the bigger one leap into the living room and look at the three little ones while they were sitting up on the floor, shaking their dizzy little heads.

The little one with the golden dot in the middle of its forehead had been turned around, and never saw the broom coming. It jumped up and harrumphed in a girly, high-pitched voice. Then, the golden one slapped the closest little creature next to her.

The poor little creature, dazed from tumbling across the floor, was stunned. Its eyes spun in a circle and rolled back into its little head, then it fell backwards onto the carpet. Mable slammed the door as the bigger creature roared with anger and lurched down the hallway toward her.

Mable leaned against the door as the full force of the creature slammed into it. The monster dug at the door with its claws, and it grated on every nerve in her body as she grabbed the phone from her pocket. She put it up to her ear to listen for a dial tone. At some point, she must have pocket dialed Betty, and her friend was hearing everything that was happening.

Betty was busy screaming on the other end of the line. "Oh my God, Mable! I'm on my way!"

The dial tone instantly went dead as she heard glass and porcelain breaking in the living room. She tried the phone again. But there was no sound.

CHAPTER 36

MAX AND JEFF SEEK AND DESTROY

Everyone hopped out of the truck and followed Jeff into the house. They entered the kitchen by way of the backdoor, and everyone tossed their gear onto the floor.

Jeff motioned for Max to follow him, and, while they were leaving the kitchen, he turned toward Billy. "Hey, can we borrow a few of your salt guns? We're going to check around the house," asked Jeff.

When Billy nodded, Jeff took two guns from the bag. Then he went to his bedroom and grabbed a battle ax he had displayed on his wall. It had a neat, braided leather strap, and Jeff crossed it over his head, so the ax would fit snug against his back.

They checked the salt guns and made sure they had plenty of iodized salt in them. Then Max and Jeff walked through the living room and out the front door. Once they searched the bushes which surrounded the front porch and found nothing, only then did Jeff let his guard down. But he looked worried as he said, "I'm going to be so busted. We left Chuck's truck in your backyard."

"Do you still have the keys, or did you leave them in the truck?"

"I have the keys," said Jeff, as he patted his pocket.

"Don't worry, we can get it later. In case Chuck looks for the set of keys, put them back where they belong and just keep the key for the truck. As long as Chuck finds his truck in one piece, I don't think he'll care," said Max.

Movement caught Jeff's eye as he furrowed his brow and cocked his head to one side. He watched the old neighbor lady run down the sidewalk with a tennis racket in her hand. But he was still thinking about the truck. "I hope you're right." Then he moved to the center edge of the porch and watched the old lady run up to her friend's house and frantically bang on the door.

Max stepped forward to watch the commotion. Then a sense of foreboding was felt when they heard the concert in the middle of town begin. Even though they remained calm, they knew it was fixing to get real.

"Shit is about to hit the fan," said Max.

"Help! Somebody please, help me!" Betty yelled, hoping a neighbor would come to her rescue.

With an ornery expression, Jeff asked, "Should we?"

"We should." Max cocked the gun. "Let's kick some ass!"

They jumped off the porch and sprinted across the street. A few seconds later, they were standing next to the frantic lady. They could hear things shattering and falling as a woman screamed inside the house, while a Vandalow viciously clawed at the other side of the front door.

"We're going around back. Stay here and stop banging on the door. They're attracted to noise," said Max.

"What do you mean?" asked Betty, looking befuddled.

"Please stay here, ma'am, and we'll help your friend," said Jeff.

The boys jumped off the porch and jogged around to the backyard. They unlatched the gate and slipped through, shutting it behind them.

"The noise from the concert should draw them away if we can get them outside," whispered Max. Then he slowly looked through the brightly lit glass door.

Kitchen chairs were knocked over, and the floor was covered with shattered plates. Little figurines were chipped, broken, and strewn everywhere. They looked like little soldiers laying all over a battlefield.

"I don't see any Vandalow inside the kitchen," said Max. He placed his hand on the sliding glass door and was surprised when it slid open. He pointed with two fingers, as a sign to show they were a go.

Max went in first, and Jeff followed close behind. The kitchen was trashed. The refrigerator and cabinets were scratched and completely ruined. It was a total disaster area. They heard more breakables being shattered in a frenzy in the living room, while a woman continued to scream somewhere in the house.

Max motioned for them to get closer to the action. They stepped carefully through the broken glass with some difficulty. Only making a few crunching noises along the way, as chaos continued on the other side of the wall.

Max peeked his head around the corner, but he couldn't see anything. It was too dark in the rest of the house. But he could hear a big one jumping around and wreaking havoc on a door down the hallway. Then he heard something squeaking behind him to his right as something broke.

After Max pointed at himself, he then indicated that he would take care of the Vandalow down the hall. He motioned to Jeff and signaled for him to go right.

"We have to turn the light on," he whispered to Jeff. "Ready?"

Jeff nodded with a sheer look of determination.

Max flipped the light on, and everything stopped.

He looked around the corner and saw a Vandalow in the brightly lit hallway. It was standing there, shielding its eyes from the light.

"Let's go!" said Max, as he jumped out into the living room and turned toward the Vandalow. He moved closer to it, as the Vandalow dropped its hands and ran toward him. He yelled, "DIE SUCKER!" as he fired salt rounds at the vicious beast.

When the salt hit the Vandalow's skin, the reaction was instant. Every area it hit let off puffs of smoke, and it burned their skin like acid.

Max stepped to the side, as the Vandalow ducked and ran past to his left. Then it turned and ran into the kitchen. He kept a steady barrage of salt, flying toward the creature as he stepped back to the doorway. "Jeff, we need to kick them out the backdoor!"

Jeff was busy firing shots. "There's three of them!"

Max glanced over to where Jeff had three smaller Vandalow huddled together in the corner. They looked like baby Vandalow!

"Keep firing at the big one and I'll take the little ones!"

They switched places, and Jeff kept a continuous volley of salt going, as he backed the larger Vandalow into the middle of the kitchen and stepped forward.

Like a magician, Max yanked a pastel yellow tablecloth off of a table and felt quite impressed with himself when a few figurines remained.

"Get that one out of here, and I'll bring the little ones right behind you!" Max yelled. He chucked a few throw pillows on top of the Vandalow and blanketed them with the tablecloth while they huddled together in the corner. Max gathered the tablecloth, picked them up, and only took two steps before a long black claw stuck straight through the top of the cloth. It happened right in front of his face, and when he looked at it, his eyes practically crossed, as he stared at the needle like nail.

"Hurry Jeff, I'm coming!"

Jeff took two more shots, and the Vandalow staggered back a foot shy of the back door, while grabbing its shoulder.

"Coming throoough!" Max yelled.

Jeff stepped out of the way at the last second, as Max threw the balled-up baby Vandalow right into the middle of the bigger one and bowled it over out the door. Then Max slammed the door and locked it. He put his hands on his knees to catch his breath and panted for a few seconds. "Jeff, go get the lady on the front porch!"

Jeff ran to the front door and let Betty inside. Then he locked the door and took a moment.

Betty quickly ran inside, then immediately stopped, and gasped, "Oh my stars, it looks like a twister tore through here!" She was completely heartbroken when she saw the complete destruction of Mable's keepsakes. "Mable? Where are you?"

"I'm in here!" came the muted reply from down the hallway.

Betty hurried toward the sound of her voice and said, "It's okay, Mable, you are safe now."

"Are you sure?" Mable's muffled voice asked, before opening the door.

"Yes, I'm sure." Betty stopped and patiently waited.

Mable opened the door and ran into Betty's arms. "Oh my God, Betty. I was terrified!" They hugged each other for a good, long minute. Then Mable looked up and saw two teenage boys standing in her demolished living room.

"If you don't mind me askin', who are you?" asked Mable.

"They are the ones that came to our aid. By the way, what was in your house?" Betty asked, wide eyed as she took in the scratched-up doors, walls, and devastation. "Your living room is tossed upside-down."

Mable ignored Betty's question and stepped forward. She took Max by the hand and said, "Thank you so much. You saved my life."

Max didn't know what to say, so he warned them, "Don't go out in the dark. Don't make loud noise, they are drawn to it. In the daylight, put salt in a line around your property. They don't like it and they can't cross it."

"Oh my," said Mable, as she looked around the living room. "Did any of you see a cat and three kittens?"

Max hated to give her more bad news, but she needed to know. "Those creatures, the Vandalow, they used to be your cats. I don't really know how to explain this, but the new cats that you've seen in town. Are now turning into these little monsters."

"Oh, my goodness!" Mable gasped.

"You should stay with your friend tonight," Jeff suggested.

"I need to get home to James, since he's been sick. We need to call someone for a ride," Betty said.

"We can't call from here. The phone's dead," Mable said.

Max stepped up and set forth a plan. "Okay, this is what we're going to do. We need to weapon up, because we are going to walk to Jeff's house and get you a ride."

After gathering a few weapons, Max stood at the front door. Then he turned around to look at the motley-looking crew that gathered behind him. Betty was carrying a huge square flashlight in one hand and one of Mable's canes, from when she had knee surgery, in the other. Mable had a smaller flashlight, and she sported a wooden walking stick.

"Remember, no noise, and stick together. We are one unit. Jeff, you stay at the back. Betty, you need to look to the right, and Mable, you take the left," said Max.

Then he opened the door.

CHAPTER 37

SUGAR BEE TAKES A HIT

While Midnight sat at the table drinking coffee, he watched the boys refill their salt guns and enjoy a coke. "You guys did a superb job back there. The guns were a nice touch. I didn't even know they made salt guns."

Billy looked troubled as he walked over to the landline and picked up the cordless phone.

"Yeah, Billy found them at the hardware store," said Butch, as he smiled and picked up the saltshaker from the center of the table. He unscrewed the lid and poured the salt into the compartment of the gun. "I'm glad they worked so well."

"Who taught you guys to work in formation?"

"We play 'first person' shooter video games. It taught us everything we know." Butch flashed a smile.

"Really, well that's impressive. You guys handled yourselves like a trained unit." Midnight relaxed and took another sip of hot coffee.

Troy spilled the salt on the table while pouring it into his weapon. He took his hand and swiped it onto the floor as he asked, "How many do you think we caught?"

Midnight thought about it for a few seconds. "There were at least fifteen in the car, and seventy in the trailer. They were milling about pretty quick, but I'd say that we captured around eighty-five to one hundred of them."

Billy was thinking about his mom as he carried the phone into the living room. Worried that she would leave work because they weren't answering the phone, he dialed her phone number and let it ring. For the second time today, he heard her frustrated voice. "Billy?"

"Yeah."

"Where are you? Where is your brother, and why aren't you answering the phone?"

"Mom!"

Lana fell silent, and just by the tone in that one word, she could tell something was wrong. Mom mode kicked in, and she could feel mama bear's protectiveness come out of hibernation, as she asked, "What's wrong?"

"We're fine Mom. We're over at Jeff's house." How did he explain the situation? It sounded like a made-up story. "Max is hanging out with Jeff, and we're staying inside the house."

"Well, good. I'm glad. Please don't go outside tonight," said Lana. But she could tell something was up. Billy never called her unless it was an emergency.

"I need you to listen to me. There are…little gray creatures running around town," Billy said as he cringed and waited for the fallout.

"I knew it! I'm coming home!"

"NO! Mom, you need to listen to me. Stay in Ska Dale. Go to your friend's house and sleep there, then come home tomorrow. We're staying the night here," Billy lied. "We'll stay in the house. I promise."

"Okay, you stay there and don't you dare go outside of that house. I saw what those things can do. I took care of a bite victim this morning and it was bad." Lana was worried.

"We are in for the night. I Promise."

"Okay, I love you."

"I love you too," said Billy. He hung up first and felt better knowing that he kept his mom safe and out of town.

Lana hung up the phone and then dialed a number, but nobody would answer.

"Seriously?" she grumbled with frustration, as she remained on hold for the Pope County Sheriff's Department. Impatient, she hung up and called another number, two rings later, and a man said, "Hello."

"Pete, I have to leave. It's an emergency," said Lana.

* * *

Billy walked over to the table and sat down next to Dean. Everyone was sitting around the table talking and relaxing.

"Is everything okay?" asked Dean.

"Yeah," Billy said, looking grim, "I had to call my mom. I didn't want her to show up at home and get attacked."

"It was a good idea to call her," said Midnight, as he took another sip of coffee.

Then, the muffled tempo of a bass guitar resonated through the kitchen. The concert had started.

Max, Jeff, Betty, and Mable crowded up to the front porch. Jeff opened the door, hurried them inside, and locked it.

Midnight heard the commotion and stood up to check the perimeter. He rushed to the living room and stopped at the sight of them.

He noted two older ladies standing there with Max and Jeff.

One lady wore a nightgown, and the other had pink curlers in her hair. They were looking wide eyed and shell-shocked.

Max looked at Midnight and said, "They were attacked by four Vandalow at a house across the street."

The rest of the boys rushed into the room and gathered behind Midnight.

Betty saw Midnight and immediately recognized him. "I remember seein' you yesterday mornin'. You were over there, next to Luther's hardware store. I don't know who you are, Mister. But if these boys trust you, then so do I. Would you please give us a ride? It's not far, and I need to get home to my sick husband, and get my friend settled. She has had such a terrible fright."

"Yes ma'am, I sure can," answered Midnight, as he motioned to Max and Jeff.

"Boys, help me get them to the truck. We're going for a quick ride. Everyone else, prepare yourself. When we come back, we need to go help the others."

Max turned to Jeff and said, "Don't forget about the keys."

"I already hung them up," said Jeff.

The younger boys walked into the kitchen first. They stepped aside and watched as the old ladies, Max, Jeff, and Midnight, trailed out of the backdoor.

They gathered in a circle as Billy took their weapons bag and opened it.

"Well boys," Billy said, "or should I say, men. Since we've seen battle. We have prepared for this as best as we can. And even though I don't know what's going to happen next. I know that every one of you has my six, and I'm glad to call you...my friends. And I just have one question." Billy lifted his gun and asked, "Are you all in?"

Butch grabbed his salt gun and replied, "I'm all in!"

Troy picked up his baton and slung it out, making it telescope to its full length, and said, "I'm all in."

Everyone stopped and looked at Dean.

Dean shrugged, picked up his gun, then crossed it over his other arm as if he were holding a football and said, "I am feeling a little salty at the moment! So, I say," he held his gun up into the air by the handle, and yelled, "It's time to scorch these suckers!"

Everyone cheered and Billy yelled, "Yea-Yeah! It's time to kick some butt!"

At that very moment, they heard the truck pull up to the outside door. It was time to test their merit once again as they gathered their gear.

Midnight, Max, and Jeff were in the front seat, and the boys, feeling anxious and eager, gathered into the back of the truck cab.

Midnight threw the truck in reverse and quickly backed out. He barked his plan out loud to them, making sure they heard every word.

"The way I figure it, we have little time to prepare! We are going to need to set up quick! I need everyone to lay salt in a fifteen-foot diameter all the way around the truck! We need it to be a solid line! It can't have any breaks in it! I'm going to park the truck on the curb at the Northwest corner of the park!

"Max and Jeff, take these two knives. Be careful, they're sharp! I want you to start with the bags of salt that are open first. Hand them out, and then open the rest. Set them up as good as you can, so they don't spill.

"I need the rest of you to make a large 'U' shape in the intersection. I am hoping we can trap some of them!"

They sped around the corner and Midnight popped the tires up onto the curb, then stopped abruptly. Everyone jumped out and went to work while Midnight watched for movement.

"So far, so good! I don't see them yet!" Midnight yelled over the blaring music.

* * *

An entire stage was constructed in front of the gazebo, with a complete sound system and full concert lighting.

Excitement filled the air as the crowd stood elbow to elbow, gathered around the front of the stage. The fashion for the evening was western wear, and the cowboy hats were almost forty people deep all the way across the main event area. Farther away from the ruckus, some of the audience set up lawn chairs and were enjoying the concert at a leisurely distance.

A concession stand sat to the right of the stage, several yards away, and the merchandise table was set up next to it. The enticing aroma of popcorn and hotdogs filled the surrounding area, and it brought a hungry crowd. They sold several varieties of pop, beer, stickers, T-shirts, and ball caps, and the line of customers eagerly awaited their turn at the counter.

There was a brief pause in between songs as the front man for the headliner spoke. A few notes were strummed on a guitar, and everyone cheered as they sang along and bobbed their heads to the beat. Several couples grabbed their partners and danced to the cheerful tune.

* * *

The boys double timed it, as they laid salt in smooth lines and made sure to leave no gaps.

Midnight watched while they followed the plan. Like a sentinel, he kept a keen eye open for any form of movement as he scanned the area. He paid close attention to the streetlights as they lit the ground. He had a feeling they were going to be there any second now.

Then he saw something flutter. He trained his attention to the area and saw the form of a Vandalow walk under the light.

"Heads up! They're here, about a block away!" He tried to yell over the music. He slapped the side of the truck to get their attention, but two of the boys didn't hear him. Billy and Dean were too far away.

Dean was on the far side of the intersection with an empty bag. He looked up when he finished pouring the last granules of salt, and he saw them!

They filled the road, and it looked like they were hopping and dancing to the music in their own parade of ghastly ghouls. Wherever these creatures manifested from, it was definitely a place that Dean never wanted to go. The spectacle sent a chill down his spine, as he waved at Billy to get his attention and yelled, "They're here!"

Billy finished pouring out the last contents of the bag when something caught his eye. He looked over, and a Vandalow was coming straight for him! Billy froze. He wasn't prepared for the attack.

With its hinged jaw opening to show its nasty looking serrated teeth, the creature reached out its arms and spread its black claws. Billy could only imagine the grisly sound of the Vandalow because the music was deafening. But then it recoiled and ran off to the right. Smoke radiated from its chest, and then swirled behind the Vandalow as it streaked away.

Billy let out a breath he'd been holding and swiveled his head to the right.

Max was standing there panting, with another handful of salt at the ready. Billy could barely hear him over the din of music, but he got the gist of what Max was saying. "RUN!"

The horrific scene played out as the group of Vandalow jumped forward and ran. Their speed was impressive, but the sheer number of them was what gave Billy pause. They spread across the street as they maneuvered toward them. Billy and Max ran toward the truck, while Midnight, Jeff, Butch, Dean, and Troy came forward in a perfect wedge formation, weapons at the ready.

Midnight pulled out his telescoping baton and picked up momentum. He swung the metal weapon and connected with two of the Vandalow as they flew to the side. One got up on all fours, shook its head, and ran toward the music.

Jeff took his battle ax and swung it at a Vandalow, but it ducked, and the two beside it received the full brunt. They were laying in pieces on the ground and immediately turned into a greenish-gray viscous like gel.

The rest of the boys were shooting salt at the onslaught of the Vandalow. The spray was deterring the creatures, and they ran in a wide circle around them. A few were stuck in the 'U' shaped trap as Max took a bag of salt and closed it at the bottom of the curve. It was a decent plan, but it didn't catch as many as they had hoped. The rest of the Vandalow, which evaded the trap, were now jumping up onto the stage.

Midnight yelled, "Everyone! Fall back! Get to the truck!"

Jeff's mom, Ava, and her boyfriend Chuck were standing up-front and center stage. He put two fingers in his mouth and blew a loud whistle, as Ava jumped up and down while Chet Brown sang their favorite song. Suddenly, a small gray creature ran across the stage in front of the drums and full-on attacked a speaker.

Chet Brown was still singing, and the drummer, bassist, and guitarist remained playing as the crowd stood stock still.

The band didn't see what was happening behind them, but it was as if the people were set in stone.

The crowd was watching in awe as three more appeared and attacked the same speaker. The first creature used its claws and dug into the center of the massive amplifier.

Chet Brown turned his head toward where the crowd was gawking, and pointing, and saw the Vandalow. Frightened by what he was seeing, he stopped singing into the microphone.

As the music kept playing, Chet Brown yelled, "What in the hell is that?"

The drummer, who was playing his heart out, turned his head to see a Vandalow standing there staring at him. It cocked its head to one side, and he jumped up from his seat, and threw his sticks at it, then ran off the platform.

At the loss of the sound of the drums, Chet Brown turned around and saw a creature sitting in his drummer's place. The Vandalow picked up the sticks and banged on the drums as another slammed into the drum set and wiped out the cymbals. They fell with a loud clang.

The bassist and guitarist turned in unison and upon seeing the Vandalow, they immediately dropped their instruments and ran offstage, dragging Chet with them.

It was suddenly eerily quiet as the crowd stood confused by the scene. Then a woman screamed! The crowd, which was frozen only moments ago, rapidly dispersed into every direction. Screams and chaos erupted as several more Vandalow ran onto the platform and destroyed the sound equipment. One slid across the stage, taking out the fiddle and steel guitar, which sat leaning against a stand.

The rest of the Vandalow were at ground level. They ran around the stage, across the green grass, and chased the crowd.

Frightened, people darted to their cars for safety as the creatures chased them and jumped on top of their vehicles. In a panic, they called for help.

A man ran past Chuck and Ava, while they stood frozen like statues, completely in shock. A Vandalow was sitting on top of his cowboy hat as the man screamed.

The Vandalow fell off, taking the owner's white hat with it. Curious, it stood for a moment and looked at the hat. Then the Vandalow stuck the hat on top of its head, and as soon as he plopped it onto his noggin, he sauntered off like a cowboy in an old western movie.

Another Vandalow swung across the stage by a cord from the lights above and slammed into the stacked guitar amplifier.

Two Vandalow were sitting in the popcorn machine, and one wore popcorn on its head as it came up from the unsalted treat. They laughed as they watched the swinging Vandalow, Tarzan, into the solid stack.

A Vandalow picked up a guitar and swung it around in a circle, while sparks flew across the stage from the electrical panel attached to the lights and sound system. Followed by an electrified Vandalow which shot halfway across the platform. It stood up and twitched all over. Then it tried to take a step as it wobbled back and forth and walked right into the path of the swinging guitar. The sound could only be described as *THWACK!* As it flew like a beach ball out onto the ground in front of the stage.

The two Vandalow, which were sitting in the popcorn machine, were busy munching away while watching the mayhem. They stopped chewing in sync and looked at each other, then laughed hysterically. A car screeched around the corner, and it caught their attention as they watched it speed by.

They saw a Vandalow in the driver's seat. The car rocked and swerved as it sideswiped cars parked along the curb. Then it stopped abruptly when it hit a streetlight.

Midnight and the boys retreated behind the salt line. They fought the Vandalow as the creatures hopped and scampered passed on their way to the park.

Midnight shook his head and said, "We need to relocate to the other side of the square! Get in the truck!"

Breathing heavily and tired from the adrenaline rush, they jumped in and slammed the doors. Midnight threw it into gear and made a U-turn, running over a few speed bumps. Those speed bumps were once Vandalow.

One little monster jumped into the back of the pickup and screeched as it landed in salt. Smoke drifted from its skin as it immediately jumped out of the truck bed.

Midnight decided they were too close to the bedlam, so they took the alleyway behind the stores on the east side of the square.

The boys were busy reloading their weapons, and salt poured onto the seats as they bounced around.

Midnight made certain to park at the end of the alley, blocking its entrance behind Luther's hardware store. Several cars were dangerously speeding by on the road right in front of them.

"We need to put salt around the truck to protect it," said Midnight.

"I've got it," said Dean. At some point, a full bag of salt ended up on the floorboard, right under his feet.

Everyone hopped out of the truck, and they kept a watchful eye for any movement while Dean poured the salt. They could hear the large painted windows being shattered on the other side of the building.

After the truck was circled with salt, Dean threw the bag into the back of the truck. Then he picked up his crowbar and gun and said, "Ready!"

With Midnight in front, they formed a line and snuck around to the side of the building, where earlier that day they had parked their bikes. It seemed so long ago now.

Midnight approached the corner and gave the signal to stop by making a fist and holding up his left arm. Everyone halted behind him.

Like a cuck-coo clock striking one, Midnight popped his head around the corner and pulled it back and said, "Let's clear Luther's store, so we will have a place of command."

Following Midnight, they slipped one by one around the corner and went into Luther's. The boys split into two groups and went down the first two aisles.

In the far-left corner of the store, they could hear items being broken. They were not alone. Both groups reached the back of the store and observed two Vandalow jumping up and down on top of a glass counter. Another Vandalow, holding a hammer between its teeth, crawled up the side of the counter and stood on top. It took the hammer and lifted it over its head and swung down hard. The glass shattered and all three of them ended up inside the gun case. One picked up a gun.

Max and Jeff came running out of the aisle to the left of the group. They were both packing salt pistols. They had one in each hand as they let loose, rapid fire at the intruders.

Billy smiled when he heard Dean say, "Cool!"

Everyone watched as they kept the barrage going, hitting the Vandalow several times. They saw how the

Vandalow reacted like they were being actually shot. Everything happened quickly, but the entire scene played out like it was in slow motion. The Vandalow felt the coarse salt from the CO_2 cartridges sting their flesh and burn like a bullet.

The first one to get hit fell out of the glass counter. Vandalow number two was getting away, and it was unceremoniously shot in the butt. It yipped and screamed all the way out of the front door. The third one, which was holding a gun. Pointed the empty weapon at Max.

Max shot it right between the eyes at close range. Its eyes rolled back, and it fell over and turned into a smelly gel.

Max spun the guns and stuck them into his holsters, which he had also sequestered from aisle number four.

"Holy shit! That was so freaking cool!" said Butch. He couldn't believe what he had just seen.

Billy's smile was a real beamer. He had never been so proud of his brother.

Midnight being all business said, "Good job! We need to block the entrance and check the back door!"

Max said, "We've got the back door." Then Max turned toward Jeff and said, "Let's go!"

"I brought salt," said Billy, as he showed Midnight his tube socks. He had taken them off, filled them with salt, and clipped them to the back of his belt loops.

Midnight couldn't help but to be impressed by this kid, as he said, "What a great idea, Billy. Come on, let's get the front of the store secured."

Midnight couldn't believe how amazing these kids were. They kept surprising him at every turn, and they were always at the ready. They rolled with every attack and were knowledgeable in tactics to facilitate a positive outcome at pivotal moments. He felt fortunate to be surrounded by every one of them.

Then why did he feel so guilty? They handled themselves like actual soldiers. Midnight knew the truth to the question, but it was hard to face. It was because they were just boys, and he knew it. None of them even had a choice. It was to defend or be defenseless.

He watched as Billy poured salt at the front door entrance, where the glass door had been cracked down the middle. It looked reminiscent of a lightning bolt. Billy continued to pour salt across the sill where the display window had been, while the other boys stood guard. Then Midnight went to the back of the store to check on Max and Jeff.

Billy was busy pouring salt when he heard a girl cry for help. He looked out the window and saw a Vandalow. His heart rate went into overtime as the Vandalow stood panting, and then it growled. It was stalking someone, who was standing against the building wall. The person was trapped between this store and the next, and the creature was creeping forward.

"Guys," Billy whispered, "somebody is out there. Right outside the door! They need our help!"

The boys gathered behind Billy at the door, ready for battle. They quickly rushed out and shot at the Vandalow.

It yelped, then jumped and ran away. Billy saw Katie standing there, plastered against the building. Her hands, which had once been clinging to the brick façade, shot out and wrapped around Billy in a hug.

"Oh, thank you Billy! You just saved my life!"

He could feel her body shaking from fear as she cried. Then she quickly recomposed herself and drew away.

Billy smiled and said, "I'm just glad I was here to help."

A man ran towards them and said, "Katie! Come on, we have to go!" He took her by the hand, and together they ran to a car which pulled up and sat idle, waiting for them to get in. The boys helped guard Katie and her father while they jumped into the car. Then sped off around the corner and disappeared.

The boys went back inside and worked on barricading the big hole where the picture window used to be. They used pallets and wood with the help of Max, Jeff, and Midnight. They had found the pallets in the back room of the store.

Midnight watched as they moved as a perfect unit. Maybe someday, when they were older, he just might hire them and bring them into the fold of his company. They would be perfect for the job.

When everything was secured, and the last nail was in place, all eyes turned toward Midnight.

CHAPTER 38

MIA AND COOP GO TO A CONCERT

The phone at the station would not relent. Mia was already on a call, trying to make sense of the hysterical woman, when suddenly every line lit up!

Coop looked at Mia, and she motioned for him to pick up a call. Coop picked it up, "Pope County—."

"Look! You need to get down here to the Chet Brown concert! Ack!" Then the phone went quiet.

The screams in the background were still echoing in his ear, as he said, "We need to weapon up and go to the concert right now!"

Mia grabbed the keys on her desk and said, "Help me get the weapons and ammo from the cabinet. I don't know what's happening, but we may need riot gear."

Coop met her at the gun safe and took a 9-millimeter and a shotgun. Then he grabbed ammo for both. They put bullet-proof vests on that read, 'SHERIFF' on the back, and prepared themselves for a possible skirmish.

Coop loaded the weapons and made quick work of it. He grabbed a few extra magazines and filled them. Then pocketed the shotgun shells.

"I'm going to take my truck, and you can take the Sheriff's car."

She grabbed her gear, and they split up, going different directions.

Mia stopped and turned around. "Meet me by Luther's and be careful."

"Okay, you be careful too." Coop hit the door and ran out to his truck.

Coop was in front of Mia, as her siren and lights were going full tilt all the way there. He wondered how many tongues would be wagging the next day at the thought of Mia chasing him throughout the town.

They pulled up at the side of Luther's hardware store at the same time. But when he slowed down to park close to the corner, she whipped around him and stopped short, right on the corner. Now, from her viewpoint, she could see the square and the storefronts. He watched as she turned her head to the right and then he saw her physically lean against the door.

A small shadowy figure jumped at her car and climbed to the top. Then another sprang up onto the car and stood next to the first one. Suddenly, there were ten, no twenty covering her cruiser. The little beasts were jumping up and down and scratching at the top of the car.

He watched in horror as they kept attacking the lights, hood, and front bumper. His adrenaline kick into overtime as he grabbed the shotgun and put his hand on the door handle to get out. Then, to the right, he saw Midnight stride with purpose out onto the sidewalk, holding a sawed-off shotgun.

Midnight fired at the creatures, but no thundering blast came from the gun! The sirens were still blaring in Mia's car and Midnight signaled for her to kill the noise. He moved to the side as Max stepped forward with two six shooters in hand, firing away at the creatures on the hood. Again, no loud report was heard. But a few creatures clutched their wounds and fell over.

Then he saw several boys shooting the same type of weapon Midnight held in his hands. The ugly little creatures were jumping from her vehicle, evading the assault.

Coop took the shotgun and hopped out of his truck. A snarling creature ran up to him and he whacked it with deadly force as he kept walking towards Mia's cruiser.

Finally, Mia shut the siren off.

Coop marched up to the driver's side of her cruiser, while Midnight and the boys were on the other side. Blow by blow, he hit the Vandalow with the butt of his gun, knocking them from the car. Feeling like he was just dropped into a sci-fi movie, Coop watched people run for their lives as they were being attacked by the creatures. He couldn't risk shooting and hitting someone. So, he continued to use the gun as a club.

Mia grabbed her shotgun and got out of the car as soon as it was clear to do so. She stood next to Coop and looked around the square.

It was pandemonium. People were screaming and being attacked. She bent down and reached for her CB radio.

"This is Deputy Mia Romero. I need full support in Sugar Bee!" She let off the button and listened, but the radio was dead. Then she threw it down and slammed the door and strode over to Midnight. While the boys had spread out and were defending the front of the store.

Midnight handed Coop a salt gun and nodded for him to help the boys and said, "Remember, no sound. They are drawn to it."

Coop looked toward Mia as if asking, do I take his order? Mia gave him a 'go ahead' signal with a nod and a head tilt. Coop stepped into the place where Midnight had been positioned and shot at anything that moved.

Max stood next to him and said, "It's salt."

"What?"

"You're shooting salt," Max said while blasting another creature, as it fell over and turned into gel.

"Really."

"And that's a Vandalow," Max nodded toward the one he had just shot.

Coop felt like he was in a surreal situation. He could either fight it and go crazy, or just go with it, so he chose the latter. "Okay, where can I get some pistols like those?"

Max shot at another Vandalow and hit his mark. "In aisle four, on an end cap. They don't like salt and they can't cross a line of salt either," he nodded to the front entrance, "So, watch your step."

Coop glanced at the door and saw the salt crossing the entrance on the floor.

Max shot one more and signaled a retreat, as he said, "Go ahead, Coop! Get inside! We need to reload!"

The boys backed up, and turned one at a time, to step over the salt boundary to get inside.

Max was the last to go in. Then he looked at Coop and said, "Come on, I'll show you where the salt weapons are."

Coop handed Midnight his gun and uttered, "Thanks." Then followed Max.

Midnight was busy talking to Mia. He gave her an update on all of the activity and what they did to prevent such a massive attack.

"We still need to help the people out there, but we are doing everything that we can," Midnight stated.

He turned to the boys. "We need to gather the rest of the salt weapons. Then help the people by handing them out and telling them the rules of the Vandalow."

Billy nodded, "I'm on it!"

Coop came back carrying a few plastic hand pistols and shotguns.

Mia gave him an incredulous look and said, "You've gotta be kidding me."

Coop looked at her with a dead serious expression on his face. "I couldn't shoot at the Vandalow when they were attacking your car. But I can shoot salt at them."

"That makes sense," Mia said, as she quickly took the offered weapons.

"Get ready. I think they're going back out soon," said Coop, while he rechecked his guns. He shot each of them a few times to make sure they were in working order, and Mia did the same.

CHAPTER 39

LANA AND THE CONVICT

Driving her old red and black Camaro SS, Lana sped all the way to Sugar Bee. She was alone and freaking out as she yelled, "I'm going to beat those boys into next week. And they better be at Jeff's house!"

Lana turned up the volume and listened to her favorite speed metal song from those boys in black. If she was going to get caught speeding, she might as well be listening to some of her favorite tunes as she broke the law.

Lana let off the gas and relaxed as she took the off ramp to Sugar Bee. Her white knuckled driving had her peeling her fingers, one at a time, from the steering wheel, leaving impressions.

As soon as the curve straightened out, she dropped her lead foot down, and the car revved as it shot forward. The digital clock, glowing from the dash, informed her she had broken her current record for leaving work and making it to the off ramp.

"Damn dawg!" she slapped the dashboard. "Good job, Rosie. That was our best time yet!"

Then she let off the gas and with a practiced hand; guided the car into the front parking space of the Sheriff's department.

Lana wanted to know if it was safe to pick up her boys and take them home. What better way to know than to ask the authorities?

She hopped out of her car and was instantly startled by a gigantic dog. The canine was black and hard to see at first, and she heard its dog tags jingle before she saw it.

Her heart skipped a beat and her hands shot out as she watched it run towards her.

"Please, oh please don't attack me," she said. But it didn't stop in front of her. She watched as it completely ignored her, dashed around the car, and continue down the road, away from Sugar Bee.

Lana put a hand to her heart, "Ay Dios Mío! Oh my God!" she whispered as her breath left her lungs. Shocked by the sight of a large pack of dogs silently running through the parking lot. She stood stock still and watched until the last dog, a big round bulldog, snorted and puffed as it trailed behind the rest. Lana paused for a moment, waiting to see if anymore were coming. Then she ran to the door and shoved it open.

Upon walking into the office, the first thing she noticed was the broken picture frames. The shattered glass was spread about the floor and the varnished wood was splintered apart. The phones were ringing, but nobody was there to answer them, and the potted plants were tipped over with dirt scattered everywhere.

"Hello?" she waited for an answer, but there was none. She walked past the counter farther into the office and saw file cabinets opened and paper strewn everywhere. The place looked like someone went crazy and ransacked the office. Then she realized the phones didn't sound right. Lana looked toward the desk and saw the warbling phone was tipped upside down. She peered around the room to make sure no one was lurking, waiting to attack her. Then Lana tiptoed slowly up to the phone and carefully turned it over.

The phone bank looked like a dog had mauled it. Then she recoiled, realizing she had seen those bite marks before. Lana looked around, then quietly slipped over to the cabinet, hoping to find a weapon. She peeked inside and saw a long-handled baton. Lana picked it up and stuck it under her arm as she held it to her side. Next, she found what she was looking for.

She picked up the tazer gun and looked it over. Lana saw the step-by-step instructions on the door of the cabinet and found several cartridges. Before she stuck one on the end of the gun, she flipped the safety button up and saw the red light turn on. It would be ready as soon as she attached the cartridge to it. She stuck one onto the end of the gun and pocketed the extra cartridges. It was now ready to fire.

Lana was keenly aware of her surroundings, but the incessant ringing of the phones grated on her nerves. She walked over and unplugged the cord from the phone banks.

Now it was quiet, as she straightened and looked around. Lana carefully stepped back out of the office as she placed the baton on top of the file cabinet for easy access and held the gun with both hands.

Down the hall to the right, she heard a muffled sound. She looked into the room with a table and chairs, but it was empty. As Lana turned to face the front of the building, she heard the noise again, but it sounded more like a whimper. She snuck to the door on the right, and it turned out to be slightly ajar. Which made her positive something was in there. She readied herself and stuck her shoulder to the door. Then slowly pushed it open.

The room was inexplicably dark. The lights were out, save for two emergency lights from above the door. They must have been on for a while, since they flickered, and the light was dim as it barely lit up the room.

Then she heard a whimper come from a cell. But she couldn't see and there was no way in hell she was going in there without knowing what she might run into. Lana backed out carefully and ran to the cabinet for a flashlight. Then returned to the door and again she pushed it open with her shoulder and pointed the flashlight into the darkness.

Lyle sat trembling while hugging his knees, but he looked up when he saw the light shining from the door.

"Help me! Please!" He didn't yell for fear of exciting the little gray beast which stood along the wall in the far corner outside of his cell.

Lana's flashlight met Lyle's eyes as she shined it directly at him. The man was frightened as he huddled in the farthest corner of the room on top of a cot.

He took the pillow and held it out in front of him, because it was the only weapon he had. He slowly pointed with a shaking finger to the corner of the room. Lana trained her light over to where he pointed, and her heart jumped into her throat. It was a gray creature!

The creature was standing there, while its shoulders worked up and down with each quick breath as the monster opened its teeth with a growl. Then it raised its pointed hands towards her as it lunged forward.

Lana screamed, and a stream of Spanish words involuntarily came out of her mouth, "Muere perro feo!" which translated to, "Die, you ugly dog!" As she pointed the gun and squeezed the trigger.

The tazer prongs shot out instantly. One hit it on the top of the forehead and the other struck it on the stomach. Its growl started from a low octave, and its voice began to tremolo into a loud soprano. The Vandalow's eyes grew wide, and its whole body shook for only a moment from the electrical current. Then it burst like a balloon filled with water, into a gel onto the walls and floor.

Lyle sprung from the cot and ran to the cell door as he whispered, "I thought I was going to be safe in here! But I was wrong! Get me out of here!"

Not expecting the thing to explode, Lana whispered, "Ay Dios Mío," as she carefully looked at the gun. She shut it off and pulled the cartridge from the end. Then quickly replaced it and flipped it back on.

Then she looked at Lyle. "How am I supposed to get you out of there?" she asked.

"There is a key box on the wall just outside the door! Please hurry!"

Lana stepped out into the hallway, paranoid she might be attacked. She found the box and opened it. There were several sets of keys, and she grabbed them all.

Lyle's hands were gripping the black bars as he waited and watched for the woman to come back. He was momentarily worried she might just leave him there like a sitting duck. But soon his fears were squelched when he saw the door open.

With her flashlight in hand, she took one key at a time and tried to unlock the door.

"Please hurry. I don't want to be in here if they come back."

"I'm hurrying as fast as I can!" Lana tried another key, but it didn't work. She dropped the worthless keys onto the floor and tried the next set.

Lyle watched as she struggled, trying to fit the next key into the lock. Then he noticed, out of the corner of his eye, the bright hallway light and the door started to close again. He whispered, "Another one just walked in!"

Lana left the key hanging in the keyhole and grabbed the tazer from her pocket. She turned around and shined her bright light at the Vandalow as it advanced. The creature winced from the brightness of the light, then lunged. She took aim and shot it as it leaped into the air and exploded all over her.

The gel like substance clung to her hands and clothes, as Lana grimaced and said, "It smells so bad!" She wiped her hands onto her pants and reloaded the weapon again. Then turned back to the lock. "This is the last key; I've tried them all. And if this doesn't work, I'm going to have to leave you here and go find help!" she whispered.

She took hold of the key and turned it until she heard a click. Shocked that it unlocked, they stood there for a second in disbelief.

Lana grabbed the heavy door and swung it open while she said, "I can't believe I had to go through every single key to find the right one!"

In a hurry to leave, she turned around as Lyle stepped out of the cell and grabbed her. Not expecting to be clung to, she instantly went rigid. Lyle gave her a hug and cried, "Thank you so much. You saved my life."

CHAPTER 40

MIDNIGHT HAS A PLAN

Midnight, Coop, Mia, and the rest of the gang were busy battling the Vandalow as it grew later into the night. They brought people into the store, which would otherwise be left hurt and unable to defend themselves in the park. The store was looking like a triage tent.

Midnight watched as the boys brought in another casualty. They looked weary and battle worn.

Troy had a close call when a Vandalow crawled up on top of an awning hanging from a storefront. It had miscalculated and jumped off too early, and as it fell to the ground, it sliced his cheek. The kid was tough. After the initial shock of the attack wore off, all he said was, "This little beauty mark will make me look like a badass."

Max walked up to Midnight and said, "We've cleared most of the Vandalow out of the stores and the park. I'm sure we have some stragglers, but Jeff needs to go get his mom's boyfriend's truck."

"Let me take you guys. I want to check on our traps and see how they are holding up," Midnight said.

Midnight, Max, and Jeff let everyone know where they were going and, in formation, left the store.

As Midnight drove away from the alley, he clocked the devastation which rippled throughout the next few blocks. Smoke billowed up from several houses, creating a foggy scene throughout the neighborhood. He observed neighbors carrying weapons still wondering about as Midnight sped up. Then he parked by stomping on the brakes in front of Auntie's house. Fully aware of a set of headlights coming from the opposite direction.

"Oh, man! I'm pretty sure that's my mom," Max said, as he recognized the headlamps and the speed at which the car was driving. Max pulled out his weapons and jumped out of the truck, and Jeff followed suit. Max walked into their front yard and stopped her before she could park in the driveway, which would have blocked Jeff's ability to get the truck out of the backyard.

Lana slowed to a stop, and Midnight watched the confrontation.

"Oh, boy!" said Midnight as he watched the woman's hands flying around in the driver's seat. He kept the headlights on as he took his salt weapon and left the truck. Wearing his 9-millimeter handgun on his hip for extra protection, he hobbled quickly down the driveway, which was partially lit by the security lights from the shed.

Surprised they were still working, he snuck to a vantage point to see the passenger door on the old automobile had been opened recently. The Vandalow were still hopping out of the old rust bucket.

Midnight stepped to the right and hid behind an extensive set of bushes, which belonged to the house next door. Then crept forward to see if the trailer doors were still shut. After he got close enough, he was pleased to see they were still closed.

As he watched the Vandalow milling about, he saw the one thing that was definitely going to ruin his night. The trailer door slowly swung open. Midnight gritted his teeth and backed quietly away.

What a bonehead snafu! The perimeter of salt should have been placed around the trailer after the initial setup, before the cats arrived. He let himself get too close to the situation to see this coming. He'd also been living in constant pain since the wreck and the surgery, which made his intellectual aptitude suffer. With his disappointment compartmentalized, he hurried toward the front yard, as he remained seething at the blunder.

Lana was pissed! Max just got out of a stranger's truck, and she was busy tearing him a new one. Then she noticed the guy running with a limp up to her car.

The stranger looked at Max and Jeff and said something that she didn't quite catch.

He then looked at Lana and quietly said, "Ma'am, please keep your voice down."

"Oh, ho ho! Are you freaking serious right now? I could get you charged for kidnapping! Who the hell do you think you are?" Lana yelled.

"I'm the guy you call when little gray creatures called Vandalow escape from the underworld and wreak havoc in your town," said Midnight. He clamped his angry mouth shut! He hadn't meant to say that. Then he cleared his throat and started over.

"My name is Midnight Leõn, and we need to leave now, or we're going to be in danger. They are also drawn to sound," he said with an intense demeanor.

Max looked at his mother as he backed away with a few hops and said, "Listen! This guy he is the real deal!" Then Max ran off with Jeff around the corner of the house.

"Where in the hell do they think they are..." But she stopped talking as soon as she saw them come bounding out of Auntie's driveway. Silently, she pointed across the yard.

Midnight looked and saw three of them. Then said, "Do me a favor. If they get close to me as I head to my truck, make some noise, then take off. We will meet you at the back of Luther's hardware store."

Lana was left stunned. Her jaw dropped open, and she made no movement at all, but her window rolled up, and her doors automatically locked. Then her temper flared, and she scoffed, as her hands flew up in the air as she said, "Would you look at the cojones on this guy?"

How was she going to make a loud noise? She could use the horn, of course. But how much noise did she need? She queued up her favorite song and got ready to push play. Then she cranked up the volume. She waited as they drew closer to Mr. Big Cojones.

BOOM!

She jumped in her seat and watched a truck speed out of her driveway. The backend shuddered as the tires skidded sideways on the pavement around Midnight's truck.

"What in the...," she exclaimed as she realized Midnight had made it to his truck. When he fired it up, he peeled out and drove past her.

Then she saw a massive crowd of Vandalow. They came bounding out from her driveway, and the neighbors' front yard was now full of them.

She shoved her car into gear and took off like a shot! Before she careened around the corner, she looked back. Lana saw Midnight apply his brakes. She knew he was watching to make sure she had safely made it out of danger. Then she thought, maybe he wasn't such a bad guy after all.

She heard another loud *BOOM!* Jeff's truck must be backfiring, she thought as she put her foot down and raced to the other side of the square. She couldn't believe the things she saw on the way to Luther's, as she pulled up in a daze to the side of the building behind a shiny pickup truck.

Midnight parked in the salt ring, then jumped out and grabbed a bag of salt from the bed of the truck as Max and Jeff pulled up behind him. Jeff's truck backfired again as he shut it down.

Frustrated, Midnight shook his head as he turned to look at them. They ducked their heads, both from embarrassment and worry by the all-encompassing sound, and then jumped out with weapons at the ready.

Midnight walked to the back bumper of Lana's car and began to place salt in a circle around her car. He stepped to her window and said, "Don't get out yet." Then he completed the circle.

Max, Jeff, and Midnight walked up to her door on high alert. Max knocked on her window while facing away from her as he kept guard. She opened the door, and they hurried her inside Luther's store.

She felt shocked by the scene as they came around the corner. Poor Sugar Bee took a hit, Lana thought as they rushed her inside. Then she noticed the injured people and her heart fell. She automatically went into nurse mode and asked two young ladies if they would help her out.

They said, "Yes, of course."

Then Lana took the lead as she said, "Okay, we need first aid kits and alcohol, if you can find any. We also need water and blankets."

The girls began to search.

Lana saw Max freeze when they entered the door. She followed his eye line and noticed he was staring at one of the pretty girls she had asked to look for supplies. She grinned and made a mental note to talk to him about girls later.

Billy walked up to her and gave her an enormous hug and said, "Oh, my gosh, mom! I'm so glad that you're here!"

He told her the rules of the Vandalow and to be careful of the salt at the entrance to the building. Then he went and grabbed a T-shirt from a shelf and told her where the bathroom was located.

"What are you trying to say, Billy?" Lana feigned hurt as Billy turned red. "Are you telling me I smell bad?"

Billy nodded. "Sorry Mom. But yeah, you do!"

She smiled and hugged him hard. Which made him grimace and squirm. "Thanks, I needed a clean shirt."

Then she made her way to the bathroom and Billy went back to his friends.

Midnight decided they needed a plan. They couldn't bring help in until they got rid of the Vandalow. He knew they would be following the sound of Jeff's truck, and it was time to finish this. He walked over to Coop and talked to him for a few minutes.

Coop nodded and looked toward Mia and Lana as Midnight kept talking. The conversation ended, and Coop walked over to Mia.

Mia had been watching them converse and as Coop walked up to her, she asked, "What was that all about?"

"Midnight has a good plan. But we're going to need some help," Coop explained.

* * *

Midnight stood alone for a few minutes, deep in thought. They only had a few hours until the Vandalow would go to ground at dawn and this town had already suffered enough.

Then Midnight walked over to the boys, as they stood guard. They were looking out the window between the gaps in the slats of wood, covered in ooze from the plasma of the Vandalow, and they smelled to high heaven. The odor which permeated from them was likened to the foulest smell of refuse and sewage mixed together. It smelled like death. The boys had fought hard and paid for it with a bit of bruising and blood of their own.

"Listen up fellas, I want to talk to you, man to man. You guys have outdone yourselves. I have a military background and believe me when I say you have far exceeded my expectations. I have never seen a more skilled, or tougher, unit of men.

"You guys have given it your all, and I know you are tired. I have no business to ask anymore of you, but I could use some help with one more task," said Midnight.

There were no more smiles and their expressions had grown solemn.

As Billy slowly stood up, he said, "All in."

Dean nodded and said, "All in."

Troy's injured cheek had been cleaned and properly bandaged, as he stood up and replied, "All in."

Butch turned tired eyes to Midnight. "All in."

Midnight was proud of these guys. He was touched by their commitment to duty. He'd seen boys younger than these guys pulled into war, and it had deeply bothered him.

But out of necessity, they must become men. He gave a heartfelt salute. "Thanks boys."

They saw it; he knew they did by the gleam in their eyes. A little choked up, he excused himself and said, "Give me a second." He walked to the small office at the back of the store to regroup.

These kids, they got to him, and he felt responsible for their safety. He did his best to keep them safe and vice versa. He never would have been able to accomplish all of this by himself, and if the guys at the company could see him now, what would they say? Suck it up Midnight!

His phone vibrated, and he cleared his throat before answering, "Midnight, give me good news."

* * *

Billy smiled when he watched Midnight walk toward them with purpose as he said, "He's coming back, and he's got game face on."

The boys turned toward Midnight to see for themselves.

"Yep! He's back," said Butch, as he checked his salt gun for the hundredth time.

Midnight was on the phone and, as he stepped up to them, he uttered his thanks to the person on the other end.

He shoved the phone into his back pocket and smiled. "We need to find a place to talk. Let's go to the back."

Billy checked the salt perimeter before leaving his post. He rolled his eyes at his brother when he walked up to Max and Jeff and realized they were busy acting tough for the girls.

"Come on guys, Midnight has one more plan," said Billy.

They walked to the back of the store and went into the small storage room. Located to the left, a closet sized office remained open with a small wooden desk sitting inside.

The night had been so long it seemed like the daylight would never come. Exhausted, every single one of them sat on anything they could find. Midnight took the black office chair and had taken a seat.

The bags of feed were stacked on two pallets, and the height was perfect for sitting. Billy sat down next to Butch, onto the plastic feed bags, and Max and Jeff sat next to Billy. Troy and Dean were sitting on 5-gallon buckets which were flipped upside down.

They were so tired nobody talked. They didn't even see Coop standing at the doorway, where he leaned against the frame.

"Alright guys, I have one last plan and it's going to take everyone doing their part. I am hoping to set a trap that will keep the Vandalow there until daylight. We will more than likely use every bag of salt with this plan, save for a few bags for our weapons," Midnight said.

The boys remained silent.

"We need an open space to set the trap, and we need to drive our vehicles through it," Midnight explained.

"There's a park south of here where I play football," Dean informed him.

"There's also the High School football field, but it may be too difficult to use," said Max as he shrugged one shoulder. "They positioned enormous boulders to block the high schoolers from driving out onto the field," he explained.

Midnight gave a slight nod. "I believe the park on the south side of town will be a prime location to initiate the plan." He took a wearied breath and said, "Okay, now here's the rub."

* * *

Lana saw the boys and Midnight walking toward the front of the store. She watched as Jeff handed Midnight his keys.

As Max walked toward her, she asked, "What are you boys up to?"

Billy snuck by behind Max as he stopped to explain. "We've got a plan."

Lana shook her head.

"Look before you say 'no'. I want you to know that we've been battling the Vandalow all day and night long. This is the final plan to trap them so we can call in help for these people and save the town." He shrugged. "Or what's left of it?"

Lana's expression was grim as she said, "Please tell me you and your brother will be careful."

"We'll be careful, Mom," Max replied, then gave her a hug.

Which surprised Lana, but she savored it as she put her arms around her oldest boy. Ever since her ex, his father, hurt him. He had become withdrawn from her and wasn't very affectionate. She thought, for the longest time, he was mad at her. But somehow, whatever emotion it was that kept him aloof must've broken loose and changed him during all of this madness. It was hard to let go of this moment, for it dawned new hope in Lana. There was an essence of a new beginning with her boy, and her heart cried for the little boy that he was, to the man he was now becoming.

They ended the hug when Max pulled away.

Relieved, Lana smiled sweetly. She sniffed as she kept her hand on his shoulder, and said, "I am so proud of you... my boy."

She watched as they readied themselves and was surprised when Midnight looked her way and walked over to her with a sober expression.

"I will do everything I can to keep them safe. I also wanted to ask if you might want to help with the rest of the plan?"

Inquisitively, she tilted her head as she replied, "Sure, what do you need?"

Midnight looked amused and said, "Your driving skills."

CHAPTER 41

FROM MIDNIGHT TO DAWN

With eyes peeled, Midnight sped to the park. He stopped at the entrance and the boys hopped out.

Max and Jeff jumped into the back of the truck with the bags of salt and cut them open. Then, they set them up against the tailgate, as the other boys and Midnight poured the bags along the edges of the wide driveway, toward the open field.

"I will never look at salt the same way ever again," Billy said, as he lined the last of the gravel driveway and proceeded into the grass.

"Me either," said Butch, as he walked past Billy. Butch continued pouring the line where Billy's bag coughed up its final contents. Butch went left, while the boys on the other side of the gravel drive hit the grass and turned right.

Part of the plan involved making an enormous circle of salt directly inside the white, acrylic, painted lines of the football field. Then, when they draw the Vandalow inside, they will close it and, if they are lucky, trap them until daylight arrives.

Midnight kept watch and then hopped into the cab of the truck and fired it up. Max and Jeff sat down on the tire wells and held on tight, since Midnight seemed to always drive, like a bat out of hell. He stopped in the middle of the field and hopped out. Max and Jeff jumped out as well and grabbed two bags in each hand.

Everyone was on the field now, working diligently, when Midnight answered the phone, then made a beeline towards the road.

Billy emptied another bag and started toward the truck when he saw the exchange. Someone had pulled up in a car and Midnight spoke to them for only a minute. The windows were tinted dark, making it difficult to see the person inside. Then Midnight held up a hand, and the car sped off.

Butch walked up behind Billy and said, "I wonder who that was."

Billy shrugged and said, "Who knows? But I'm ready for this to be done and over with." Fed up and feeling low on gas, he hefted another bag from the truck.

Butch sighed, then said, "Me too."

The boys finished laying the salt and went back to the truck.

On the way back to town, Midnight saw movement in the bushes on the side of the road. He stomped on his brakes when a man stepped out into the lane, carrying a woman.

Jeff leaned forward and yelled, "That's my mom and Chuck!"

Chuck stumbled to the truck on the passenger side, and Max and Jeff bailed out with their guns.

"Get into the front!" Jeff yelled as he and Max shot the Vandalow, which had been dogging his mom and her boyfriend. It yelped and ran off into the night. Max and Jeff hopped into the back of the truck, and Max banged on the cab to signal to Midnight that they were ready.

When they made it to Luther's store, Midnight parked in the space next to the side of the building. They carefully helped Chuck and Ava inside.

Lana took one look at the couple and said, "Oh my goodness! Who got it worse?"

Chuck carefully sat Ava down on the counter and said, "I'm okay. But she was bitten on the leg."

"Ava, don't you worry one bit. We'll get you cleaned up and bandaged and soon, we'll get you to the hospital," said Lana.

A young lady handed Chuck two bottles of water.

"What were those things?" Ava shrieked.

"Let me explain to you what we know about those little ugly dogs. First, they are called the Vandalow," Lana said, explaining the situation while she helped her friend.

Billy and the boys were keeping post when Billy noticed an influx of Vandalow. "Hey, Midnight. I think some of the escaped Vandalow have made it to the square. We've seen some movement."

Midnight stepped forward and looked through the open slot of wood. He stepped back, looked at the boys, and said, "I think it's time."

The boys hopped up and seemed to have caught a second wind.

Midnight looked over at Lana and asked, "Are you ready?"

She smiled, pulled her keys out of her pocket, and shook them. "When it comes to driving, I'm always ready."

Midnight smiled at her spunk as she walked over to him. Then he grew serious as he handed her a two-way radio and said, "Be careful and don't let them get too close."

He spoke into his own two-way radio, and she could hear his voice crackle through the speaker, as he said, "Check… Check…" He took his thumb from the button. "You're good to go."

She nodded and grabbed a salt gun and a bottle of water.

Worried, Billy walked up to her and said, "Mom, please be careful."

His little voice touched her heart as she put her hand on his shoulder. "Don't worry, son, I'll be fine."

Chuck ambled up to Midnight, wearing salt pistols and leather holsters on each hip.

"I've been shooting handguns since I was knee high to a grasshopper. I'm a deadly shot, and I want in," said Chuck.

"Okay, shoot out the eye of that bear over there on the wall," instructed Midnight.

Chuck whipped out the gun and shot twice. Then he slipped the plastic gun back into the holster. Where the eyes used to be, there were now two holes.

Impressed, Midnight said, "You're going with Lana."

* * *

Midnight and the boys made sure the coast was clear and guarded Chuck and Lana to her car. Lana gave a small wave and drove off.

Ever vigilant, Midnight searched the area as he saw two Vandalow pop up their heads at the sound of Lana's car.

They stepped back inside and readied themselves while waiting for everyone to get into place. A few minutes later, the radio crackled.

"I'm over here in the eastern section of town, and I'm ready to roll," said Lana. Her voice crackled over the radio.

Midnight spoke into the radio. "Sound off when you are ready."

"I am ready," said Mia, as her voice hissed through the speaker. She was out by the High School.

"I'm almost in town from Curtis's, and they're following me. Okay, I'm in place. It's pretty busy over here on the west side of town," Coop yelled. His voice was almost drowned out by the loud music playing and a honking horn.

The tension in the air surrounding the boys and Midnight was palpable. The boys were getting jittery and were ready to go, but Midnight waited.

"I'm good to go." An unknown man crackled through the speaker. His voice was laid back and smooth, with a hint of an accent.

Midnight's lips quirked up at the corners for only an instant. Then his expression turned resolute as he yelled, "Go! Go! Go!"

The boys were surprised! They had more help, and he was one of Midnight's friends.

Midnight looked at the boys and asked, "Are you ready?"

A unanimous, "Hell yeah!" came from the boys as they gathered at the door.

"Wait! I think Coop took some cats to the mill yesterday morning!" said Billy.

With furrowed brows, Midnight stopped and turned to Billy. His gaze was intense as he asked, "Are you sure?"

"Yes, but it was only two pet carriers. So, that's what? Maybe four to six cats? Ask my mom if JP was her patient yesterday morning. If it was JP, then there are over six Vandalow out there."

Midnight put the two-way to his mouth and asked, "Can anyone tell me if JP was attacked by the Vandalow yesterday?"

"Yes, he was attacked the night before and when he got to the main road, he lost his brakes and hit Sheriff Halsey," Mia answered through the loud background noise.

"Four vehicles making noise to draw the Vandalow won't be enough!" Midnight shook his head in frustration and said, "We need a fifth vehicle!"

"Midnight, take me to my house. My mom's car should be there," said Jeff as he stepped forward.

Midnight nodded his head. "We need to double time it! Let's go!"

They formed a line in a hurry and ran to the truck. Luckily, they didn't run into any opposition as they hopped in.

Midnight threw it into drive, and they peeled out. They were at Jeff's in less than a minute. He pulled into the driveway and made sure they got the keys and were in the car with it started before he took off.

Jeff adjusted the seat and threw the car into reverse. Then it died. Jeff jumped up and down in the seat and yelled, "Start! You piece of shit!"

Max punched the dash. When he looked up, he spied the same Vandalow he shot earlier, at Mable's house. It had a peculiar amount of purple to it, making it easy to distinguish from the rest.

He put both hands on the dash and gritted his teeth as he said, "Start the car, Jeff!"

Jeff pumped the pedal once and turned the ignition as the Vandalow crept closer and closer. He tried the key one more time as she lifted her claws and prepared to jump up onto the hood. They noticed the three little ones behind her closing in.

The car finally started, and Jeff ripped the shifter into reverse. He stomped on the gas as the big Vandalow jumped, then missed, and landed on her face. The car was moving fast as Jeff turned sharply and hit the mailbox on the way out of the driveway. They ended up in the street, facing the direction they needed to go.

"OOPS!" Jeff's eyes were wide as he chuckled, then he threw it into drive and gave it some gas.

They drove quickly out of the neighborhood and only hit a few Vandalow on the way to the mill. It was creepy driving out there on the dark, deserted road, wondering if they might hit something bigger as they sped through the night. The road ended as they entered the gravel parking lot and stopped for a moment.

"Whatever you do. Don't shut the car off," said Max.

"Agreed!"

"Just honk the horn and see if they'll come out."

Jeff started laying on the horn. It was so annoying. But after a few minutes, they saw a few Vandalow come out into the parking lot near the building. Then a few more showed up.

"There is maybe six, no ten, no, no, no," said Max repeatedly as at least thirty Vandalow walked into the dim light of the parking lot.

"Turn around Jeff, they're coming!"

Jeff floored it and spun around, turning back toward the road. He honked the horn once every other second and asked, "Are they following us?"

Max turned around and put his knees in the seat. He could see them, but they were so far away.

"Stop for a second and let them catch up."

They had no way of knowing how many there would be, and they didn't have a phone or a two-way radio to let anyone know what kind of trouble they were in.

"We need to make noise and lots of it." Max turned on the radio and some country yokel was singing.

They both cringed and said, "Yuck!"

Max turned to the ultimate radio station and found some good heavy metal music playing. "Hey Jeff, roll down the back windows about three inches."

Jeff rolled them down. "How's that?" he asked as the car crept forward.

"Perfect! I'm going to turn it up and watch them. Just maintain the speed that you're going right now!"

Jeff looked at the speedometer. "UGH! I'm literally at a crawl. Like fifteen miles per hour. This is gonna take forever!"

Max yelled, "Get ready! We're going to crank this shit up to ELEVEN!"

Max turned the music up at almost full volume. It was a great tune, and he really enjoyed it. Jeff joined along as he honked the horn with the beat.

Max stared at Jeff, and Jeff glanced over at Max, and they began to laugh deliriously.

Max looked out the back window again, and the Vandalow had almost caught up to them. They were practically on the bumper!

"Go! GO! GO!" Max screamed. Jeff put his foot down, and the car shot away from the approaching Vandalow.

Max turned down the music for a second, so he could be heard. "Apparently, they like our music and your horn. They definitely sped up when we did that. So, let's give them what they want." He turned the music back up, and they made decent time to the road which led into town. Max hoped they would all meet up at the same time, but for now, they couldn't do anything but wait and see.

Jeff made a right turn onto the road toward the park. The field lights were on, and the entire field was lit up. But nobody was there yet, except Midnight and the boys hiding under camouflage netting.

"Stop!" Max yelled. "We have to keep going. Back up and go down the main road until we run into someone that can take them off of our hands."

Jeff slammed on the brakes and backed up too far, which brought them closer to the Vandalow.

Max screamed, "Oh shit! They're right on us! Go Jeff! GO!"

Jeff peeled out, but it was too late. Two of them had jumped onto the trunk and were hanging on for dear life. Max and Jeff heard their claws scratching across the paint, and it ramped up the anxiety level in the car. But they couldn't do anything about it, except continue driving north toward the center of town.

Jeff kept an eye out for someone coming their way. "I see your mom. Oh, and there's Mia in the cop car!"

Max faced forward and saw his mom pass in front of Mia, since Mia had stopped for a second, giving her the right of way. Lana had several Vandalow following her, but Mia had more. "Jeff, kill the music and stop honking the horn!"

Jeff shut the music off and sped up to get out of their way, so they could carry on driving south, and turn left toward the park. Unfortunately, Lana and Mia were going to run into the thirty Vandalow, which followed close behind them.

"This is turning into a real shitshow!" said Max as he gripped the dashboard. "Jeff, flip a U-ey. Mow over the Vandalow and clear the way! The others will be coming soon, and I'll bet they have even more of those little mongrels than Mom and Mia."

Jeff nodded and swerved hard to the right. Then he jerked the wheel to the left and turned around. He sped up and hit those suckers hard! It was as if he were the King Kong of all bowling balls and the Vandalow were bowling pins as he mowed through them.

THWACK! THUNK, THUNK, THUNK! Was the sound they made as the car jostled over them. A few of them got lucky and rolled up onto the hood. But only one stuck to the windshield wiper, and it was busy hanging on, like a fat tick on a dog, as Jeff drove into the park driveway and through the field. They stopped before the salt boundary and Max leaped out with a baseball bat and gave it a *Whack!* Knocking it from the windshield.

The others had fallen off when Jeff had made the U-turn like a lunatic. Max jumped back in, and Jeff rolled carefully over the salt line to make a touchdown on the opposite end of the field. He turned the car around so the headlights would shine across the park.

Next were Lana and Chuck. She drove through the field and trapped several Vandalow which were following her. Then she drove around Jeff's car and pointed her headlights at the field as well.

Mia, by far, had the most. Her siren on the cruiser pierced the air as she drove through the field and rolled up next to Lana's car. The Vandalow kept following until they reached the salt barrier.

Max noticed several Vandalow had jumped onto her car, but immediately jumped off as if they were burned. He walked up to his mother and pointed to Mia's car. Lana yelled, "We mixed washable white glue with salt and painted the vehicles with it!"

"That's genius!" he yelled.

The little monsters jumped up and down. Max and the rest of the group could only assume they were hissing and growling by the angry movement of their mouths, and the vibration of their upper lips, since Mia had left the siren going. A few tested the border, but backed up as soon as they were burned. It was getting to be quite the crowd, and they looked sinister as their yellow eyes reflected off the headlights, and their teeth glinted and dripped with drool.

Cooper Daniels came rolling through next. He drove at a slow pace and the count behind him was incredible. They bounced up and down while they followed his honking horn. There must've been quite a few Vandalow out at

Curtis's farm and, collecting them with the hoard from the from the west side of town, created a massive crowd.

Max was awestruck! He'd never seen so many before, and the number was truly daunting. He watched as Coop turned to the left on the 40-yard line to avoid the crowd which gathered in front of him as he stood watching the number grow.

The Vandalow ignored Coop's truck and hopped toward Max, because they were still drawn to Mia's siren.

Midnight and the boys watched behind the salt line as the number of Vandalow grew and grew with each passing car.

Max and Jeff knew the trap was holding, and they were too excited to stand still, so they got into the car to drive over to Midnight and the boys. Chuck walked up and opened Jeff's door.

Jeff looked up at the big man.

"Hey, do you suppose I could ride with you?" He yelled.

Jeff nodded as he pointed and shouted, "Sure, we're going over to where the guys are over there."

Chuck nodded and got into the backseat. He was such a big man that his knees pressed into the driver's seat in front of him, so Jeff moved his seat forward.

Jeff backed up and drove over to where Midnight and the boys were standing at the ready.

Billy couldn't believe how many there were. They just kept coming. Max walked up next to him and bumped him with his elbow. Billy looked up at Max, and Max smiled, a genuine smile at him.

Midnight scrutinized the scene. "Get ready boys!" he sounded off. At least they weren't standing right next to the siren, but it was still tumultuous.

Midnight was on full alert as he declared, "Here comes the last vehicle!"

They could see the headlights first, then they actually heard it over the siren. It was loud, and he was rolling slowly as to collect the last of the Vandalow. As he approached, the sound grew even louder.

"Holy shit!" Max yelled; he was impressed as he watched the truck roll into the driveway.

Chuck's eyebrows knitted together, and suddenly shot up in surprise! "Hey, that's my truck!" he blurted at the top of his lungs while he tapped Jeff's shoulder.

Jeff stiffened, and turned pale, and with wide eyes he looked over at Max.

Max was busy looking down, but when he looked up, he grinned like the Cheshire cat. His smile was electric. They hid their laughter until they saw Chuck's dumfounded expression, and since they stood in front of him, they looked forward and lost it.

Max watched as the truck grew closer. A spiked cage was built over the cab, and several fence panels were attached to long metal bars covering the loudest speakers he had ever heard. The music was a heavy crunching metal song, and the scene played out, looking post-apocalyptic.

"That shit is MAD MAX!" he yelled. Instantly knowing exactly what he wanted to do when he grew up.

Max stood awestruck, as he watched the truck roll into the field and stop well into the center. The driver vaulted out of the truck and ran about five yards. He secured his exit by shaking salt across an eight-foot-wide path before running off the field. It was something they must have planned for and created, while Jeff and Max were busy getting the Vandalow from the mill.

"GO! GO! GO!" Midnight barked while using a hand signal. The boys ran forward as the enormous crowd of Vandalow finished entering the field.

Between the speakers playing heavy metal and Mia's grating siren, the Vandalow became frenzied as they crawled all over each other and the truck. The noise was so cacophonous, it was loud enough to wake the dead.

Upon seeing Midnight's hand signal, the boys got cracking as they poured the salt to close the gap in the line.

Max lagged behind for a moment to watch the stranger get out of the truck. He wanted to know how he was going to escape the Vandalow. When he was sure the stranger was safe, he turned and ran towards Billy. But a Vandalow ambushed him.

He saw it coming from the corner of his eye. Unprepared, there was nothing he could do to avoid it. So, he braced himself and waited for the hit.

Suddenly, Mr. Grimm slammed into the side of the Vandalow with its four paws, knocking it to the side. As the Vandalow jumped up to run away, it wobbled, and leaned too close to the sodium chloride, and stung its toes. Mr. Grimm chased it as it followed the salt border, trying to get away.

Butch saw the Vandalow run toward Billy, and he reacted by knocking him out of the way as he threw salt at it. The little creeper winced as the tiny white granules landed on its skin. Then it fell through the small opening left in the trap. The boys fired a barrage of salt at the Vandalow, as it ran away into the field toward the others.

Billy finished closing the gap, and after it was done, he walked over to Mr. Grimm and picked him up.

Max, Jeff, and the stranger continued to guard the boys until they were safely behind the salt border which surrounded Midnight's truck.

Mia shut off the siren, and the Vandalow continued to crawl all over Chuck's truck. Everyone stood exhausted as they watched the Vandalow. The music skipped, and came back on, and skipped again. It did that a few times and then died altogether.

At the same time, the first rays of sunlight glowed in the eastern sky. The Vandalow grew wild and started to tremble and shudder. As they shook violently, they began to burst into a liquid blob and immediately harden into a shell. As the sun rose higher, the shells cracked open and disintegrate into dust. Leaving behind the sacrificed animal. They watched in disbelief as a few deer appeared from the dust.

"Hey Jeff, look!" Max said, as he put his hand on Jeff's shoulder and laughed. He pointed to a mother and three baby bunnies as they hopped away.

Billy couldn't believe his eyes, as he and his friends watched rats and mice run every which way. They saw grasshoppers and frogs, and lizards too, and a few very confused-looking chickens.

Midnight smiled when his friend walked up to him. They shook hands and patted each other on the shoulder.

Billy and the boys, along with Max and Jeff stood, and watched the exchange of camaraderie.

"Boys! Meet Lucius Marcellus. One of the best men I know," said Midnight.

The guy had tanned skin and a white smile. He wore a camouflage boonie hat and green army fatigues.

"It's Lu for short, and I'm sorry I was late for the show. I just got stateside this morning. But I heard you guys were doing a spectacular job at soldiering," he smiled and shook their hands.

The boys were impressed. An active soldier was in their presence, and they introduced themselves one at a time.

Midnight walked up to Max and asked, "Are you good?"

Max had walked away and was watching the animals as they got a new lease on life. A second chance. He kept his eyes on the field and said, "I wondered for a long time where I fit in."

Midnight grinned. "Soon you'll be old enough. Expect a call from me."

Max looked at him, feeling hopeful. "Promise?"
"Would this 'Old Guy' lie?"

CHAPTER 42

CHAOS TO COMMUNITY

The catastrophic scene emerged along with the daylight as people appeared. Paranoid, they were careful and walked out of their homes with weapons in hand. The choice for today was the baseball bat. Other people carried with them brooms, axes, and even a few tennis rackets were seen. They looked outside their windows and saw their neighbors surveying the damage. Curiosity got the best of them as they walked outside. They bravely faced the environment that once threatened their survival, exchanging nods and waves.

Neighbors were helping neighbors with the cleanup effort, as they watched every type of emergency vehicle drive by. The Sugar Bee fire trucks sat at the center of town. The tow trucks came and went as they took away the demolished vehicles, leaving broken glass in their wake. Store owners were surveying the damage while they swept their stores and sidewalks. People from the community brought brooms, shovels, and wheelbarrows to the center of town to help aid in the cleanup effort.

The church parishioners brought covered dishes and barbeque grills to cook burgers and hotdogs. The smell filled the air as the Sugar Bee community came together.

* * *

In the backyard at Jeff's house. It resembled normalcy, and it was a pleasant place to be. Lana and Mia put bowls of prepared food on a large picnic table. While Chuck was manning the barbeque grill as Coop stood next to him, chatting away.

Midnight sat at a round patio table covered with a white, frilly tablecloth. He smiled as he sipped a beer. His buddy Lu sat next to him while they watched the boys play catch football. Even Max and Jeff were out there with the boys.

Lu could see that Midnight felt bothered by how this operation had gone. Even though Midnight smiled, there was something still eating at him.

"What's on your mind?" asked Lu.

"I almost screwed this one up, big time," said Midnight. He leaned forward, clasped his hands together, and put his elbows on his knees as he watched the boys mess around. "I can't do what I used to do. I'm hurt. My heart is in it, but my body says otherwise. I feel stunted in my abilities, and it makes me angry…to tell you the truth."

Lu knew his friend well. He had discerned, before this operation, that Midnight had been on edge and unwilling to ask for help. This job could have blown up in his face if it wasn't for the kids, and a few adults, helping him out. It very well could have gone bad. He also needed to work out his demons with what happened to Sgt. Baker. None of which was his fault.

"Well, maybe it's time to start the next chapter of your life. You've always been great at ordering me around." Lu chuckled.

"I think you've found your niche with these kids. It's time for you to take command and be a strategist. You can always be in the field. But from a better viewpoint. You've always been clever at tactical organization." Lu patiently waited for his reply.

"You know what? I think you're right. You've met Max?"

"Yeah, he reminds me of you," Lu said.

Midnight grinned at that. Because that kid had moxie, and he was all heart.

"He's almost eighteen, and he wants in. I'm going to take him under my wing." Feeling resolute, he looked forward to the next phase of his life. "And since L&M is shorthanded, I'm going to recruit and get some new blood into the company."

Lu smiled, "Good! Does that mean I'll get a vacation sometime soon?"

Billy looked toward the front of the house and jumped up and down as he yelled, "They're here!" He ran up to Betty, her husband James, and Mable. "Hey y'all! Here, let me help you carry those," he smiled, as he took the two bowls of food from the ladies.

"Well, aren't you the sweetest little thang? Why, thank you for being such a gentleman," Betty smiled while handing over her dish.

Max was right behind him, grinning as he took one bowl from Billy and carried it to the table.

Lana was busy yelling from across the yard, "We're so glad you're here! Oh! you didn't have to bring anything but thank you. It was so sweet of you both. Please, have a seat at the table."

The boys played football for a while until they grew tired and took a time out to catch a breather. Then they grabbed drinks from the cooler and strolled over to sit and listen to Mable and Betty tell their story about their experience with the Vandalow.

* * *

Coop wore a shy expression as he walked up to Mia. He handed her a little blue jewelry box. "I believe this belongs to you." He beamed a hopeful smile.

Mia eyed the small box, unsure about such a gift. But she was curious, so she opened it.

He watched her eyes light up and smiled.

"Oh, my God!" she said, as she looked up at him with tear-filled eyes.

"How did you ... You don't know what this means to me." Mia wanted to put it on, but she held the lid in her other hand.

"Here, let me help," Coop offered.

Mia held out the box as Coop picked up the delicate necklace by the chain. Mia closed the box, turned around, and held up her hair, as Coop place the silver necklace around her neck and closed the clasp.

She turned to face him and smiled. Then she gave him an enormous hug. "Thank you, Coop. This necklace belonged to my mother," Mia sniffed. A few tears brimmed before escaping down her cheeks.

"She passed away just a few months before my purse went missing." Mia put her fingers around the sterling silver petals of the daisy and held it up to look at it.

It was just as she had remembered it. The center was filled with tiny yellow sapphires, and it shimmered as it caught the light. "When I lost this. It felt like I had lost her all over again."

Coop felt remorseful as he said, "I'm sorry it took so long for me to give it to you. The night I found it on the ground, I put it in my pocket. I would've asked Carry to find out who it belonged to, but I don't think she would've been very forthcoming." Coop stared off, as he watched the boys play ball as he continued.

"So, I kept it in my pocket for a while and waited for someone to say something. After several months of waiting, I put your necklace in a box and stuck it in a drawer. Then I forgot about it."

Coop looked at Mia, and said, "That is, until we met at the bar, and you accused me of stealing your purse."

He was surprised when Mia leaned up on her tiptoes, put her hands on his shoulders, and kissed him. It was a sweet, innocent kiss, and his heart did a little dance.

"Thank you, Coop. I'm so glad we bumped heads at the bar, and you've been by my side ever since. I couldn't be more grateful to you."

Then Coop and Mia overheard Lana, and they paused to listen.

Lana was telling her story to Betty and Mable about the Vandalow. She was very animated as she talked about the man in the jail cell. Lana told them in great detail how she defeated the Vandalow and set the poor man free.

Mia asked, "What happened to Lyle, the guy you set free?"

Lana said, "I don't know. He took off and ran down the road toward the highway. After that, I never saw him again." She shrugged.

Coop worried his lip, and said, "At least I don't have to explain to him about what happened to his speakers."

Everyone looked at him and chuckled.

Max wore a dreamy smile as he said, "Those sure were some killer speakers. They looked so cool on Chuck's truck."

Lana shook her head and said, "Don't even think about it Mister," then her expression grew thoughtful, "but, oh my goodness, they had A-mazing sound."

"All I can say is that it was a win-win for me. Now, I can get a full night's sleep. It's so nice and quiet," Coop said with a blissful grin.

Midnight stood up and walked to the front yard, as he made a phone call.

The man on the other end of the line answered, "L&M, Incorporated."

"It's a go. Scrub the servers for anything mentioning Vandalow, Vandalows, gray monsters, demons, etcetera." He hung up the phone and returned to the backyard.

Midnight saw Ava sitting close to Chuck with her foot propped up on a pillow and walked over to her.

"Thank you for inviting us to the barbeque. I know it can't be easy with your injury." Midnight said, with a sincere expression.

"Oh, it's my pleasure. To tell the truth, everyone's been so helpful in putting this meal together, I haven't lifted a finger." She smiled and leaned back in her chair, looking fully relaxed.

"Good deal." Midnight grinned and walked back to his chair.

Troy led the boys as he walked up to Midnight, carrying the old brown book. He held it out toward Midnight and said, "I thought you would enjoy reading this."

Midnight was surprised and took the book as he read the title, 'Centuries Old, Myths, and Legends.' "Thank you. I was interested in this artifact the very second you guys mentioned it. I can't wait to read it."

Everyone sat around the table and ate a splendid meal together. They enjoyed each other's company and were thankful for every minute. For they had survived an incredible ordeal.

Then Sheriff Jake Halsey came walking around the corner of the house, and everyone turned to face him.

Surprised, Mia stood at attention, out of respect for the Sheriff.

He was in full uniform and looked a little roughed up from the wreck. There were a few bandages on his face, and he wore a cast on his right wrist.

His wife looked apologetic, and more than a little embarrassed, as she followed him into the backyard.

Halsey wore a perplexed and rather heated expression on his face as he marched up to the table and stopped. He looked at Deputy Romero and asked, "Mia, what in the hell happened to my town?"

There was a loaded pause—then everyone began to talk all at once.

Author's Note

Thank you for reading, 'Under the Magnolia Moon'. I hope you enjoyed it. If you did, I kindly ask that you consider leaving a review (no matter how short or long) at your favorite store. Reviews help readers like you discover new books, plus I'd really appreciate it!

If you would like to follow Dani Denali's updates for new books and more.

Join her email list.
Danidenali072@gmail.com
Follow on Facebook, Instagram, and X.